DRAMA ON DECK

*RelationSHIPS
can be hard*

B. JOSEPH SMITHSON

ISBN 979-8-9910561-1-3

First Printing, 2024

DRAMA ON DECK

I

CHAPTER 1

Why are these things so hard to write? I asked myself, staring at the application form.

The glow of it from my computer screen illuminated my dark hotel room as I scrolled down to see how long this was going to take. I had already filled out so much paperwork for this new job, and I was relieved when I thought I had completed it all. Now I was stumped by the section that said "Tell us about yourself." I tapped my nails on the keyboard of my laptop as I continued to draw blanks. My first day of training for this new job started in less than 24 hours, and I could feel the nerves setting in. My recruiter had told me this training class was their largest yet with over 50 people, and I really wanted to make a good impression.

What can I say that will make me stand out? I pondered.

It occurred to me that this felt very much like filling out a profile for a dating app. My roommate had made me join one not long ago and practically wrote my profile for me with some gratuitous embellishments. I smiled remembering some of the ridiculous things she had written...Not the sort of embellishments appropriate for a first day on the job orientation.

Focus Bree, I told myself.

Who knew me better than myself? I understood the qualities that made me unique and approachable, so this should be easy. I tried out several beginnings of a biography that I kept deleting after second-guessing myself, and I realized how scattered my life was. Especially now that I was making a big lifestyle change. I decided to stick to the basics of "me" and keep it fun and light. As I started typing, I imagined I was standing in front of the group and introducing myself...

My name is Breanne Bradley—a 25-year-old

Aries originally from Savannah, Georgia. Since graduating from college in recent years, I've been trying to navigate my transition from the eclectic, laid-back southern vibe of Savannah to the fast-pace and edginess of Los Angeles, California. Most of my college friends had moved to New York after graduation, but I felt the West Coast calling me. I quickly realized how different LA was...Any ideas I had of what Hollywood would be like certainly changed when I passed a woman on Hollywood Boulevard dressed like Tinker Bell sitting at a bus stop smoking a cigarette...When she saw me looking at her, she promptly told me to mind my own business—with many more expletives. That's an accurate visual for the vibe of Hollywood, but its unique charm grows on you.

Reality TV is my not-so-guilty pleasure. There's an odd satisfaction in getting tangled up in unscripted drama, like a captivating novel you can't put down. From housewives' catfights to dramatic re-couplings, I'm all in. Nature is my therapy. Hiking trails, chasing sunsets, and feeling the earth beneath my feet—it's not just fitness; it's about finding serenity in the chaos, one trail at a time. Fashion is my playground. Mixing timeless classics with the latest trends—it's my personal canvas. A way to express myself, explore styles, and keep life interesting. Happy hour is my golden ticket to unwind and catch up. It's like a pause button for the soul. Beyond all that, I love learning new things. It's a journey, whether diving into mind-bending books, savoring thought-provoking conversations, or simply learning from the twists life throws my way.

I thought that was a pretty good start. It got me thinking about my life back in LA, and why I applied for this job in the first place...

Los Angeles was a challenging city in which to thrive. Since I moved, I encountered more roadblocks than I ever anticipated. The job hunt in the "City of Angels" proved to be more daunting than I had expected. Applying for a job became a job all on its own, and then going on the endless number of interviews, only to be left in a state of limbo, while I hoped to hear back was maddening. The glamorous facade of LA had cracked a bit, revealing the struggles beneath—including a recession and numerous entertainment strikes. I found myself in these jobs that barely paid the rent and had no clear future. Even with my college degree, I was finding that I was, according to the hiring managers, either over-qualified or under-qualified —there was no in-between.

Yet, from this mix of uncertainty, a surprising opportunity emerged—a chance to embark on a journey of a different kind. I saw a job listing that sounded completely different from the listings I had been applying to with no luck, so I decided to apply for it. I didn't hold much hope that I would hear anything back, and I had forgotten about it shortly after. So, I was surprised when the email came and offered me a position with an art gallery that staffed the major cruise lines. I knew that working on a cruise ship was a bit unconventional and out of the realm of what I thought I would be doing. My friends in LA certainly voiced their thoughts. I went to happy hour with my roommate at the bar around the corner from our apartment to break the news to her that I would be moving out.

"I'm confused...You're going to do what?" she asked, as if it was an utterly unheard-of thing. But I saw it as a lifeline amidst the tumultuous job market...not to mention an opportunity to bank all my earnings. I did have my reservations about living at sea, but the more I thought about it, I decided I was okay if the ocean was to become my temporary refuge. At least it would offer a respite from the relentless job rejections on solid ground. Also, the idea of getting to travel for free was very enticing to me. I told myself I would do it for a year and then return to California and see if the job market was more favorable.

I sold my car, put all my belongings in storage, and hopped on a plane to attend the two-week training course in Florida, trading in the dry heat of Southern California for the humid heat of Miami. It finally felt real being in the hotel room, and preparing for the first day. The company, Landmark Quest, specializes in fine art sales and live art auctions onboard cruise ships.

"They do art auctions on cruise ships?" was the response I received from everyone I told about my new venture, but to me, it seemed like a perfect fit, given my artistic background and my degree in Art History. I had felt a rush of excitement as my plane touched down in Miami, and anticipation for my new adventure. However, when I started training the next day, I quickly discovered what an intense experience it turned out to be. Admittedly, the prospect of public speaking made me extremely nervous, and I soon realized that the trainers were laser-focused on my presentation and sales skills.

As I stepped on stage on my first day, I felt my anxiety rising. I stood in front of the microphone and forced myself to stop staring at my shoes and look out to the crowd. The black blazer I had bought for the training suddenly felt tight, and my hands started to sweat. I ran them over the matching skirt, trying not to fidget. I began to deliver my presentation and realized halfway through that I was speaking so rapidly that surely no one could understand what I was saying. As I walked off stage, I breathed a sigh of relief.

At least I wasn't as bad as the guy who had a panic attack, dropped the microphone, and ran off stage, I thought.

As the first day came to an end, I contemplated if I had made a wrong decision in coming. However, I decided to stay the course, and with each passing day, I found myself improving. I even ranked among the top three in my class, which filled me with pride and affirmed my decision. I refrained from divulging this opportunity to my family, fearing it might jinx it. I did, however, call my parents to share the good news once I had completed the training, though their reception was lukewarm. They had always encouraged me to explore opportunities outside of Los Angeles, but a cruise ship differed from what they had in mind. Nonetheless, they supported my decision, for which I was grateful. Pursuing an art career made them uneasy; after all, my dad was a firefighter, and my mom was a computer programmer —quite different careers. No one knew where the "art gene" within me came from, but I decided to follow my intuition, determined to forge ahead.

The job promised to push me out of my comfort zone, which I felt was what I needed. My tenacity, adaptability, and affinity for connecting with people all lined up perfectly for the position. So, I was thrilled when I was assigned to Vivace Cruise Lines on the Vivace Vision, sailing from San Diego to Hawaii. Vivace was known as one of the more affluent cruise lines and boasted an impressive fleet of cruise ships. It was also the cruise line that was rumored to be the best to make good money on. The rumor among the training group of newbies was that you didn't want to be put on a "Shun Ship."

I looked confused when the girl next to me whispered it. She explained that one particular cruise line was difficult to make money on, and all their ships had names ending in "tion." The Innovation, the Navigation, the Temptation, to name a few. So, I felt accomplished when I had avoided the "Shun Ships" and was assigned to Vivace. I was super nervous but also excited. Getting through the training course had been a harrowing experience in itself, and that wasn't even the actual job. There was abundant material to familiarize myself with regarding the artists whose artwork I would be selling. My recruiter informed me that a gentleman from the company, Bradley Smith, would join the ship on the same day as I did. I felt hopeful when I learned we were both Bradleys and took it as a sign of good things to come.

As the plane rushed down the runway and took off from Miami, I flipped through my training manual, trying to absorb as much of the artists' backgrounds and accolades as I could. I found it difficult since I couldn't help but reflect on the blur of events from the Miami training and wonder if it was all a dream now that I was flying back to California. It felt a bit chaotic flying across the country twice in two weeks and then joining a cruise ship to sail over to Hawaii. I had never been on a cruise before, and I had heard horror stories about them —not all of them unsettling, but those are the ones that stood out. I had a few wines during the flight to calm my nerves and quiet my thoughts. It didn't help that much, as I was still thinking about the job as the wheels hit the ground in San Diego.

During the flight, I had heard several people seated around me talking about how they were going to sail on the Vivace Vision, and I couldn't help but wonder if they could possibly be one of my first big sales. I tried to make note of their faces as I waited patiently for everyone to disembark the plane. My recruiter had given me Bradley's phone number, and he and I coordinated to meet at baggage claim and travel to the ship together.

Standing at the baggage claim belt, I watched a ton of luggage that wasn't mine pass by. The unimaginable idea of my bags being lost and my having to start this new job with only the outfit I wore began to creep in. As employees of Landmark

Quest, we weren't required to wear the shipboard uniforms—a fact I was happy about since I packed all my best outfits—but if my luggage was lost, I had no idea what type of uniform would be waiting for me. Better than nothing, I figured. My anxiety was starting to rise as I listened to the continuing whir of the luggage belt and the garbled airport announcements overhead. More bags passed me by.

Packing only two bags at fifty pounds each for my entire 6 month contract onboard had taken forever. Honestly, I couldn't stay under fifty pounds. I had to flirt with the gate agent at the Miami airport to let me slide. He had winked at me as he applied the fluorescent "heavy" tag to my bags. I began to look around the baggage claim area to see if I could pick out Bradley from the crowd. He said he would be wearing a suit, ready to step on the ship. There were several men in suits. One was on his cell phone, speaking in Spanish. I didn't think that was him. Another older man in a suit was coughing loudly and sneezing multiple times.

Please don't let that be him, I thought to myself.

I looked back at the luggage belt and was relieved to finally see the neon "heavy tags" on my matching bags moving toward me. I struggled to get my first bag off the moving ramp—it was heavier than I remembered. Suddenly, a tall man appeared behind me and helped me yank it off. He also grabbed my second bag and placed it next to the first.

"Damn, girl! They might be heavier than mine!" he exclaimed. "How many outfits did you pack for one contract?"

I paused and looked at him in his slim-fitting three-piece suit, and it dawned on me...this was Bradley. I shook his hand as I introduced myself and asked how he knew it was me.

"I already stalked you on Instagram," he said with a grin.

I wondered why I hadn't thought of that as we rolled our luggage away from the baggage claim area. Bradley told me he had already scheduled an Uber, but he looked at the size of my bags and said, "We may need to upgrade to an XL." He got on his phone and began texting away.

It was bustling outside in the pick-up area, and we had some time to kill while we waited for our car. I stood next to Bradley, who was seated on top of his suitcase among our considerable mound of luggage. He was tall and slim with very angled features and long dark hair neatly pulled back. I noticed he gestured with his hands a lot as he told me about himself and how he had come to work for Landmark Quest. Our conversation flowed easily, as if we had known each other for a while already. We laughed at how we shared the same name, which happened a lot, leading Bradley to adopt the nickname "Smitty" to differentiate himself from the multitude of Bradley Smiths out there.

I really liked the nickname and told him I would refer to him as "Smitty" moving forward and he could call me "Bree." We were also both from Los Angeles, not that far from each other, so we commiserated over the challenges of finding stable employment.

Smitty's journey took an unexpected turn when a summer production internship turned into an accounting job, despite his admitted lack of math skills, which didn't help him last long there. He even tried modeling, only to be rejected due to his impressive height of 6'4".

"I've never heard of a height limit for male models," I said, surprised.

He shrugged. "That's the way it is. I'm starting

my third contract today on the Vision. My previous contract was on a Vivace ship, and I did very well. You must have done well at Miami training since the Vision is one of Vivace's newest ships and amazing for the art department." Smitty began to give me the lowdown on ship culture.

Once our Uber arrived, we loaded our bags and departed for the port. The air conditioning was very welcome after waiting in the heat, and the car's interior smelled like fresh leather mixed with the scent of a fruity air freshener. As we drove away from the airport, Smitty continued telling me what I was about to experience.

"Life at sea is filled with many rules—both official and unofficial," he explained. "There's a weekly practice called 'boat drill,' where the entire crew simulates a ship sinking. Each emergency has its own code name and protocol to follow, and we can be randomly tested on this information. Failing to recall the codes results in being summoned to something ominously called 'Captain's Court.'"

"That sounds chaotic and bizarre," I remarked.

"There's also a ridiculous restriction: wine can only be purchased between 3 p.m. and 4 p.m. We call it 'Wine O'Clock,' and I even set an alarm on my phone for it."

I was surprised to learn that random breathalyzer tests were conducted on the crew, with a strict limit of only 0.02. It was astonishingly low, barely allowing for a single drink.

"Even with this rule," Smitty mentioned, "most of the crew frequents the crew bar each night. If security calls for any reason, the unspoken agreement is to feign ignorance of each other's whereabouts."

He continued on, "The crew is divided into two categories: 'Staff' and 'Crew.' Those of us in the Art Department, along with Spa, Hotel, and Entertainment, fall into the 'Staff' category, which grants us additional privileges. However, this creates a divide with the rest of the crew."

"It almost sounds reminiscent of high school," I commented.

He gave a knowing wink in response. There were more details to absorb, but they eluded me due to the overwhelming amount of information I was hearing. One aspect that made me nervous was the room accommodations. Smitty referred to the crew cabins as "broom closets."

Surely, they can't be that bad, I thought to my-self. However, the notion of having only one closet was disconcerting. Adding to the challenge was the fact that I would be sharing the aforementioned "broom closet" with another girl. Smitty mentioned that he would be sleeping in his boyfriend's cabin, as he met him during his previous ship contract.

His boyfriend happened to be the main singer in the production cast, allegedly named Dan Holiday—a name that I thought must have been a stage alias. Smitty assured me that it was his real name but said that everyone called him Holiday. Even more outrageous was that they met at a holiday crew party.

"If we were to break up," Smitty joked, "it would have to be on a holiday to maintain the absurd level of synchronicity."

I couldn't help but wonder if Smitty's attraction to Holiday was solely based on the spacious cabin he enjoyed as the main singer. It was unclear whether Smitty's affection for Holiday extended beyond the practical benefits. The dating scene on ships appeared to be a game where winners reaped the rewards and confirmed the similarity to high school dynamics, an environment in which I didn't excel.

Smitty had completed two contracts and had ample experience in shipboard relationships. He confessed that he was not allowed to date models, singers, or dancers—a self-imposed rule he consistently broke. He amusingly shared that all his ex-boyfriends were his passwords for various accounts, with one serving as his bank password and a previous singer-boyfriend who ghosted him acting as his Apple ID.

"It is certainly a fun trip down memory lane," he said with a smirk.

It sounded like a world filled with curious twists and turns, where boyfriends became passwords and your connections onboard dictated your lifestyle. I tried not to let myself feel overwhelmed with everything I was hearing. I knew this was going to be a major lifestyle change, and I reassured myself that I was up for the task. I had done well during training, which was hopefully a sure sign that I would excel in this new position. Still, I couldn't help but wonder what kind of world I was stepping into. While I looked out the window, I saw the ship appear as our car drove over the bridge that led into the cruise port.

II

CHAPTER 2

Upon arriving at the port, we were met with absolute chaos. It looked like a massive crowd at a theme park, with some passengers complaining to the port workers about the time it took to leave the ship, while others who were beginning their cruise were frustrated by the prolonged wait to embark. The size of the ship eclipsed the distraction of the altercations—it was beyond huge. It dwarfed the rest of the ships lined up in the port. I tried to tune out the din of the people around me and the loud alarms sounding from the ship as we collected our luggage before it was run over by the numerous taxi cabs dropping people off. The sun's heat was beating down, and I was starting to sweat, pulling my bags and regretting packing so much. The whereabouts of the crew entrance was a mystery to everyone we asked, but fortunately, Smitty's keen eye spotted a group of individuals carrying TJ Maxx bags who turned out to be fellow crew members.

I asked him how he knew, and he replied with a mysterious smile, "It's a crew thing."

This is it, I thought to myself. It was finally real after two weeks of training for it—all of the gossip and talk about the job and what would happen once I was onboard was floating through my head. It must have resulted in a nervous look on my face as Smitty looked at me and made us pause.

"It's all good. Just take a breath and relax. You're going to kill it, girl. I can already tell," he said and then continued to roll his bags again.

As we approached the security gate, manned by two officers engrossed in their conversation in Italian, they initially ignored our presence. However, Smitty did not back down and interrupted their discussion, telling them our names. Glancing at a stack of papers on a clipboard, they informed us that our names were not on the sign-on list and went back to their conversation. Smitty rolled his eyes dramatically, muttering about the notorious forgetfulness of Landmark Quest's recruitment department. He interrupted the officers again and clarified that we were the new sign-ons for the art department, emphasizing the agency's tendency to overlook adding names to the security clearance list. I watched as Smitty conveyed all this in his designer sunglasses and stylish suit. I wondered if I should have changed into something more professional, but no doubt, with how stuffed my bags were, everything would need to be steamed before wearing.

As Smitty continued to explain the situation, I observed crew members already bustling past us, flashing their crew ID badges and heading towards the ship. Each one carried numerous grocery bags overflowing with items. It turned out that "embark day," as they referred to it, marked the transition between one cruise ending and another beginning. The crew used this time to venture into town, stocking up on personal supplies and snacks before returning to work and hitting the metaphorical reset button. It was clear that a well-coordinated dash to replenish provisions was the norm.

Despite Smitty's best efforts, the security guards remained unyielding. He even dropped Dan Holiday's name, which made me smile. It was funny how I already felt a connection to someone I hadn't even met. I also attempted to reason with the guards, but they responded by smiling and looking me up and down before exchanging a few words in Italian. I couldn't tell exactly what they were saying, but it was clear they were talking about me in a suggestive manner. My ship experience was off to a rocky start. Smitty saw them staring at me, rolled his eyes again, and snapped his fingers to bring their attention back to him.

Fortunately, our predicament caught the attention of a woman in a white uniform adorned with striped epaulets on her shoulders. She approached us and inquired about the situation. We explained that we were new sign-ons for the art department. She grinned and remarked that we looked like "Questies." I turned to Smitty, perplexed by the term, and he clarified that "Questie" was a nickname onboard for people who worked for Landmark Quest. The woman introduced herself as

Ziwe and mentioned that she was the assistant to the Hotel Director. With a confident air, she instructed the security guards to make a phone call and have someone come to assist us. One of the guards nodded and promptly contacted the designated number she provided.

Ziwe reassured us, saying, "No worries... your department head will be out to get you." With that, she walked away towards the ship, leaving us with a sense of relief that our situation was being addressed.

I could sense Smitty's flustered state, annoyed that he had failed to gain us entry, but he swiftly composed himself, smoothing his hair calmly. Then, he turned his gaze towards me, lowering his sunglasses and flashing a nervous but excited smile.

"Prepare yourself," he uttered before raising his mirrored shades back up.

Subsequently, he divulged his knowledge of our Gallery Director. Her name was Georgette Day; she was apparently a British "glamazon" associated with Landmark Quest for numerous years, boasting an esteemed reputation within the company. Smitty rattled off a list like a fan girl.

"First, Georgette is hailed as flawless, always in

impeccable and fierce outfits. She is the company's darling, capable of choosing any ship assignment she desires. Second, with over 100,000 followers on Instagram, she holds influencer status. Being both stunning and able to document her world-wide cruise ship travels on social media earned her collaborations and a plethora of free swag. Third, she is from an illustrious family with a rich English heritage, and they own a grand estate."

It was clear that Georgette was essentially the queen bee of cruise ships. I tried not to let Smitty's Wikipedia-style rundown of this woman unsettle me. Battling self-esteem issues had always been a personal struggle, particularly the feeling of inadequacy in comparison to others. Though I had been working on it, it was a daily challenge.

I've got this, I reminded myself, using those words as my anchor.

I had only just regained my composure for around thirty seconds when I caught sight of her. Georgette emerged from the ship's gangway. "Glamazon" didn't even begin to capture her essence. The California sun illuminated her blonde hair, styled in a sleek, short haircut out of a magazine. Her silk wrap dress clung flawlessly to her supermodel figure. As she drew closer, I couldn't help but notice her perfectly manicured nails, clutching a Vivienne Westwood handbag. I observed Smitty straighten his posture, a wide grin spreading across his face as if he were encountering a Hollywood celebrity. Then it struck me—she probably was, at least to him.

Georgette reached the security gate, pausing momentarily. Even the security guards appeared awestruck, although one managed to offer a smile and greeted her with a charming "Ciao Bella." She paused briefly, gracefully removing her Prada sunglasses, and slightly reciprocated the smile. I discovered his name was Lucenzo, or "Lucenzo, Darling," as Georgette addressed him in her posh English accent. She explained that it had been a busy morning, implying that he surely wouldn't want her to have to endure the scorching sun while navigating the red tape required to facilitate the entry of her two new team members. With a manicured hand slipped into her handbag, she retrieved a small flash drive and extended it towards him.

"For your trouble," she declared.

Things took a positive turn when Lucenzo allowed us to pass through with all our luggage.

The contents of that flash drive certainly did the trick. Within seconds, I found myself standing in front of Georgette. She was slightly taller than me but not as tall as Smitty. Her glossy stiletto heels certainly gave her a boost.

How did she walk down that steep gangway in those? I asked myself.

Georgette cast her discerning gaze over us, lingering on Smitty before focusing on me. I felt my anxiety rise a bit, but I kept an outward calm.

Finally, Georgette spoke, "At last, the Americans are here." She instructed us to leave our luggage in the crew loading area and follow her up the gangway. It appeared that we had a series of stops to make.

Navigating the interior of a cruise ship proved to be quite bewildering. In the crew areas, all the walls were painted a glossy white and seemed indistinguishable from one another. Crew members bustled past us, pushing large metal crates filled with luggage that made an awful clanging sound, and I had to be vigilant not to be run over. Smitty and I struggled to keep pace with Georgette, whose stilettos clicked assertively on the metal floor, the luggage trolleys parted way for her as she glided through. It was as though she owned that space—her personal runway. How she managed to walk so swiftly in those heels remained a mystery to me. She informed us that we were on what the crew called the "I-95," essentially the main hallway spanning the ship's length. Georgette described it as a place where we needed to proceed with courage and conviction. The stares from the crew members we passed left me feeling unsettled. On the other hand, Smitty seemed thrilled by the attention, explaining that we were the "new meat." I couldn't understand why he found it exciting; the situation made me even more uneasy.

Curiosity got the better of me, and I couldn't help but ask Georgette about the contents of the flash drive she had given to the security guard. To my surprise, she revealed that it contained the latest movies and television episodes, which held a particular value onboard. They were like currency since most crew members had minimal opportunity to access Wi-Fi and download them. I was fascinated to learn about these unique dynamics and what held importance within this ship's community.

Georgette abruptly turned into a smaller hall-way, nearly causing us to collide with her. She stopped in front of a door marked "Safety Office." Knocking on the door, she then turned her attention to me, confirming that I was Breeanne. Her expression was difficult to read. I nodded and gave her a quick smile. She looked indifferent...or unimpressed. It made me wonder if I had done something wrong already. I tried my best not to look intimidated as she quickly moved on to Smitty, asking if he was Bradley. Smitty replied affirmatively but added that he preferred to go by Smitty, explaining that he found Bradley Smith to be too common. He even pronounced "common" in a pseudo-British accent. Georgette's lips curved into a slight smirk before the door to the safety office swung open.

We were greeted by a very tall, elderly man who seemed unimpressed by our presence but focused on Georgette. She informed him that we were the new sign-ons for the art department and that he would be responsible for assigning our safety duties. I assumed these duties were what Smitty had told me about earlier, involving the simulated ship-sinking exercise, also known as the boat drill.

I smiled at the safety officer, but he did not smile back. Smitty saluted him with a smile, which the officer did not seem to appreciate. Georgette told us to come and find her in the gallery on deck 6 when we were done, and with a flip of her hair, she was gone.

He motioned for us to come inside, and we sat down in the chairs in front of his desk. The office was sparse, and I felt like we were in the principal's office. A map of the ship, as well as several safety slogans, adorned the wall in front of me. The safety officer handed me a card with a printed speech and explained that I would be delivering it to the passengers over a megaphone because, as he put it, "the art people usually speak well."

Smitty was given a neon yellow hat and vest, and his assignment was to direct passengers to the appropriate location for the boat drill outside the dining room. Smitty remarked light-heartedly about the hat not being his color and how it would mess up his hair. The safety officer, however, didn't seem amused and mentioned that the captain might require Smitty to cut his hair as it apparently violated the ship's "Grooming Policy."

I could sense Smitty's horror at the thought.

It was evident that the safety officer and Smitty weren't going to be fast friends, and their interactions might be strained. The officer handed us our training schedule for the cruise, which was extensive. As we left the office, I mentioned to Smitty how rigorous the schedule looked, to which he responded, "It's never-ending." Smitty was not thrilled about his safety duty and said he planned to find a way to switch it to something that didn't involve wearing a neon hat. He explained that it wasn't so much about the hat itself but rather the feeling of being told he had to wear it. He mentioned something about how it was a personal game of his to see how many rules he could "get around" during a contract. Meanwhile, I found myself reminiscing about my father and all of his rules about safety. When I moved out to California, the first thing he did was give me an earthquake kit. The safety manual I received reminded me of his thoroughness in ensuring my preparedness—he would have read it like a thrilling novel.

As we navigated the ship searching for the gallery on deck 6, Smitty was still complaining about the safety hat and remarked that he doubted Georgette would ever be required to wear a hat like his.

There was a hint of envy in his tone, and I could understand why. Georgette seemed to hold a particular position of privilege and authority within the ship's hierarchy. We finally found our way to the art gallery onboard the ship. It surpassed my expectations in terms of its size and elegance. The wood-paneled walls were adorned with beautiful artwork, as I had seen during my training. I noticed all the art was hung on a wiring system from the ceiling, and Smitty explained, "Don't put a hole in the ship; they'll absolutely freak out." He told me that the art department often was blamed for any damage found on the ship because we were "easy scapegoats" due to the large trolleys that we used to move all the art around the ship on auction days. As we explored the gallery, Georgette appeared from around the corner.

"Telling her all the gossip already are we, Smithsonian?" she asked.

Smitty smiled sheepishly and replied, "Actually, it's Smitty." Georgette said she liked 'Smithsonian' better.

Smitty chuckled and said, "That totally works too."

Georgette then noticed the neon hat and vest

that Smitty was holding. She grinned mischievously and said, "So he gave you that job, did he? I'm sure you'll look adorable in that hat."

Not too thrilled about the duty or the hat, Smitty joked back as he did downstairs in the safety office, "Safety yellow isn't quite my color, and hats mess up my hair."

Georgette mimicked the safety officer, "Well, the captain may have a word about your coiffure anyways." Smitty's horrified expression reappeared on his face.

Georgette showed me the way to my tiny cabin, affectionately referred to as the "broom closet" by Smitty. True to his word, the space was incredibly small, and I couldn't help but feel a tinge of jealousy as he reveled in the alleged spaciousness of Dan Holiday's cabin. Perhaps there was some truth to this notion of dating the managers for better accommodations. However, I was unsure if having a boyfriend just for his cabin was a path I wanted to venture down. My roommate was Georgette, and she kept the cabin impeccably tidy. As I glanced at her neatly arranged jewelry and perfumes on the small desk, I couldn't fathom how she fit all her free influencer swag and clothes in this minuscule space. When I asked about it, she revealed her secret—she kept a week's worth of clothes in the cabin and stored the rest in the female dancer's dressing rooms. It seemed she had several arrangements in place, including a deal involving the dancers' favorite television episodes on a flash drive.

I had yet to meet our boss, Theobold Thorne, another Brit and the head of the Art Department. Eager to gather some information, I asked Georgette about him. However, my pronunciation of Theobold with a pronounced "th" sound didn't go unnoticed by Georgette. She quickly corrected me, informing me that the "h" in Theobold was silent. Georgette described him as direct but fair and advised me to focus on getting the work done and selling the art to avoid his interference. She emphasized that she would be my main point of contact as the Gallery Director. As Georgette gracefully slipped out of her silk wrap dress and donned a sharp-angled black pantsuit that accentuated her enviable figure, I couldn't help but feel self-conscious. While I thought I had a decent body, standing next to the statuesque Georgette made me reconsider. I would need to step up my game and find my confidence in this environment. She instructed me to change into my work attire and locate Smitty, who seemed to have disappeared with his boyfriend. Gallery hours began at 6, and she expected us to be ready by 5:45, suited and booted, to prepare for the evening. I was not particularly fond of the term "suited and booted," as it reminded me of the repetitive jargon used by the managers during training. It was a Landmark Quest thing, apparently. Despite the overwhelming nature of this new environment, I was doing my best to stay calm and composed. I sincerely hoped I made the right decision by embarking on this adventure. It was too late to turn back now—I had sold my car and stored all my belongings in LA. Fortunately, San Diego was our home port, and if things didn't work out, I had the solace of knowing that LA was just up the coast.

III

CHAPTER 3

After a long afternoon of sign-on procedures and meeting various crew members, I stumbled upon Smitty in the crew bar. He was with none other than the infamous Dan Holiday. As I quickly discovered, the crew bar was the hub of activity for the crew, where they gathered each night to unwind and socialize. It was mostly empty at the moment, but Smitty assured me that it was always busy at night.

Holiday appeared true to Smitty's description – charming, charismatic, and just as tall as Smitty. They did make a gorgeous couple. He regaled us with stories of his time at sea, praising the camaraderie among the crew. He had spent an entire decade singing on ships, which amazed and bewildered me.

As we chatted, several crew members came in, and I couldn't help but notice the diverse mix of nationalities around us. Several different languages were spoken throughout the bar, and everyone seemed to be in their own little worlds. Time seemed to slip away, and just as I began feeling more at ease, Smitty checked his watch and realized we had to head to the gallery. Before we left, Holiday grinned mischievously and hinted at a significant surprise awaiting us. I exchanged a curious glance with Smitty, wondering what more could possibly be in store for us on this eventful day. Frankly, I wasn't sure if I could handle any more surprises.

When we arrived at the gallery, Georgette was waiting for us. She effortlessly retrieved a set of keys from her Chanel handbag that perfectly matched her sleek black outfit. There was an air of sophistication about her as she uttered the words, "Theobold will see you now," which had a hint of theatricality to it, reminiscent of the famous line from The Wizard of Oz - *The wizard will see you now.*

I couldn't help but be intrigued and slightly apprehensive as Georgette slid open the gallery doors, and we followed her inside. My mind raced with anticipation and curiosity. The surprise that Holiday alluded to was unveiled when Georgette glided toward the back of the gallery, revealing the presence of Theobold Thorne. He was seated at an ornate desk and rested comfortably on an equally ornate chair, framed by the numerous artworks on the wall behind him.

Smitty and I were utterly stunned, our mouths likely hanging open in disbelief.

"Gorgeous" seemed an understatement to describe Theobold, who resembled a living embodiment of a Tom Ford advertisement. With his impeccable suit, blonde sleeked-back hair, and chiseled jawline, he exuded an irresistible charm. Both of us stood rooted in place, seemingly enchanted by his presence. Theobold motioned for us to approach, and we obeyed his command almost as if under a spell.

"Welcome onboard," he greeted us with a posh accent rivaling Georgette's, who gracefully made her way behind the desk and sat beside Theobold. The two of them appeared like a match made in heaven. At that moment, I couldn't help but wonder if they were a couple, given how impeccably they complemented each other's appearance. However, I quickly shook off the thought and refocused my attention.

Focus, Bree, I reminded myself.

Theobold gave us the schedule for the cruise and described how he ran his program, explaining that he preferred to avoid involving himself in the day-to-day affairs and that Georgette would be our main point of contact.

"She is, after all, the queen of this floating empire," he mused, a playful grin directed at Georgette. She remained silent, her gaze fixed ahead. He mentioned that the company only sent him the best-of-the-best when it came to associates, so he had high expectations of us. The team that was on the Vision during the previous season had done extremely well, and he wanted to break their record. He explained how he and Georgette had arrived to the ship earlier to get the gallery and everything ready to begin the current season. He also gave us our individual sales targets – Smitty's goal was higher than mine since this was his third contract. Nonetheless, Theobold's expectations were intimidating.

Am I really the best-of-the-best? I asked myself, and then I reminded myself how well I had done at training. I was half in my thoughts and half listening to Theobold. I wasn't sure if I was distracted from tiredness or his beautiful features.

Soon, Theobold rose from his chair, announcing his departure to prepare for the champagne reception later that evening. With a sweeping gesture akin to a performer on a grand stage, he bid us welcome once more before exiting the gallery. Georgette watched his departure, her gaze lingering on him momentarily before returning her attention to the two of us.

"Well... Now that that spectacle is over... time for GTP," Georgette declared, rising from her chair. Her words snapped us back to reality, reminding us of the task at hand.

"GTP", as I discovered, stood for "Guess the Price." Smitty gave me a nonplussed look as he grabbed a wooden box with a slot in the top of it. It turned out that Guess the Price was a nearly daily event onboard, where we were tasked with standing next to an artwork by one of the more popular artists we represented, which we had to set up in a public space and ask passengers, as they passed by, to guess its retail value. Initially, this sounded manageable to me. However, my optimism waned when I inquired about the duration of this activity.

"Until your soul is crushed... until your feet fall off... until the hideous outfits of 95% of the passengers assault your eyeballs..." Smitty responded with a touch of cynicism. He explained that, at the beginning of their first contract, newcomers often found GTP enjoyable, only to find it increasingly grueling and torturous as time went on. While I felt the term "torture" was a bit strong, there was no denying that it was an experience in itself.

We set up a folding table in the central atrium. As I looked upward, I could see multiple decks that circled the area and a sparkling chandelier hanging in the illuminated dome above. It was large and grand, with music from a string quartet playing and mixed with the chatter of excited passengers as they explored their new floating home. I helped Smitty cover the table using a black tablecloth adorned with Landmark Quest's logo on the front. He placed the wooden box in the middle of the table and began laying out golf pencils and small stacks of guessing slips around it. Then he set up an easel next to the table and placed the artwork that people would be guessing about. I could tell this was not his favorite part of the job.

"You really have this down to a science, huh?" I joked about how quickly he had set it up.

"You have no idea..." he said, rolling his eyes, as the first passengers approached the table curiously.

Some passengers displayed genuine interest and enthusiasm for the activity. Even entire families eagerly participated. Smitty encouraged everyone to take a guess, mentioning that Georgette would keep track of the number of guesses we received each night. I adjusted the gold name badge on my lapel. We weren't required to wear a uniform, but we were required to wear a name badge. Initially, it didn't bother me, but soon, I discovered it was an open invitation for passengers to ask us anything and everything. Instead of participating in Guess the Price, most people were more interested in discovering where everything else was onboard, particularly the food.

"Where the food at?" seemed to be the most

frequently asked question, and each time it was uttered, Smitty couldn't help but roll his eyes once the passengers turned away. I lost count of how often it happened, but by the end of our three-hour Guess The Price session, Smitty had transformed into a human eye roll emoji. Despite this, he concealed his exasperation well, always responding with a charming smile and directing guests to the buffet or wherever else they inquired about. I couldn't help but wonder how he knew the ship's layout so well since we had just signed on earlier that afternoon. He explained that most ships this size were built similarly, and his previous ship had been identical. Having completed several contracts already, he had a clear advantage.

The interactions we experienced ranged from amusing to confusing and, at times, even offensive. Due to Smitty's tall stature, some passengers gasped and exclaimed, "We thought you were a mannequin!" Some passengers took an eternity to write down their guesses, and it was comical to watch Smitty politely urge them along so he could increase his guess count. However, there were less amusing moments, like when a drunk individual approached me and asked if "I came with the painting." And then some glanced at the artwork and boldly declared they wouldn't pay a single dollar for it. I believe in the subjectivity of art, but it would have been nice for them to exercise some tact and keep their rude opinions to themselves. Unfortunately, I quickly realized that tact was a virtue lacking among most cruise ship passengers. I had heard that cruising used to be chic and glamorous; however, those days seemed long gone. As Smitty and I continued with this activity, I glanced across the large open atrium at another group of crew members wearing bright red T-shirts that boldly stated 'JUST ASK' in large white lettering.

Smitty noticed my gaze and remarked, "Social staff... Never, not once, would I do that." He explained that they had to endure such questioning on every cruise, often subjected to even worse behavior than we were currently experiencing. I overheard some questions they were bombarded with: "Where the food at?" was still the most popular. "Did the elevators go to the front of the ship? Were we flown onboard to work each day?" The worst one, "Can I speak to someone who speaks English?" despite every crew member conversing in English, albeit in different dialects. As the behavior of some passengers grew increasingly concerning, I couldn't help but feel a sense of awkwardness. It became evident that Smitty and I were treated slightly better simply because we were American. One passenger even exclaimed, "Finally, someone that speaks American!" That made me cringe inside; however, amidst the less-than-pleasant encounters, there were still passengers who exhibited kindness and a genuine sense of wonder. For them, the cruise was a magical experience.

With each passing moment, Smitty and I accumulated a substantial number of guesses in the GTP box. When Georgette appeared, she opened the box and commended us, stating, "My, aren't we the over-achievers tonight." Her slight, captivating grin filled me with a fleeting sense of accomplishment. However, that feeling was short-lived as she swiftly added, "Now double that in the next hour," before gliding away. The pressure was on. All the guesses we received had the guests' cabin numbers on them, which Georgette meticulously compiled into our mailing list for the cruise. Our event attendance would directly reflect on Smitty and me. It was as if we were mere cogs in a giant machine, as Smitty had described. The significance of our efforts became apparent.

In the three-hour shift of Guess the Price, we managed to accumulate over 3,000 guesses. I considered it quite an accomplishment and congratulated Smitty and myself. He smiled at me but cautioned, "It's a bitch of a double-edged sword, girl." Confused, I didn't fully grasp his meaning until Georgette summoned us to the gallery, addressing us as "Smithsonian and Miss Bradley." I entered alongside Smitty, and it was evident that Georgette could sense my dissatisfaction with being addressed as "Miss Bradley." She inquired about my preferred name and how she should address me. Smitty, always quick with a playful suggestion, chimed in, proposing that since his first name is Bradley and my last name is Bradley, she could call us "The Bradleys!" We shared a lighthearted moment, but Georgette did not seem amused.

She paused before responding and looked at Smitty, "No, Smithsonian." I quickly requested that Georgette call me "Bree." She repeated the name in her posh accent but with a cool undertone, then nodded. Georgette proceeded to eliminate duplicate cabin numbers, reducing our count almost by half, which deflated my earlier pride of a higher guess count. Finalizing the mailing list at 1,567 cabins, she announced her departure to change her outfit and host the champagne toast with Theobold. Addressing Smitty, she asked, "You know the drill, right?" Smitty nodded in understanding, and Georgette bid us both a good evening as her statuesque silhouette departed down the hallway.

Upon hearing about Georgette's need for yet another outfit change, I couldn't help but marvel at the vastness of her wardrobe that must be stored in the costume room. I felt disappointed that we weren't part of the champagne reception, as it sounded like much more fun than "GTP." Nevertheless, I shrugged it off and eagerly glanced at the clock, announcing that we had only one hour left of work. Smitty raised an eyebrow, curious about my excitement. Then, I remembered his earlier comment about the double-edged sword. Smitty proceeded to explain the remaining tasks we had to accomplish. We needed to print the 1,567 letters, personally sign them in Theobold's name, stamp each one with the cruise logo, put them into envelopes, and deliver them throughout the numerous decks of the ship. Initially, it sounded like a joke to me. It seemed utterly ridiculous, considering we only had one visible printer in the gallery. However, Smitty pulled out a second printer from a cupboard. Two printers still didn't sound like enough to handle over 1,500 letters.

"...And Georgette and Theobold don't assist us with this?" I nervously asked. Smitty laughed and assured me that he had it all under control. As the final hour in the gallery slipped away, my enthusiasm dwindled, realizing that an all-nighter awaited us. We also had to be up early the next day for safety training. My face must have shown my exhaustion and dejection.

Sensing my mood, Smitty stepped in to offer reassurance. "Don't worry, I've got this," he said as he picked up the gallery phone and dialed a number. "Hey babe... Are the troops ready?" he asked the person on the other end. He placed the phone back on its receiver and instructed me to grab the second printer. We were about to pay a visit to Holiday's cabin. Curiosity and an increasing weariness coursed through me as I followed Smitty, ready to discover what lay ahead in Dan Holiday's domain.

As I peeked into Holiday's cabin, I was blown away by its sheer size, which was twice the size of mine, complete with a queen-size bed and a full couch. There were colored mood lights in the corners of the room, illuminating it in a warm, balanced glow. It was in stark contrast to the harsh fluorescent lighting in my cabin. A humidifier and aromatherapy diffuser bubbled on a table by the bed, giving the room a delicious vanilla scent. I couldn't help but feel jealous that Smitty enjoyed such luxury. The whole "boyfriends for passwords" mantra suddenly made more sense. "Can I just please stay here and sleep on your couch?!" I pleaded to Holiday jokingly.

"You have no idea how many security guards I had to bribe to get the humidifier onboard," Holiday said, explaining that he finally had to declare it an essential item to his position as a lead singer. Several wine bottles were on his desk across from the bed, and stacks of blank letters and envelopes spread around. Looking at Smitty and Holiday curiously, I couldn't help but wonder what was happening. They exchanged laughs and motioned for me to join them inside the cabin. To my surprise, five other people burst into the room behind me, all talking excitedly about a "cabin party." It turned out they were the dancers from Holiday's cast, and little did I know, they were about to save the night.

Smitty and Holiday proceeded to explain the ingenious system they had devised during their time on their previous ship, aiming to save time in Smitty's schedule for more private time with Holiday and ensuring that he wouldn't be a "huge tired bitch in the morning," as Holiday humorously put it. Smitty raised his eyebrows, agreeing with the comment, and retorted, "Except for the huge part... rude." They divulged the details of the operation: Smitty and I would fire up both printers and take charge of printing the letters, keeping them in order. Then, two dancers would fold each letter in half, passing them on to Holiday and the dance captain, who possessed elegant handwriting. These "autographers" would sign Theobold Thorne's name at the bottom of each letter. The folded and signed letters would then be handed to two more dancers, who were responsible for placing them in envelopes, sealing them, stamping them with the cruise logo, and sorting them by ship deck. Throughout the process, everyone indulged in copious amounts of wine from the crew bar while exchanging gossip about the previous cruise and drama from other departments.

I was absolutely amazed. It was a boozy assembly line that not only saved my sleep schedule but also provided a fantastic opportunity to bond with the dancers. Two of them, Sergei and Alina, the dance captain, were a ballerina couple from Eastern Europe. The other three female dancers hailed from Scotland, Australia, and New Zealand, respectively, named Eryn, Anna, and Erika. I was so intrigued by the many nationalities in one room. These countries were places I had never been to, and I had so many questions for each of them. The girls gave Smitty a big hug and said how much they had missed him. I realized they had all been on the same ship during their previous contract. They warmly welcomed me into their circle, asking personal questions about my life that went far beyond the typically shallow questions people asked in Los Angeles. They initially asked about my relationship status, whether I was single or dating, and then moved on to other topics. The girls appeared particularly excited when they learned it was my first contract and first cruise ship. It felt like I had learned more about the dance cast in that short period than some of my friends back in LA. Eryn seemed to be the rowdiest of the group, while Anna was more laid-back and gave off a more chill, bohemian vibe. Erika was the most elegant of the three – even the delicate way she handled the letters, slipping them into their envelopes, appeared refined. Together, we managed to complete the task of all 1,567 letters, fueled by wine and a sense of camaraderie, in less than two hours. I felt elated, but then the realization hit me as my half-drunk and tired brain finally processed the information —we had to deliver all these letters tonight. I asked Smitty how long it usually took to deliver this many letters by hand. As everyone erupted into laughter, I couldn't help but join in, even though I wasn't entirely sure what was so funny.

Continuing with the ingenious machine that Smitty and Holiday had concocted, the next step involved Erika and Anna's boyfriends, who happened to be two of the captain's officers onboard. They entrusted the letters to them, and as they conducted their security rounds on each deck, they would deliver the letters to their designated cabins. Once again, I was amazed by how different crew members worked together so seamlessly. Curiosity got the better of me, and I asked why everyone was so willing to help us. Erika and Anna explained that Smitty bought all the wine, ensuring the cast could drink for free. Additionally, the girls playfully revealed that they used the power of withholding sex from their Italian officer boyfriends as a motivating factor for their assistance. They mentioned that withholding sex from Italian men could be a pretty persuasive tactic, which left me intrigued, considering my limited experience with relationships outside the US.

"So, it's a machine fueled by booze and sex," I remarked. Everyone laughed and agreed, adding that Georgette's flash drives also played their part. It reminded me of my earlier conversation with Georgette, and I turned to Smitty, shocked. I asked if Georgette knew about the whole operation. Smitty explained that keeping secrets onboard a ship was nearly impossible, and Georgette didn't care about the details as long as things got done. As the dancer girls giggled at the mention of Georgette, I couldn't help but be intrigued by their comments about her being the "Ice Queen of Glamor."

Erika leaned in and explained. It was a playful nickname that the dancer girls had given to Georgette, highlighting her fierce and glamorous persona. They said that Georgette had a reputation for being assertive, demanding, and highly particular about everything related to the style, fashion, and aesthetics of the job...and how unpleasant she could be if displeased. The girls commiserated with me that I had to share a room with Georgette, saying that if she "took that silver spoon out of her ass," then maybe she would have a manager's cabin to sleep in as well.

"Oh, so Georgette and Theobold aren't a couple?" I asked. The girls exploded in laughter, answering my question. I was incredibly impressed by the resourcefulness and coordination of everyone involved, especially Smitty. It was only our first day, and he had already set everything in motion.

Smitty abruptly exclaimed, "Okay, bitches! Everyone out!" as he clapped his hands and rose from his seated position on the floor. The dancers filed out of Holiday's cabin, holding all the letters. I was the last to leave, turning around tipsily and saying, "Good night."

Smitty responded with a playful wink, saying,

"Day one done, bitch," before closing the door. I stood outside, slightly buzzed from the wine and filled with a sense of admiration for the incredible teamwork and creativity I had witnessed. It was certainly a memorable introduction to my new home.

IV

CHAPTER 4

I went to the crew mess for a late afternoon lunch, still trying to process all the information from this morning's safety trainings. We had an entire week of early morning courses training us in emergency procedures should the ship sink. Smitty dragged me to the crew mess, schooling me on the "what not to do" when interacting with others in the mess. The divide he had mentioned on our way to the ship between the "Staff" and the "Crew" was indeed a reality. The crew mess looked much like a high school cafeteria, with a tall stack of colored trays at the beginning of a long food assembly line. Long cafeteria-style tables were scattered throughout the mess, and everyone sat with their own departments. The engine department was all burly guys, and Smitty warned me that sitting there meant being hit on nonstop. The housekeepers were the largest group, but they only spoke in their own language amongst each other, which was not exactly my go-to for making conversation—same deal in the galley department. It felt like all eyes were on me, like I was the "new kid" on her first day of school. Smitty suggested if I wanted the freshest gossip onboard, I should sit with the salon and spa girls. And if I was up for some "nonstop bitching" about the cruise, he pointed me to the front desk crew or, even better, the kid counselors.

"You can find out whose teenagers are making purple," he said as I looked at him, asking what 'making purple' was. He explained, "Boys are blue, and girls are pink, and when they hook up... Bam! You get purple." I grinned, and off he went, leaving me with a snarky remark about upgrading to better food upstairs with his boyfriend.

I grabbed a tray and a plate as I looked to see what food was available. The crew mess had a unique smell that I thought might be some type of fish. It wasn't the most appetizing smell, so I decided the salad bar seemed sufficient for me. I put together a salad and then surveyed the sea of tables, Smitty's advice echoing in my head. Luckily, I spotted a hand waving at me in the far corner of the mess. A familiar Scottish brogue rang out, "Oy! New girl, over here!" It was Eryn sitting with Anna and Erika. Excitement bubbled up in me; seeing them and having "friends" to sit with was great. Nothing was worse than being the new girl no one wanted to hang out with.

Eryn and Anna sat on one side of the table, with Erika on the other. As I approached, Erika quickly switched so all three girls were on the same side, facing me as I sat down – as if I was about to be on trial. They all smiled and stared at me, but there was an odd expectation in their eyes.

"So..." Eryn drew out the word, looking at me.

I repeated the word back to her in the same drawn-out manner. Then, in unison, they all excitedly asked about my first night rooming with Georgette.

"Oh, that," I said. They wanted a story, so I decided to spill the beans. I began the story by telling them it had taken me a while to find my way to my cabin since all the crew hallways looked exactly the same and also being slightly drunk. Eventually, I did and tried to enter the room quietly. It was a bunk bed setup, and Georgette had claimed the bottom bunk. She'd gone all out with silk sheets and a stunning array of throw pillows, now scattered on the ground as she was already in bed with a sleep mask over her eyes. I quickly changed and got ready for bed. Coming out of our tiny, triangle-shaped bathroom, I assessed the situation. There was no ladder up to my bunk. I eyed the desk with all of Georgette's perfumes and jewelry and decided to go for it. Quietly, I grabbed the top bunk, put one foot on the corner of the desk, and hoisted myself up. Georgette stirred slightly. I laid down and let out a sigh of relief—not only for not waking her below me but also because I was exhausted and couldn't wait to sleep. I hadn't shut my eyes for more than a few seconds when the loudest noise erupted somewhere in the room. I jumped up and smacked my head on the ceiling. As I rubbed my head, the noise persisted, loud and annoying.

What is it? A vibration? I thought, and then I saw it.

On the other side of the desk, in the shadows, was what looked like a large cell phone vibrating and ringing so loudly that it was moving across the desk. I wasn't sure what it was until I heard that posh accent below me.

"That's for you," Georgette murmured sleepily.

What? Who's calling me? I asked myself as I tried to reach the phone and nearly fell from the top bunk. Grudgingly, I got down and retrieved the phone, figuring out how to answer it. I said hello, but there was no one there. After no response to my second hello, I ended the call. Georgette raised one-half of her sleep mask to look at me.

"You might as well sleep with it, darling. You are going to be fast friends," she said, lowering her eye mask and rolling over and offering no further explanation.

As I finished my story, the three girls across the table cackled loudly, especially Eryn. After they calmed down, they explained that it was a "deck phone," part of the ship's internal communication system. It had a deafening ring, and, unfortunately, I was stuck with it. Georgette was pulling rank, and Smitty told me, "Sorry girl... shit rolls downhill."

Eryn explained, "It only rings when someone has a gripe about something."

Great, I thought. I told them that no one was on the other end, and the girls said it likely wouldn't ring all that much because people thought Georgette still had it, and a lot of the crew were terrified of her.

"I wouldn't call her!" Anna exclaimed.

I looked at them and asked if that was why they let her keep most of her wardrobe in the dressing room.

"It's best to have one of the most intimidating people onboard on your side," they said.

"And maybe she'll let me borrow a frock one day!" Eryn exclaimed. Anna and Erika joked that Eryn's boobs wouldn't fit into any of Georgette's outfits.

"Oh yeah, I forgot she has no tits!" Eryn said, laughing at her own statement.

The women continued, gossiping about the crowd at last night's show as I ate my salad.

Eryn commented, "I hope you like it because it's

the same bloody thing every day down here." I suppose my facial expression left much to be desired, and they giggled. They explained that I should sit with them each day because the art and entertainment departments got along well and were an "alliance."

"Safety in numbers, right?" Anna said, more as a statement than a question. I suppose they were right. I felt I was also right about this environment being like high school. At least I already had an "alliance," but it was an alliance against what exactly?

The next day was a day at sea, which meant it was an auction day, our busiest days in the Art Department. Smitty and I had to wake up at 6 a.m., which was brutal since neither of us were morning people. Our task was to lead a team of galley workers, hired by Georgette, in unloading artworks from storage lockers in the lower decks and transporting them to the lounge on deck 7, where the auction would later take place. Doing this at 6 a.m., when most passengers were still asleep, made the job easier—seeing the ship so empty after witnessing the previous day's crowd felt odd. We then set up easels and strategically placed the artwork around the Explorer's Lounge, turning it into a makeshift pop-up art gallery. It took about 2 hours to set up around 300 artworks. Afterward, we could return to our cabins for a nap before preparing for the auction. Smitty returned to the Holiday residence while I returned to the sleeping Georgette.

She lay on her back like a corpse, hands over her chest and a designer eye mask in place. She didn't move as I climbed back into my top bunk and drifted back to sleep. Two hours later, when I woke up, she was gone. Her bed was perfectly made, and all her throw pillows were in place like something out of a designer magazine. I showered in our tiny triangle-shaped shower, a mission due to the curtain sticking to my wet body and the nonexistent water pressure. Remembering all of Georgette's outfit changes the day before, I aimed to at least try and emulate her. I put on a tailored black blazer with a matching pencil skirt and black, glossy heels.

Here we go, I thought as I left the cabin.

Getting lost in the endless white crew hallways was becoming a daily occurrence. Eventually,

I found the crew elevator. Another rule was that crew members couldn't use passenger elevators but instead use one of the two elevators at the front or back of the ship, leading to constant overcrowding. On my third try, I squeezed in, only to find myself next to the Safety Officer who asked, "And who are you?"

I cheerfully responded that I was Bree from the Art Department. He tapped his name badge, questioning, "And how would I know that?" That's when I realized I had forgotten my name badge, a significant faux pas. I grimaced and pressed the button back to my floor, thinking at least I'd figure out how to get back to my cabin without getting lost this way. Fifteen minutes later, I finally made it to deck 7. Walking to the Explorer's Lounge, I heard the chime of the announcement system. Georgette's melodious voice invited the whole ship to the upcoming art auction, ending with, "I so look forward to the pleasure of your company." I approached the lounge and saw a folding table covered in the Landmark Quest tablecloth with Eryn, Anna, and Erika's familiar faces sitting there. As I walked up, I heard them mimicking Georgette's announcement in an over-the-top recitation of "the pleasure of your company," and laughing. I greeted them as I approached, and Eryn cheered, "Time to sink or swim, girl!" Already feeling nervous about the first auction and wanting to prove myself to Georgette and Theobold, I agreed and made an anxious face. The girls reassured me and clued me in on their system to help us out. Theobold had hired the dancer girls to register each auction attendee and hand them a bid card with a bold number from 100 to 300. Those who had bought art before got numbers in the 200s, and those who had purchased a lot or were wearing luxury items got numbers in the 300s.

"So be sure to hit those people up first when the auction starts," Anna said.

Erika also added, "And Eryn won't be handing the 300s out just to the hot men this time..." raising an eyebrow at Eryn.

She defended herself, saying, "I'm just trying to help her out! Besides, I think the average age on this cruise is 65, so we're all out of luck. Anyways, you'll see the Italians circling your space soon enough."

Confused, I was about to ask a question when Smitty, walking up behind me, answered, "I told you that you were the new meat," with a smile and a wink. Apparently, the Captain's Italian officers were known for chasing after any new female crew members who joined the ship.

"Don't worry... We'll be your wingwomen," Eryn said. Georgette's voice, which I just heard over the PA system, was suddenly behind me.

"Yes, well, all that will have to wait until after the business day, ladies," Georgette stated. "Shall we, Miss Bradley," she said, motioning for me to enter the lounge. It seemed like she was purposely ignoring my request to call me Bree. I gave the dancers one last smile as I walked in. Georgette's eyes followed me as I entered, and then she gave a knowing glance to the dancers and glided into the lounge after me. It was time to go to work.

The entire auction was a blur. After getting registered, the guests entered the lounge, which was quickly filled with people milling around and looking at the art. I remembered the dancer's advice and began first talking with the 200s and 300s. It was a bit difficult to speak with people at first because I kept getting interrupted by other guests constantly asking where the free champagne was...to which I did not know the answer. At one point, I approached the bar to inquire, only to be sidelined by Georgette, who told me that under no circumstances was champagne to be served until Theobold had started on the mic. Her tone changed, "If I see you passing out champagne to people, I will be very displeased," she said ominously, disappearing into the crowd.

I remember Smitty coming up and saying it was always a great motivator if we turned this moment into a friendly game to see who could outsell the other. I agreed, and we dispersed into the crowd. I tried to recall all my training leading up to this, and I ended up selling two artworks for $1,500 before the auction started. I didn't beat Smitty, who had sold four for $5,000, and Georgette, who had sold a massive original painting for $12,000, which she placed on the stage to begin the auction...I had some stiff competition. She reached into her designer handbag and retrieved a microphone as she welcomed everyone and began to introduce Theobold. She was so calm and serene on stage, and I only hoped I could achieve that level of stage presence one day.

"Ladies and gentlemen, I give you Theobold Thorne," Georgette finished her introduction as he walked out. Theobold looked like he had just stepped out of a Prada advertisement and onto a runway. He looked so handsome, and it was then that I realized I had a slight crush on my boss.

Everyone was clapping as I stared and then realized I was not clapping. I saw a cutting eyebrow raise from Georgette standing on stage just behind Theobold, and I frantically started clapping. The rest of the auction went on for over two hours. Theobold commanded the stage as he stood, illuminated by the bright stage lighting. He brought his gavel down with an electric crack on the podium as artworks of all styles and sizes passed behind him. The free champagne started flowing, and bid cards flew up in the air all over the room. The crowd became more excited and engaged as an artwork sold, and then another, and another.

Smitty and I were meant to go to the bidders and encourage them to raise their card again if they were outbid, so I ran throughout the room the entire time. I regretted wearing heels immediately. By the end of the auction, $55,000 worth of art had sold. I was in shock. I had heard how big and successful the auctions could be, but seeing it actually happen was surreal. The guests began shuffling out of the lounge as I waved goodbye...until Georgette appeared next to me, started collecting the bid cards back from the guests, and promptly started shuffling them into my hands.

"You do realize Smithsonian and yourself will be preparing new cards if you let them walk away with the whole stack," she said while smiling at the exiting guests. Once the guests were all gone, her smile disappeared as she closed the doors and clapped her hands twice. The helpers from the galley appeared in their coveralls in a flash and started breaking down all the art, easels, and tables like a well-oiled machine. As I watched them, I heard Georgette, "Breakdown is not a spectator sport, Miss Bradley," she commented as she walked over to the galley team.

"Thank you, darlings," she said, handing them envelopes with cash and another flash drive. They all had huge smiles, like they were looking at a supermodel.

How many flash drives did she have? I asked myself.

"Smithsonian, you're in charge...See you shortly in the gallery", she said, exiting the lounge.

Behind me, I heard a quiet "Pssst!" Turning

around, I found Smitty tucked into a corner be-hind the bar. I joined him as he flashed a sly grin and placed two glasses on the bar and a half-empty bottle of champagne.

"Can't give it all away to these people. Plus, we have to celebrate you losing your auction virginity!" he said excitedly as he poured. "And look at you, selling on your first one...I have seen some newbies go through an entire cruise and not sell anything," he said as his phone alarm started going off in his inside blazer pocket. Smitty pulled out his phone, and I saw the alarm name, "Wine O'Clock" - the one hour a day we could buy wine from the crew bar to take away to our cabins, which was essential to keep our boozy late-night letter-folding parties going. "Duty calls!" he exclaimed as he downed his glass of champagne and entered crew quarters on his way to the crew bar. I watched as the break-down crew quickly returned the Explorer's Lounge to its usual state, and I felt a sense of pride for my performance.

At least I'm not going to be the newbie who didn't sell anything the entire cruise, I thought.

V

CHAPTER 5

Gallery hours that evening were insane. If I thought the auction was a blur, I certainly wasn't ready for the checkout process for all the auction sales. We had to set up folding tables throughout the art gallery, each with a laptop and printer – a one-stop shop to upsell everyone who had won a bid at the auction. There was a whole hierarchy already in place for who handled which client. Theobold and Georgette dealt with the higher in-voice amounts. Smitty managed the overflow from them, and I, being the newest, was relegated to upselling framing.

Some of the raffle prizes given out during the auction were free artworks, and it turned out that these prizes were a royal pain in my ass and my sanity. Ideally, these freebies would give us more opportunities to sell; however, most of these guests were pinching their pennies hardcore. I discovered these freebie artworks weren't even onboard with us but had to be shipped from the land-based facility. So, there I was, the lucky one, informing people who thought they were quickly collecting a free prize about the situation. After breaking that news, I got to offer them an option of a $15 shipping tube for an unframed artwork, or they could frame it and have it shipped for free.

I had never heard so many elaborate excuses not to frame, especially how everyone seemed to have a personal framer. My thoughts were becoming more and more frustrated with these passengers, and I tried not to let it show on my face. After my tenth appointment, my patience was beginning to wear thin. But amidst all the framing talk, several tall, handsome men wearing white uniforms with epaulets kept walking through the gallery. It was as if they were doing laps around it, and I couldn't help but feel like they were staring at me. It was unnerving and was not helping me focus on the ridiculous framing sales pitches I was throwing out to counteract all the excuses not to frame.

There was this one man who passed through at least four times. During the last trip he made, I looked up and saw his gorgeous brown eyes. He winked at me as he walked by. As he did, his deck phone that hung on his belt went off – as loud as my annoying phone did. He answered with a "Ciao" in a delightful accent, and then it dawned on me... the Italians! Eryn wasn't joking.

I got distracted by this revelation for a moment and was interrupted by the free artwork winner seated across from me holding his bucket of beer, "Yeah, my cousin makes all my frames, so I'm not gonna do it... you sure I can't just take it with me?"

I returned to my current framing reality and repeated the same answer that I had told literally everyone that night. I did a hard eye roll towards Smitty as the guest walked away. A slight smirk appeared on his face as he sat with his client across the gallery, typing on his laptop. Georgette and Theobold were in his private office with their clients... no doubt they were having better success upselling.

Overall, the auction was a huge success, and we were already almost halfway to our sales target. Smitty said this boded well for keeping Theobold and Georgette calm and off our backs. I glanced at my appointment schedule and was delighted to see I was done for the night, even though I was slightly demoralized at my invoice pile of mostly $15 shipping tubes. I was going to have to work on my framing game.

I leaned under the table to unplug the printer and saw a pair of white shoes appear under the tablecloth as someone sat across from me. Most likely, it was yet another person asking where the nearest restroom was – it is one thing I learned very quickly on this ship because I was asked at least every twenty minutes by a guest looking like they urgently needed one. I had my prepared response on autopilot, about to voice it to the person when I sat back up in my chair, but I went mute when I saw the handsome Italian man who had winked at me before was seated just opposite me. Caught off guard, I smiled and ran a hand through my hair.

He grinned at me and said, "Ciao. You caught my eye, and I simply had to come and introduce myself... I am Serge."

I must have smiled like a schoolgirl and introduced myself as, "Bree... well, Breeanne, but you can call me Bree."

"Piacere, Bree. You are new, yes?" he asked, leaning forward in his chair. I nodded and gave a hopeful, very abridged version of how I came to be onboard.

Serge smiled and stated to himself, "Of course, American." His large eyes were a deep, dark brown, and his even darker medium-length hair was combed back behind his ears. His uniformed shirt fit him like a glove around his defined chest and arms. My eyes snapped back up to his face, and I realized he was also staring at my body, then met my gaze again.

Then, a loud noise sounded. When the deck phone blared, I practically jumped out of my skin. I was convinced it was my own for a split second, but it was his. Without missing a beat, he answered with a casual, "Ciao," and dived into an animated conversation in Italian. As he chatted away, he kept his gaze locked with mine, and I faked flipping through invoices to appear busy. I could sense an energy between us that felt like it was pulling me across the table towards him.

I glanced at Smitty, who had just wrapped up with his client, shooting me a sly smile and wordlessly mouthed, "Hot!"

After Serge ended the call, he announced he had to go but promised to swing by sometime soon.

"Great!" I blurted out way too eagerly.

Effortlessly, he reached across the table, took my hand, lifted it to his lips, and planted the softest kiss there. He released my hand, which hung in midair momentarily as he strolled away with a parting, "Ciao Bella."

I couldn't help but follow him with my eyes until he disappeared. Then, there was Smitty, casually hopping over to my table and plopping down cross-legged.

"I told you! Fresh meat! And look at you, lady... straight to the top!" he exclaimed, winking at me with infectious excitement.

Apparently, Serge was the First Officer – the second in command under the Captain.

Meanwhile, Theobold and Georgette were wrapping up their appointments. Georgette had traded her earlier ensemble for a cream, angled pantsuit, a white blouse, and stilettos – another effortlessly chic look. I still sported my now slightly disheveled outfit from the auction. She sifted through the invoices on Smitty's table, grinning in approval.

"Not too shabby, Smithsonian," she praised, and Smitty responded with an even broader grin, declaring, "I know, right?!"

Georgette's approval seemed to light up his world. However, the moment she approached my desk, her expression shifted. She shuffled through my invoices and remarked, "We shall have to work on your framing skills, Miss Bradley." She still refused to call me Bree. I explained the framing struggle, mentioning how everyone seemed to have a personal framer.

She retorted, "I highly doubt that with most of this crowd, darling."

Theobold emerged from his office, extending congratulations to all of us. "The Americans came to slay!" he proclaimed as he walked over.

I asked myself why everyone kept emphasizing Smitty and my American citizenship, and it suddenly dawned on me – besides Dan Holiday, we were the only other Americans I had encountered onboard so far. Theobold seemed satisfied with the day's outcome, expressing his anticipation for a repeat performance at the next auction in two days. With a suave farewell, he left us to our evening.

Two debonair exits by handsome men within the hour. Life at sea isn't looking too bad for a girl, I thought to myself.

After we closed the gallery for the night, Smitty said we were heading to the martini bar to meet Holiday and the girls. As we ascended the sparkling crystal staircase in the central atrium to deck 8, I watched the couples dancing together as a musician played a romantic tune on the piano.

Okay, so there is still some glamor left on cruise ships, I thought. The ship was buzzing with energy, and people were out and about. As we neared the martini bar, I heard a raucous laugh that could only belong to Eryn. She spotted us as we approached and jumped up from her barstool, "The artisans are here!" she exclaimed loudly.

I could tell that the dancers were a few martinis in already. Holiday got up to hug Smitty, and they exchanged a kiss. He smiled at Smitty,

"Someone made some money today," he said, looking at Smitty, who smiled back and nodded.

Anna and Erika shuffled down a few barstools

to make room, and another handsome Italian officer in a white uniform brought up another barstool for me. Erika introduced him as Marcello, her boyfriend and the Third Officer. I received another, "Ciao," and a big smile.

I replied with my own, "Ciao," and Smitty just couldn't wait.

"I'm not the only one having a good night!" he blurted out to the whole table. "Somebody got clocked by the first officer hard... and I do mean hard," he drew out the last word. Everyone's attention turned to me.

One of Eryn's prominent red eyebrows angled high on her forehead as she looked at me, "Oy, let's have it then!"

I blushed slightly and recounted the rendezvous with Serge. Anna mentioned something about Italians wasting no time, and Marcello responded, saying that beautiful women were their weakness as he put his arm around Erika and squeezed her. She looked up, smiling at him, and they kissed. I could tell they were very into each other. I thanked him for being our postman and delivering our invitations during his security rounds. He said it was no problem at all.

Smitty ordered us two spicy martinis, which were delicious. Crew members got half-off drink prices at the passenger bars, he explained excitedly, to which Holiday responded, "And yet they still end up on my tab," as he winked at me. Everyone laughed and raised our martini glasses to cheer each other.

It was then I realized that these would be "my people" onboard.

VI

CHAPTER 6

Reaching the Hawaiian Islands took several days at sea from San Diego. I had never been to Hawaii, and I absolutely could not wait. Since we had so many sea days at the beginning, most of our auctions were at the start of the cruise. Then we reversed the route to go back to San Diego—the old passengers left in Honolulu, and the new passengers came onboard to cruise the islands on the way back to San Diego. I thought it was pretty fabulous for my first contract itinerary. We had our second auction, almost a repeat of the first one with different artworks. We didn't do as well as the first, but Smitty said that was normal for the middle auction, and the final was usually the windfall. Theobold expected us to be 75% towards our final goal by now, which we were over currently. So Smitty was right; he seemed very satisfied. In fact, I didn't see him very much if it wasn't an auction day. I decided to keep my slight crush on Theobold to myself – especially since my interaction with First Officer Serge the other night. It was only my first few days onboard, and I already was developing crushes on two people. It was very unlike me, which was slightly confusing.

I had seen Serge passing by the gallery several times and giving me his enchanting wink and smile. As new crew members, Smitty and I had early morning trainings that stretched through the day, going straight into Guess the Price and gallery hours in the evening, so I had little free time to pursue anything further. Our final training was up on the pool deck the next morning, and we were meant to pretend the ship had sunk and we were stranded in the ocean. For our water test, we had to tread water for thirty minutes in the pool. I figured it would be my cardio workout for the day.

I was so thankful to have Smitty to go through

these trainings with me. He was constantly cracking me up with his quips to some of the trainers who seemed very disenchanted with their jobs and didn't have too much love for the art department. They thought we didn't work very much, which was obviously false. I was also thankful we were not required to wear the ship uniforms.

As I sat in the trainings, trying to absorb all the information, I became distracted by how ill-fitting they were... at least on most people. Serge looked terrific in his... in fact, the whole "Italian Mafia," as they had been coined, looked amazing in their uniforms. I suspected they had them tailored – which I wasn't mad about. The Captain's officers appeared to all keep themselves fit, unlike many of the other officers and crew. They did work long hours, so I supposed it was difficult to fit the gym into their schedule.

Smitty and I had been doing workouts in the gym at night. Luckily, as Staff, we could use the passenger gym after it closed to the guests. It was hilarious because Smitty was so tall that his head hit the ceiling when he tried to run on the treadmill. So, he was forced to run in an awkward hunched-over motion. The ship did have an outdoor running track, but it was too wet to use safely while cruising at sea. I was shocked that I hadn't felt the least bit seasick, and it was bizarre that some of the guests were horribly sick but refused to take seasick medication. Some crew members even got quite seasick, so I was unsure how they could do an entire work contract. I actually enjoyed the feeling of being rocked to sleep by the ocean each night in my little top bunk bed.

Georgette and I hadn't broken the ice much as roommates. She usually came back to the cabin and went straight to bed. She was good enough to let Smitty raid her master hard drive with all the recent movies and shows, which he then gave to me. So, on quiet nights, I could just watch something on my laptop and slip off to sleep.

I begrudgingly crawled from my top bunk at 6 a.m., not looking forward to my fake ship sinking.

What do you wear for a planned sinking? I asked myself, but then decided I was too tired to care. I threw on my one-piece bathing suit and a hoodie, walked to the crew elevator, and realized I had forgotten my name badge—again. Back in the cabin, I used my phone flashlight to sift through yesterday's outfit to find my badge. The whole time, I tried not to wake the fabulous corpse in the bed next to me. Finally, I found it and grabbed my largest sunglasses, popped both on, and headed back out.

The sun was beginning to rise as I walked onto the pool deck, the deflated husk of the lifeboat floating in the pool. I saw a group of crew members and headed over. Not being a morning person, I wasn't feeling very social and didn't see anyone I recognized. So, I stood there, staring at the wooden, teak planks of the pool deck, waiting for the drill to begin.

Where is Smitty? I thought.

I wondered if I should have gone by Holiday's cabin to ensure he was up. Before I could finish the thought, I saw his tall, slender frame walking through the glass sliding doors. I felt a smile immediately come to my face despite my tiredness. Smitty wore a silk robe hanging open, revealing nothing more than a neon yellow speedo as he sauntered over to me. He also had sunglasses on, which he pulled down slightly when standing beside me.

"Isn't it a fine morning to drown in Hawaii," he joked.

"Well, you definitely dressed for the occasion," I responded.

He quipped, "Hello... It's safety yellow! It matches my safety hat. I feel like it's pretty on-brand for me. But let's keep it real... if this ship is sinking, I'm grabbing the largest Picasso artwork with the thickest frame to float on and pulling a Rose from Titanic... And no, there won't be room for you, Jack."

We giggled as the safety officer arrived on time and took a roll call. The cool, early morning breeze was blowing and making Smitty's robe billow like he was on set for a photo shoot. The officer paused when he got to Smitty and me and looked up from his clipboard. Smitty saluted him with a cheeky grin and pose, which made me giggle even more. I saluted as well.

We may as well have fun with it, I thought.

"The art department... Unique as always," the officer muttered as he put his clipboard away.

The drill commenced, and we were instructed to stand beside the pool and fall in sideways. As I stood on the edge of the pool, it felt awkward to make myself purposely fall sideways. When I hit the water, all the breath was knocked out of me –

it was freezing! I swam to the surface as quickly as I could and immediately wanted to get out, but then I remembered we had to stay in for half an hour. It felt like it was going to be the longest thirty minutes of my life. I hated being cold – It was one of the reasons I loved Southern California. Treading water, I turned around to find Smitty.

"So, I know I was joking about Titanic a minute ago, but this water is making it real," he said as his teeth chattered.

I let out a small laugh through my shivers and turned around to look at the rest of the scene in the pool. It was slightly chaotic, and several people immediately went for the raft to inflate it. Smitty's head was bobbing in the water, and he raised his eyebrows.

"Looks like the men have it covered," he said as the initial shock of the cold was wearing off. He swam to the other side of the pool, floating gracefully on his back like he was at a resort. His neon speedo glowed from beneath the water, matching the yellow life raft as it became fully inflated.

Behind me, I heard a scream, and I turned around while still treading water. One female crew member was freaking out and flailing in the water.

The safety assistant immediately pulled her out and made her sit on the wooden deck.

I swam over to Smitty, who commented," Damn, I didn't realize we were in the Hunger Games..." I laughed, still staying afloat, and hoped I wouldn't be pulled from the water. I was a decent swimmer, but I never tested myself to stay afloat for half an hour. As the minutes passed by, several other crew members were pulled. By the end of thirty minutes, about 70% of the group was left... including me, for which I was pretty proud.

By then, the sun had fully risen, and the golden rays warmed my shoulders as I floated in the pool. It was my first day in Hawaii, and we were docked in Maui. Even though it was early, I felt excited and wanted to get off the ship immediately. Unfortunately, crew members had to wait until the passenger lines died down, which wouldn't be until a few hours later. I returned to my cabin, changed into dry clothes, climbed back into my top bunk, and drifted back to sleep.

The sounds of the bathroom door and the shower turning on woke me. I excitedly hopped out of bed and started getting ready, choosing a bikini over the one-piece for my first time in

Maui. Georgette came out of the bathroom with wet, slicked-back hair and a silk robe, very similar to one Smitty had on earlier, wrapped around her. I told her she and Smitty were "twinning" this morning.

To my surprise, I saw a slight grin on her face, and she responded, "He can only wish."

I told her I was meeting some of the cast at the gangway to go to a beach club and asked if she wanted to come. She said she already had plans and placed a giant sun hat on her head. "Besides, I doubt your new girlfriends would want the 'narcissistic ice queen' cramping their style," she said as she flashed a knowing look my way.

Of course, she knew what the girls were saying, I thought to myself. I was about to respond with something like that's not what they said, but the announcement system piped into our cabins, announcing that the crew was allowed to get off the ship. I noticed Georgette had a very large bag packed for just herself, but I didn't give it much thought as I said goodbye and left the cabin.

Walking toward the gangway, I spotted a long line of crew members. Smitty and Holiday were there with the dancers, so naturally, I went to join them. Something felt off; everyone was quiet. Curious, I asked what was happening. Eryn turned to me, her voice hushed, and spilled the tea—they were being silenced.

My face must have shown confusion, and Holiday jumped in to explain that the security guards were very strict and not very friendly when dealing with the crew. Right in the middle of his explanation, a security guard showed up at the front of the line, screaming at everyone to be quiet, confirming Eryn's story. The line moved at a snail's pace as security allowed one crew member to go at a time. Hats, bags, and shoes all had to go through the security machines, and each person had to endure a thorough pat-down. Male crew members got one of the male security officers, while the females got the only female security officer, making our line even longer. Eryn hinted that the line was longer because the security woman enjoyed taking her sweet time on the pat-downs, especially with "us curvy girls." She demonstrated with a sexy pose, running her hands over her boobs and down her butt.

The loud security officer returned, yelling for everyone to have their "I-95s" out. I had no idea what he was talking about until I noticed everyone holding small folded-up forms. An "I-95," I discovered, is a crew member landing form to exit the ship in the US. Smitty, Holiday, and I, being American citizens, didn't need one, hence my unawareness of this rule.

I went through the motions, putting my shoes and belongings through the machine and waiting for my pat-down. The security lady took more time with Eryn than with me, but it seemed like Eryn didn't mind the extra "hands-on" time. The last step was scanning my crew card with the final security officer to mark me off the ship. He didn't even look at me, just held his hand out, saying, "I-95."

I responded, "Oh, I don't have one."

He sternly told me to go back, ignoring my explanation.

Smitty, behind me, chimed in, "Hey sunshine, we are American. We don't have I-95s." Smitty grabbed my crew card, along with his, and put them in the security officer's hand. The officer looked up, glanced between us and our cards, and a disgusted smirk appeared on his face.

"Ah, American... must be nice," he said as he swiped our cards and threw them back at us.

"Well, he must be having a bad day," I said as we walked down the gangway. Smitty reassured me that they were all like that, and he and Holiday had dealt with it on his last contract. Americans were few and far between on the crew, primarily found in the entertainment and art departments, creating a bias since our departments got the most time off to go out into port.

"Don't sweat it," Smitty said as he pulled a flask from his bag, took a sip, and handed it to me. "Aloha, bitch," he winked, putting on his sunglasses as he skipped forward to join Holiday ahead. I looked up, seeing a cloudless blue sky and the warm Hawaiian sun filtering down through the palm fronds onto me, and I couldn't help but smile.

This job is awesome, I thought to myself.

A hotel on the far side of the island offered crew members discounts on drinks and food at their beach club, apparently making it the go-to spot. Our taxi dropped us off at the hotel entrance, and we walked through the open-air lobby to the back of the hotel towards the pool. As we walked across the lobby's marble floor, some front desk staff waved at the dancer girls as they passed. It seemed they were regulars. The pool area was luxurious, with plenty of loungers, tables, striped umbrellas on the patio, and a stone staircase down to the beach. I asked the girls if they knew the staff that was waving, and to my surprise, they told me that they were former crew members who had "jumped ship."

"That actually happens?!" I asked.

The girls nodded, saying it was a pretty common occurrence – especially among Americans.

"But I thought there weren't many American crew members?" I asked.

Erika explained, "And now you see why. Especially the bartenders... they make more here at the resorts than they do onboard. So, they get a free trip over compliments of Vivace Cruise Lines, and then they bail."

It sounded so odd to me. I couldn't imagine going on a trip and then just never going back, but these former crew members were proof that it happened. "Ship Life" was replaced by "Island Life."

We walked over to the patio, and Smitty and

Holiday started pushing tables together for everyone. We all sat down, and everyone immediately began pulling out their tablets and laptops. For crew members, Wi-Fi was gold, and fast Wi-Fi was a well-guarded secret. The ship did have Wi-Fi for the crew, but it was expensive and barely worked long enough to check your email. Eryn stuck her earpods in, held her phone up to her face, and let out a loud, excited shriek. She jumped out of her seat and walked a few steps away as she talked with the person on the other end. Holiday told Smitty and me that she called her sister whenever they came here.

"They are super close, and she is coming to cruise in a few weeks, so we had best prepare our eardrums... Can you imagine Eryn's energy doubled?" he said lovingly.

"Well, look who's back again," the waiter said as he came over with a big smile. "The usual for you ladies, I assume?" The girls nodded excitedly and introduced Smitty and me to the waiter. It turned out he was one of the crew members from the Vision that jumped ship. He used to be a bartender onboard and decided to quit halfway through his contract.

"I had enough of all the ship rules and dealing with the drunk passengers," he said. I gave him an understanding nod as I remembered the first auction and how I was getting hounded for the free champagne. It all seemed to have worked out because he said he couldn't be happier with island life. "And I get to see your beautiful faces every few weeks," he said to the dancer girls but focused more on Erika.

"Easy baby... She's halfway up the aisle," Anna said about Erika as she blushed at the comment.

The waiter commented what a shame it was and said he would get their drinks out soon. He handed Smitty and me the "special menu," as he called it. As I looked down the drink list, I realized each cocktail was named after a job onboard the cruise ship.

From the "Hotel Director," a stiff Long Island iced tea, to the "Tiny Dancer," which was a sex on the beach. As I read the name aloud, Anna rolled her eyes and told me to turn the menu over. The first drink on the back was the "Land-mark Questie." I laughed out loud and showed it to Smitty.

"Of course, we are dirty martinis," he commented.

Holiday was typing away on his laptop as Smitty reached over and started massaging his shoulder.

"Can we get out of manager mode, please?" he asked Holiday.

Smitty explained that he had been sending emails all morning to Vivace corporate headquarters. Holiday continued to type as he explained that the ship management was trying to schedule the dancers for extra social duties and library shifts. They also wanted the ballroom couple to teach several more ballroom dance classes for the passengers. And finally, they wanted Holiday to host the backstage tour of the Stardust Theater.

Holiday explained, "It clearly says in our contracts how many duties we are required to do, and none of those things are listed. If we say yes to any of it now, they will just keep asking for more. So, if I have to go to war with ship management, then I will," he said as he finished typing his email.

"Great. But do we need to start the war right now, babe?" Smitty asked.

Anna laughed and said Smitty and I were lucky

that we were "Questies" and not direct employees of Vivace.

"Otherwise, the same thing would be happening to you," Erika said.

I asked Erika where Marcello was, and she said he had to work but was planning to join us later. Then, a sly smile appeared on her face as she looked at me.

"What?" I asked. She said that Marcello mentioned that Serge had asked him if I would be with them.

"Seems like somebody has a little crush," Erika teased.

Now, I was the one who was blushing.

"Yeah, you better make that happen," Smitty said. "Because if you don't hit that, I totally will!" Which earned a raised eyebrow from Holiday. "What?! His cabin is bigger than yours, and he has a balcony!" Smitty said playfully, trying to get a rise out of Holiday.

"And how would you know he has a balcony?" Anna teased him with the question.

"Oh, she's sassy today," Smitty retorted at her.

A dirty martini didn't seem like a daytime drink, so I ordered the "Spa Girl," a piña colada, while Smitty and Holiday ordered the "VIP Concierge," a mimosa. The group continued discussing the pros and cons of Holiday's cabin versus the officer's cabins. The concept of dating crew members with their own cabins was not just a rumor; it was a real thing, and the nicer the cabin, the more competition. Eryn had finished her video call with her sister and returned to the table, joining in the conversation, saying that if I got with Serge, it would be an upgrade from bunking with the ice queen. I mentioned that I had invited Georgette, but she had declined.

"Shocking!" Eryn said facetiously. The girls went on to divulge the gossip about Georgette. She always got an Uber and disappeared for the whole day, and she was never seen at any of the crew hangouts, so the rumor was that she had a lover on the island. I remembered seeing Georgette's oversized bag and thinking it was a lot for just herself.

"Allegedly... and unsubstantiated," Holiday responded.

"I bet he's a hot Instagram model... or maybe a strict daddy... I can totally see her being into dominance," Eryn said. According to the girls, Georgette had never been with anyone onboard – no one was good enough. Smitty said if anyone knew, it should be me – her roommate. But I told him we didn't talk much; when we did, it was about work and nothing personal.

"To be continued," Smitty said as he downed the last of his mimosa, which was the first of many as the day went on. Smitty, Holiday, and I dipped in the pool while the girls sunbathed. I took time to call my parents and fill them in on everything. My mom seemed fascinated by the unique aspects of "Ship Life," while my dad was fixated on the safety drills and was grilling me with questions, just like the safety officer onboard. I joked, telling him that he was missing a career opportunity.

When I got off the phone, I turned around and realized many more crew members had shown up, including Marcello, laying with Erika on her lounge and caressing her leg. I got a bit excited and looked around to see if Serge was there, but I didn't see him. Eryn and Smitty laughed loudly at the swim-up bar – I had lost count of how many mimosas he had. "Ship Life" seemed to adhere to the common phrase "work hard, party harder."

Even with as much as Smitty had consumed, he was nowhere near as drunk as I would be if I had as many drinks as he did. Smitty was even more fun when he was tipsy. On our ride back to the ship, he cracked jokes and asked the Uber driver to turn up the radio while he sang along to the top forties.

Eryn was also less than sober as we walked down the pier back towards the ship, Smitty and her teetering with arms around each other and laughing loudly. Holiday was next to me, and I told him I hoped they didn't have a show tonight, to which he laughed and agreed. He told me the show that night was a guest entertainer and that it should be interesting because the woman called herself "Ventriloquist Barbie." That piqued my interest, but then I remembered Smitty and I had Guess the Price duty tonight.

Holiday laughed again and said it would be his job to sober Smitty up before then. But first, we had to get him and Eryn past security. As we neared the gangway, Holiday walked up to Smitty, took his arm from Eryn, and held his hand. "Just make sure she doesn't trip in front of security," he said as they walked on.

Eryn paused as they passed until I was at her side. She tilted her sunglasses down to look at me. "Hey, sexy bitch," she said, lightly smacking my behind, and we both laughed. "Sorry your boyfriend didn't show up today, but I have a feeling you'll see him sooner than later!" She playfully said and handed the security officer her crew card.

I noticed the officer looking suspiciously at her, so I quickly threw my card into his hand and gave him a big smile, asking how his day was and trying to make small talk, which earned me nothing but a deadpan stare. Security, indeed, was not very friendly, but at least I accomplished my task of getting a drunk Eryn onboard without too much suspicion.

In the past, some crew members had gotten so drunk while out in port that they were flagged and breathalyzed when going through security. In fact, some had missed the ship altogether. That could be another reason some crew members came to live on the island. You were immediately fired if you missed the ship or blew over the limit. You got what was called the "Six O'Clock Knock," which meant you got a knock at 6 a.m. in the next port of call and were kicked off the ship and left to figure out your situation.

That thought scared me a bit, and as I watched

Eryn walk towards the pat-down lady, I panicked. Eryn's turn came up just as I reached her. She strutted up to the female security officer, threw her hands up, and said melodiously, "Assuming the position!"

My anxiety flared but dissolved quickly as the officer finished the pat-down and let her move on. Eryn could keep it together when she needed to. I picked up my bag as it popped out the other end of the security scanner. Smitty was waiting for me as I came through.

"See you at GTP in an hour," he said as he smiled at me.

I giggled and asked him if he would be able to do Guess the Price that soon, to which he raised an eyebrow. Then he popped his sunglasses back on, saying, "I do my best work with a buzz," as he sauntered on.

VII

CHAPTER 7

Guess the Price that evening was hilarious. Smitty wasn't wrong about doing his best work while buzzed. He was practically dancing around the table, throwing the tiny guessing slips into passing hands and encouraging them to take a guess. I joined in with his antics because it certainly made the time pass quicker. We were set up in the central atrium, so there was a lot of activity and live music. The ballroom-dancing couples were back, putting the rest of the passengers trying to dance to shame. Some elderly ladies approached Smitty and pulled him onto the dance floor. He didn't put up too much of a fight, and I laughed and clapped as I looked on.

"Smithsonian certainly is the crowd-pleaser, isn't he," a voice said behind me. Startled, I turned around to see Georgette in another killer outfit and a slight grin on her face. "It's difficult to reprimand someone when they look so effortlessly happy... do try to help him reign it in," she said to me, placing a stack of newly printed guessing slips in my hand and grabbing the written guesses out of the box as she glided away. Then I remembered we were supposed to be doubling our number count from the previous session. I walked back to the table and placed the slips out nicely on the table.

I was startled by another voice behind me – this time, an Italian accent. "And do you come with the art, if I guess correctly?" Serge asked, smiling at me as I quickly spun around to meet his handsome gaze. "Ciao, Bella." He winked at me as I smiled and tried not to blush.

"Try one I haven't heard," I replied, having heard that line already from several male guests at different levels of intoxication. Serge was the first man that I didn't mind asking me the question. He apologized for missing me today at the beach club, explaining that he couldn't get away from work. I told him he missed a fun time, as I stepped closer to him, trying to look a touch alluring.

"Some had too much fun, no?" he said as he looked at Smitty on the dance floor. I gave a slight shrug. Serge mentioned that many of the officers were planning a night out to the passenger lounges and asked if I'd be joining. I said that it all depended on how tonight went... if I didn't get enough guesses to please Georgette, then I would probably have to do GTP most nights.

"Mamma Mia!" he exclaimed and grabbed a stack of guessing slips from the table, beginning to pass them out to everyone in the atrium. Using all his charm and playing up his accent, he motioned everyone towards me to come and place a guess. Before long, I had a line in front of the Guess the Price table. In between speaking with the guests, I looked into the atrium, where Serge was watching from a distance. He blew me a kiss and walked on. Smitty had finished dancing with the ladies and returned, looking down the line of guests amazed.

"What are you giving away over here?!" he asked in a sassy tone. I laughed and looked on as the line Serge created grew longer, as more guests were curious about what was happening. "It's like herding cattle," Smitty whispered to me as he grabbed for guessing slips and went to talk with the gathering crowd at the end of the line.

Georgette looked more than pleased counting all the guesses from our shift. "Well done," she said with an approving look. She exuded such confidence that it was as if the sun was shining on you when Georgette showed her approval. We both smiled and thanked her, and she continued and looked at Smitty, "If this is the result of entertaining those thirsty women on the dance floor, Smithsonian, then by all means, continue." Smitty blushed just a little and glanced at me quickly. I didn't see the point of revealing my secret weapon of the attractive Italian First Officer being involved. It was a win for me as long as Georgette was happy and the team was working well.

After a few days, I realized that "Ship Life" felt like you were flooring the gas pedal and accelerating your life exponentially. Days began to blur together between my work schedule with the gallery and my training schedule for the ship. I was looking forward to our next port, Hilo, on the Big

Island. According to the crew, there wasn't much to do unless you were on a passenger tour. A small, cramped shuttle took us to the center of town, and the crew took over the local coffee shop to use the good Wi-Fi. It looked like a second crew mess with all the different departments sitting together throughout. I met several new crew members from the photo gallery and front desk.

Soon enough, all the gossip and drama about the current passengers came out – the good, the bad, and the unbearable passengers. After hearing the horror stories of the problematic guests they had to deal with, I wasn't sure how the front desk people did their jobs. So far, my biggest dramas had been over them wanting more free champagne or freebies from the art department. It began pouring down rain shortly after, so most of us went back to the ship. I was a bit disappointed with the weather, but I reminded myself that we would be back and there would be plenty of time to explore Hilo later. As Staff, we could sign up to escort the passenger tours for free, which I was very excited to do once my ship training was complete.

As uneventful as that day was, the evening that followed was unforgettable. We did our usual evening gallery hours, which mainly seemed quiet as the guests were busy with dinner and the shows and generally tired from their touring all day. Since we were so successful at our GTP shift, Georgette allowed us a "lighter" schedule where Smitty and I took turns in 30-minute shifts. This time, the table was set up in one of the hallways leading to the dining room, so we could catch the crowd as they went to dinner. It was also across from the bathrooms, and it shocked me how many people did not wash their hands. There were constant health reminders for the passengers that germs spread quickly onboard, which obviously was being ignored. There were even two housekeepers placed at the entrance of the dining rooms to spray each person's hand with sanitizer. The ladies were petite but made up for it with their bubbly personalities as they excitedly greeted every guest and sprayed hands. One of the girls even invented an impromptu tune to accompany her spraying. It honestly looked exhausting to keep up that level of energy - I probably looked like a stone-cold bitch in comparison to them. I had been accused more than a few times of having a "resting bitch face," which meant I looked angry or displeased when I simply have no expression... or at least I thought I didn't. So now I was constantly trying to be aware of what my facial features were doing... overly smiling at the guests as they walked by. Another lady exited the bathroom without hand-washing, and she got excited as she saw me and the Guess the Price painting on the easel. She picked up one of the short golf pencils on the table, quickly grabbed several slips, and turned her back to me.

I'll be sure to sanitize the pencil in her unwashed hand; I thought as she slipped at least four guesses into the box – thinking I didn't notice she was guessing multiple times. I had seen this woman each night of GTP doing the same thing. Some of these guests were comical – they loved anything free. It didn't bother me because it increased my guess count, and hopefully, they would be at the auction to see if they won... that was the whole point of doing Guess the Price – getting people to the auction.

Smitty came to relieve me and announced it was our final hour. I reached into the box and took the guesses I had accrued to deliver to Georgette in the gallery. As I did, Smitty asked if I was excited for tonight and explained that many of the

Staff picked one night for each cruise to dress up and go out to the passenger bars. Holiday and the dancers would be out along with several others. Then I remembered Serge mentioning it.

"Well, then, I am totally there!" I said as I walked back to the gallery. After we closed, Smitty said he was going to his cabin for a "costume change." I followed suit and returned to mine. Georgette wasn't there, but our cabin steward had dropped off her dry cleaning – Staff were allowed to have stewards assigned to clean our cabins – a privilege the rest of the crew did not, and another reason for the divide between the two. Managers were allowed dry cleaning, which defined the class system even more. I found it interesting what defined classism onboard a ship instead of "Land Life." I quickly flipped through Georgette's designer outfits with an enviable eye.

How did she have all these? Was it through her family money or her Instagram influencer swag? I wondered.

She was still such a closed book to me, and I wasn't sure how to endear myself more – she still called me Miss Bradley and seemed to favor "Smithsonian" over me. Smitty never had pushed back on the nickname and now even seemed to enjoy it a little.

I opened my closet door—it barely passed for a closet due to its size, but I had managed to cram most of my clothes in it. I debated what to wear for our night out and then decided on something a bit sexier in case I saw Serge—he said he would be out, so I chose my favorite blue cocktail dress. It was a vibrant shade of blue that stood out in a crowd and fit me in all the right places. At least it had always been a hit on a night out in LA.

A loud noise went off, echoing in the small cabin, and made me jump out of my skin. The horrendous brick of a deck phone was ringing. I could not get used to the horrible thing! Smitty was laughing on the other end because he knew it scared me every time it rang. He told me where we were meeting and said I had ten minutes. I took a deep breath to shake off my scare and looked at my reflection in the mirror. I ran a comb through my hair, put on a smokey eye with my mascara, and reapplied my lipstick. I finally remembered my name badge, which didn't help the look, but I had been reprimanded enough already for forgetting to put it on. I looked at the printed badge,

"Breanne – Art Associate – Hollywood, CA." It was becoming difficult not to roll my eyes when the passengers saw I was from Hollywood. I got so many remarks about "tinsel town" and glamor and how "bougie" and elite it must be. If they only knew how trashy it could be. My life in Hollywood felt so distant after only a short time onboard the Vision, I thought as I put on my stilettos, had one last look in the mirror, and walked out the door.

The metal floor of the I-95 caused my stilettos to echo loudly down the corridor, which made everyone turn to look. It reminded me of my first day onboard when Georgette clicked down the hallway as she brought us onboard. I received a few whistles and catcalls, which I ignored as I made my way to the guest area, which was carpeted and tiled. The loud clicking still echoed in my head. Transitioning from the clinical white of the crew area to the vibrant neon and bold patterns of the passenger space was always a bit jarring... like stepping into Wonderland, just like Alice. In a way, a cruise ship was "Wonderland" for the passengers... a floating theme park.

As I walked through the smoky haze and the din of Vegas-like sounds in the casino, full of people at the slot machines and card tables, I caught the eye of some of the crew. The casino seemed to be staffed mainly by Eastern European men who kept to themselves. I made my way to the Explorer's Lounge—the same lounge where we held the auctions. It looked completely different at night, without all the artwork and auction setup. Indeed, there were numerous staff members mixed in with the passengers. It was a formal night onboard, so many of the guests were dressed up. Some chose to ignore the dress code and were still wearing casual wear, but all the crew members were decked out.

The Captain's officers were adorned in gold epaulets and knots, showcasing their rank on their white formal jackets and gloves. Several spa girls were gathered at the bar in cocktail dresses, their hair swept up in lavish hairdos and entirely made-up faces. At the far end of the bar, I spotted Smitty and Holiday dressed in bowties and tailored blazers. Eryn and Anna were next to them, holding glasses of champagne. Eryn was even more poured into her dress than I was, her flowing red locks falling past her bare shoulders onto the red fabric of her dress—she looked like a real-life version of Jessica Rabbit. I admired how free she was with her body and confidence. Anna was in a black corset and tight leather leggings. She turned as I approached and outstretched an arm to hug me.

"Va va voom!" Eryn exclaimed as she saw me and took a sip of champagne.

"Tens across the board!" Holiday followed up. Smitty agreed, saying we all came to slay and gave a wink. Holiday asked what I wanted to drink and said it was his treat. Before I could answer, Smitty chimed in, "She wants a dirty martini." In no time, Smitty and I were carefully clinking our full martinis together.

"Is this meant for anyone specific?" he asked, motioning to my dress.

"Just trying to keep up with all these fashion girlies," I replied. Smitty took a sip of his martini and turned me around to survey the room, saying it was a good turnout.

The jazz band was center-stage, playing live music as the passengers and a few crew members danced. Many of the front desk staff were seated at tables to the left of the stage, dressed in their formal blue uniforms and chatting with each other. The spa girls had returned from the bar and sat a few tables away. As my eyes kept moving across the room, I saw two women at a high-top table in front of one of the many large lounge windows that looked out to the ocean. The light from a full moon glittered on the sea and silhouetted the women. Seated with her legs crossed and wearing a flowing gown of black sequins that almost touched the floor from her high perch was Georgette. She was holding a martini as well and talking to the woman seated with her.

"Oh, come on! She outdoes herself every single time!" I said to Smitty, and he replied that she couldn't help herself, saying something like, "Perfection simply can't allow itself to fail."

I rolled my eyes at him and said, "Someone is fangirling... obsessed much?"

"There are far worse things to be obsessed with," he retorted.

He wasn't wrong. If anyone embodied perfection, it was Georgette. Far be it from me to judge her for wearing a dress that looked like it belonged on the red carpet at the Academy Awards.

I looked on the other side of the room and saw Erika seated in a dark booth with Marcello and his gold epaulets. Several officers were seated with them in the booth, and I realized Serge was there as well, facing away from me. A rush of excitement filled me, which Smitty must have clocked.

"Oh yeah, your future husband is over there. I'm calling best man right now... just saying," he said as he took another sip. Some passengers approached us, recognizing Holiday and the girls from the production show, and gushed over how good they were. They said thank you, and I smiled as Smitty—not in the production cast—also said thank you.

"What? I'm cast adjacent," he joked. He did have the build of a dancer, but he had mentioned a few days ago that he lacked the coordination to pick up the choreography. I also had a similar issue. Smitty and I were alike in so many ways that he already felt like a brother to me.

The band finished their song. The singer thanked everyone for their applause. She looked stunning, wearing a tailored purple jumpsuit that beautifully contrasted her black skin and her large earrings glittering in the stage lighting. She looked over at our group and announced to the guests that they were lucky enough to have the production cast in the room. She continued on the microphone, declaring it was time for a quick break, and perhaps Dan Holiday wanted to entertain everyone with a tune. The guests started clapping and looked back at us. Holiday smiled, and Eryn patted him on the shoulder, saying, "Go and prance, my fabulous show pony!" Holiday walked up to the stage and took the jazz singer's microphone. He whispered something to the band and took center stage. After a pause, he began to sing.

Several couples took the dance floor, including Erika and Marcello. I watched them as they looked deep into each other's eyes.

"Okay, forget your wedding... those two are definitely beating you up the aisle," Smitty whispered in my ear. I gave him a light slap on the wrist, and we both giggled together. "Speaking of..." Smitty trailed off as Serge walked up to me and outstretched his hand.

"Dance with me?" he asked in his divine accent. Smitty raised both eyebrows with excitement and walked away, leaving me to be whisked onto the dance floor.

The passengers were right—Holiday did have a fantastic voice. Butterflies fluttered in my stomach as Serge's hand touched the small of my back. I could smell his cologne as he pulled me in close to him.

"I'm happy to see you don't have to do your guessing game all night," he said as he gazed into my eyes. I giggled at his calling it a "guessing game" and told him I never got to thank him for helping me with my game.

"You wouldn't need any help if you wore this dress when you did it," he said as his gaze moved over my body, making me blush.

We talked briefly about my experience onboard and how I liked the art department. I was in such a surreal moment, dancing with a gorgeous man to such a romantic song in the middle of the ocean on a moonlit night. I asked about his family and growing up in Italy. He mentioned having a large family and suggested that I should visit and experience how lovely his town was. His family loved it when he brought beautiful women home, he told me with a mischievous grin. I asked him how many beautiful women he had brought home so far, to which he laughed and said he was joking and that his family was still waiting. I had never been to Italy, and being shown around by Serge sounded idyllic. It sounded so cliché, but I was undoubtedly developing a big crush on the tall, dark, and handsome Italian first officer. It felt like a scene from an old romantic movie. We slowly made our way around the dance floor, passing Smitty and Eryn, who started dancing together and ended up next to Erika and Marcello. Erika looked over and gave me a big, knowing smile, which I returned.

Holiday finished his song. As everyone around us clapped, we stood frozen in place for what felt like forever. His hand was still on my back, and I could feel the heat from his hand through my dress. Those dark eyes continued to look deep into mine and had me slightly hypnotized. Back from her break, the jazz singer took the microphone from Holiday and began another party song. Serge finally released his hand from my back. My left hand was still in his from our dance, and he raised it to his lips and gave it a light kiss. I was lost for words as he bowed his head, then looked up and winked at me before returning to the booth with the other officers. Smitty and Eryn walked over to me.

"Wow, are you pregnant yet?!" Eryn asked and continued, "I know I would be after getting eye-fucked like that!" she laughed loudly at her own comment as we walked off the dance floor.

"Round two!" Smitty chimed as we got to the bar.

Holiday joined us and commented, "Wow... you two looked like you danced straight out of a movie."

"Okay, everyone calm down," I responded.

Eryn laughed again and, in her thick Scottish brogue, loudly announced, "Oh please, dinnae act like your panties aren't wet, you lucky bitch!"

Smitty nearly choked on the sip he just took from his martini.

My cheeks became instantly warm. "Oh my god, Eryn!" I exclaimed as I quickly looked around to see if anyone heard. Holiday laughed and said that was tame for Eryn.

She gave a playful shrug and said, "What? Mine would be soaked... that is if I was wearing any!"

I turned around to set my martini on the bar and came face to face with Georgette.

"Not wasting any time, are we, Miss Bradley," she said with a slightly raised eyebrow and a slight curve at the edge of her mouth. I wasn't sure if she was asking a question or stating a fact. I decided to move past it and commented on how stunning her dress was.

"It's Balmain," she responded and introduced me to the woman she had been sitting with earlier. She was the Spa Manager—a South African woman named Lauren. We shook hands, and she said she saw me in the atrium a few nights ago.

"You and your dance partner were drawing quite the crowd!" she said. Georgette gave me a knowing look, and I nervously laughed, wondering if my secret was out of the bag. Lauren said she gave the art department a generous discount if I wanted any services.

"Just stay away from the botox and fillers," Georgette quipped.

Smitty popped in and raised his martini to Georgette, "Fierce!" he exclaimed about her dress. Georgette raised her martini, and their glasses clinked together. Smitty said we were finishing this round of drinks and then heading down to the crew bar and asked Georgette and Lauren if they were joining.

"Not tonight, Smithsonian," she said, sipping her martini. A large ring on her finger glittered in the light as she put her martini glass down. "And do remember that boat drill is tomorrow... try and keep it to a sensible number," she said, looking at the martini in Smitty's hand. He raised his glass again, and the ladies said good night and walked away from the bar. We rejoined the dancers, who were now standing with some of the spa girls. I started chatting with one of them, Emma—she was also from South Africa and was on her tenth contract! I mentioned how impressive that was, and she said Diviner was her life.

"Diviner?" I asked, and she explained that Diviner was the name of the spa company and that it operated similarly to Landmark Quest. According to her, many spa girls transitioned from spa to art, but she was a "Diviner for life," she said proudly.

Smitty heard her and responded, "Nothing finer than a Diviner!"

"But if you want the best, go Landmark Quest!" Emma responded cheerfully. They both laughed, and Smitty raised his glass, "Cheers, girl!"

I asked where that saying came from. Emma explained it had been around forever, originating from the stereotype that the spa girls and art staff slept around a lot.

"I mean... it's not wrong," Smitty said as he

finished his martini. Eryn came over and put her arms around us, "Are we ready for the crew bar, darlings?!"

VIII

CHAPTER 8

The crew bar at night was a whole different vibe. As we strutted down the metal hallway, the clacking of our heels blended with the thumping beats from the bar. Once inside, the dimly lit space was alive with colored party lights, and the loud music made conversation a shouting match. Eryn grabbed my hand and led me to a booth near the bar, where Smitty soon joined us with more martinis, followed by Holiday with a tray of shots. I wasn't a fan of shots, but I didn't want to miss out, so I downed it while Eryn cheered – though I couldn't hear a word over the music. I was unsure what the shot was, but my disgusted face made Smitty laugh.

The bar was packed with crew members from different departments, unwinding after a long day. I was shocked when I learned about the long working hours for many of the other departments. Most of them hardly had any time to get off the ship and enjoy the ports. It made me wonder if it affected their mental health. I would be going crazy by now, I thought. It reminded me of a retail job I used to have at the Savannah Mall during college. My hours were so long, with hardly any breaks, and I was miserable. I couldn't help thinking their schedule was similar, and I had a lot of sympathy for them.

The housekeeping crew chatted over a table filled with beer bottles, and the galley crew in the booth beside them, still in their work coveralls, joined in communal cheers. Despite the warnings from my training the past mornings about alcohol limits onboard, it seemed like everyone was letting loose. In one corner, there was a glass box filled with people surrounded by smoke – Anna stood in there with several others, all smoking cigarettes, the designated smoking spot for the crew onboard.

One of the spa girls shared stories about her ex, a chain smoker who practically lived there, and how she nearly asphyxiated herself to be with him.

It was karaoke night, and Smitty leaned over to talk loudly in my ear, saying the Filipinos were all amazing.

"If karaoke in LA is like American Idol, this is Eurovision!" he exclaimed and then asked what I was going to sing. I told him it was a hard no. I was just getting comfortable with public speaking, and there was no way I would be singing in front of strangers any time soon. Georgette had already mentioned having a meeting to see which art seminars Smitty and I were going to present on the upcoming cruises, which I was not looking forward to.

As the night went on, I could feel the martinis kicking in. Smitty was right – the Filipinos were outstanding. They sang everything from current popular songs to classics from various decades. There were other microphones on stage for others who wanted to join them. I was surprised by how communal an activity karaoke was here. In LA, it was a way for singers to be "discovered," and joining in on their performance would undoubtedly get you bounced from the bar. But here, there seemed to be no such rules or boundaries.

The next song in the karaoke lineup was "A Whole New World" from Aladdin, and Smitty and Eryn couldn't contain their excitement. They erupted into screams, and before I knew it, Eryn leaped over me and dashed to the stage with Smitty in tow. I laughed uncontrollably as they struggled to keep up with the main singer, who looked slightly perturbed by their impromptu participation. But soon enough, even he was chuckling along with us at the sheer absurdity of the situation. Holiday leaned over and quipped in my ear, "There's a reason Eryn dances and doesn't sing."

I met a bunch of new faces, though their names were a blur thanks to the drinks and the loud music. As closing time approached, Holiday discreetly informed us that security would be coming to the bar soon, so we better head back to our cabins to avoid any trouble.

"Okay, Dad," Smitty joked as he stood up with Holiday and winked at me. He wasn't far off, though. His boyfriend did seem like a protective father figure to the dancers.

As I walked back to my cabin, the dancer girls

were in front of me, teetering in their stilettos. I would have been close to doing the same if Smitty wasn't escorting me on his arm. The girls turned down their hallway. "Good night, bitches!" Eryn yelled as she opened her door and fell into the cabin.

"She is a party," I said as Smitty and Holiday walked me to my cabin. I thanked them for a fabulous night as I struggled to get my key card in the slot to unlock the door. It was pitch black when I finally got inside the cabin.

I turned my iPhone flashlight on and set it on the table. I was trying to be as quiet as I could, taking my heels off, but in my intoxicated state, I lost my balance and fell into the closet door. A hushed expletive escaped my lips as I hit the door with a thud.

Suddenly, Georgette's voice in the dark broke the silence, "If it isn't Cinderella, extremely late from the ball." The lights in the cabin popped on, revealing her arm outstretched to the light switch on the wall next to her bed and lifting one side of her eye mask. I apologized and said I would try to be quieter.

"Oh, do carry on so you can see. We don't need you breaking your little neck... it's far too much paperwork for me to fill out," she said as she sat up and adjusted her satin pillows behind her. I looked at her, unsure if she was serious, and she raised her eyebrows and let out a "ha-ha."

I giggled and felt a sigh of relief.

"I assume the valiant Prince Holiday and company introduced you to the watering hole known as the crew bar...it certainly smells like it," she said. I leaned against the small desk, removed my heels, and unzipped my dress.

"You missed an enjoyable time!" I said.

She looked at me and grinned, "Yes, I'm sure Smithsonian's karaoke performance was no doubt riveting!" Then she laughed – she actually laughed! Even her laugh sounded proper. I immediately started laughing as well...almost in shock. I sat on the edge of the desk and accidentally knocked over one of her fancy perfume bottles.

"Oh shit! Sorry!" I said as I put it upright. "Where do all of these come from?" I asked as I looked at all of the perfumes and jewelry shining under the desk light.

Before she could answer, I saw an ornate gold

frame with a photograph of an elegant, elderly couple standing outside in front of a grand-looking building.

"Oh, are these your parents?!" I asked excitedly.

"Yes, that is Mother and Papa," she responded.

I picked up the frame and showered her with questions, "Are they back in England? What do they do? Is that your house?!"

Her smile faded. "So many questions for two in the morning, Miss Bradley. Please put it down," she said as she motioned back to the desk. I apologized and said I wasn't trying to pry.

She put the silk pillows flat and laid down. As she pulled her eye mask back to her eyes, she said, "Do turn out the light when you are done." She ended our quick chat with that. Even though it was fast, it was probably the most relatable conversation we had so far.

IX

CHAPTER 9

The following morning was absolutely brutal. It was my very first "boat drill." A series of obnoxiously loud horns blared from the speaker on our ceiling, jolting me awake at 8 a.m. I hit my head again, but this time much harder, prompting me to let out a string of loud expletives. My head was pounding, and I immediately regretted having that shot last night. Glancing down from my top bunk to Georgette's neatly made lower bunk, I noticed she was nowhere to be seen. The horns were still blaring as I dragged myself out of bed. After popping two headache pills, I threw on a pair of sweatpants along with my Landmark Quest polo shirt. I hastily tied my hair into a messy bun and slipped on my sunglasses. Grabbing the fluorescent life vest from the top of the closet, I headed out the door, not in the mood to simulate a ship sinking.

Walking down the I-95 corridor, I tried to recall where to go for the emergency drill. I followed the flow of crew members up a staircase and found myself back in the casino. Crew members lined up at their stations, and it dawned on me that my station was in the Explorer's Lounge, where we usually held the auctions. In this hypothetical scenario, we were mid-auction when the ship suddenly plunged.

As I entered the lounge, I scanned my crew card to be marked in attendance. The officer in charge asked for my safety card, which I had forgotten. He rolled his eyes, and I apologized, explaining it was my first drill. He asked about my department, and upon learning that I was in the art department, he thrust a binder and megaphone into my hands. Opening the binder, I found a page containing a script of emergency announcements and instructions on how to put on the life vest. He then placed a small wooden platform in the middle of the lounge and looked at me impatiently. I felt bewildered by the lack of instruction on what to do during this "sinking" while he barked at me to stand on the platform and read.

My head still pounding, I fumbled with the vest, trying to figure out how it went on and where the straps went. I managed to snap the buckle into place, but the vest felt odd. The officer sighed in aggravation and came over to adjust it, snapping the buckle in place again. He promptly grabbed my sunglasses off my face and pointed at the platform. I struggled to see my feet over the life vest as I stepped up.

This is what pregnant women must feel like all the time, I thought.

Anxiously, I opened the binder and started reciting the script, only to realize that the megaphone wasn't on. Embarrassed, I inspected it, looking for the power switch. Flipping a switch at the bottom, it screeched loudly with an awful feedback sound, making everyone wince—everyone except for me, who let out the word "shit," which echoed loudly throughout the room. Winces turned into chuckles from the crowd, mortifying me even more. I adjusted the megaphone and began racing through the script.

So much for speaking well, I thought. After finishing, I jumped off the box, rushed to the back of the room, and put the binder and megaphone on the bar. I threw my sunglasses back on in an attempt to disappear.

Can this ship just freaking pretend to sink already? I wished to myself.

After standing around for what felt like ages and enduring more announcements throughout the ship, we were led outside onto the deck, where we would board the life rafts in a real emergency. There, we were told to wait for further orders. My anxiety flared as I imagined that everyone around me was thinking what a mess I was before. I was beginning to feel paranoid and claustrophobic. Scanning the area for a path to the back of the group, I spotted Smitty and Holiday—they both stood out in the crowd due to their tall stature. I politely pushed my way over to them, finding them leaning against the wall railing with their sunglasses on. Eryn was next to Holiday, her head on his shoulder, almost looking asleep.

"Thank goodness I found you guys!" I said excitedly.

"Morning, Sunshine," Smitty responded in a less-than-cheerful tone. He was as hungover as I felt, wearing the neon yellow hat he had received on the first day, which "didn't look nearly as bad," I told him.

"I cannot be asked to care this morning," he said as I leaned in next to him against the railing on the wall of the ship's exterior. I told him how embarrassed I was about completely bombing earlier, and he chuckled.

"I would gladly speak on a megaphone than wear this ugly hat...at least with a megaphone, you can order bitches around," he said and then began chugging water from a large 1-liter bottle.

I told him I wished Georgette had woken me before she left so I could have been more prepared. Then, I remembered my conversation with her last night.

"I got her to laugh!" I told Smitty enthusiastically.

As we gazed over the water, he asked, "Are you sure she wasn't laughing at you, babe?" I clicked my tongue at him and playfully smacked the brim of his hat down.

"Hey!" he exclaimed, about to continue when a whistle sounded, and a voice barked at us to stand at attention.

Eryn's head jolted up as if she actually had been sleeping on Holiday's shoulder, and everyone stood straight up away from the railing—I followed suit. The officers formed us into straight lines with enough space between them so they could walk through and look at each of us. Several officers in white uniforms started filing through the ranks, stopping randomly at certain people and saying something to them. Being in the back, I couldn't hear the officers over everyone in front of me. Smitty whispered to me to take off my sunglasses as they approached.

"Wrong! Captain's Court tomorrow!" I heard an officer yell at a crew member a few lines away. Some people jumped at the sound of his yelling.

"What are they doing?" I asked Smitty.

He said they were randomly asking questions from the safety manual, and if you didn't know the answer, it was a strike, and you had to go to Captain's Court. I remembered him briefly mentioning it in our Uber on the way to the ship. "Captain's Court" was just as it sounded... If a crew member did something wrong, they had to go up to the bridge and have a "trial" with the Captain and his officers.

"Just for getting an answer wrong?" I responded.

"It's a total power trip," Smitty said as he rolled his eyes. I saw an officer in the corner of my eye start walking down our line. Everyone stiffened up and looked straight ahead. I suddenly got very nervous. I skimmed the safety manual when I received it, but very little stuck with me.

Just think positively, I thought to myself. *He will probably stop at Smitty or Holiday because they stand out so much, right?*

Wrong.

The white uniform stopped directly in front of me. Panic came over me instantly.

What was he going to ask me? How do I get out of it?! I asked myself nervously. My fight-or-flight instincts were battling until I noticed the exquisite tailoring on the white shirt around a pair of beautiful tanned biceps, and I looked up to see Serge's gorgeous dark eyes. I immediately relaxed a bit and smiled in relief.

"Oh, hi there!" I said to his handsome but emotionless face.

Serge did not smile or show any sign that he knew me. There was an awkward silence, and I heard Smitty hold his breath beside me. Serge started speaking with his Italian accent.

"How many lifeboats are there onboard?" he asked.

I drew a blank...I thought back to the pages of the safety manual and remembered the page with the itemized list of numbers, but they all ran together.

Think, Bree...what do I know? I asked myself. I knew there were roughly 5,000 passengers onboard...I tried to do some math but didn't remember how many people each boat held. The silence was growing louder the longer I took to answer.

"Thirty?" I finally answered, nervously.

There was another long silence as he continued to look me dead in the eyes, and then he finally asked, "You are sure?" I hesitated, about to guess again, and then thought, stick with your gut, so I answered yes. Another long pause... Smitty was tapping his foot nervously on the floor.

"Wrong!" Serge shouted. I jumped as he said

it. "There are twenty-five lifeboats onboard." I grinned sheepishly at him and asked if I could try another question. "So, we schedule you for Captain's Court, yes," he said, not as a question, pulling his clipboard and pen out. I grimaced.

This is just not my day, I thought.

Serge looked up from his clipboard, "Unless... you would rather have me take you out?" We locked eyes again, and I laughed nervously. Before I could answer, he started walking on as he whispered, "Ciao, Bella," and gave me a wink.

"You are one lucky bitch, bitch," Smitty said as we both exhaled.

Eryn leaned over in line, "He's taking you out for a private disciplinary hearing!" she whispered loudly and mimicked a whipping motion. I smiled and realized I had gone from mortified to a near nervous breakdown to being on cloud nine. My headache was gone. The ship horn blared, announcing the end of the crew drill and making everyone wince.

Smitty jumped when the horn sounded, spilling water out of his bottle. "Ugh, I certainly did not miss this part," he stated, yanking off his neon hat. I was nearly run over by a sea of bodies and life vests from the rest of the crew shuffling inside as we walked over to the ship's railing. It was gorgeous outside. I looked out and realized we were not docked, but I could see land close in the distance. I asked where we were, and, in unison, everyone answered, "Kona." I turned to Smitty, asking what we were doing today, and he took another big sip of water.

"Sleeping," he said excitedly.

"Sleeping?!" I responded, incredulously.

He wrapped his arms around Holiday from behind, "Or not sleeping..."

He winked at me. Holiday turned around and hugged Smitty back, "Plus, it's tendering today," he said.

"Tenders," I found out, were smaller boats that sailed out to our ship anchored in the deeper water and shuttled everyone over to the land, and apparently, they took forever, so a lot of the crew didn't get off the ship.

Eryn chimed in, "But we have to go find you a frock for your big date!"

Smitty looked offended, "How are you so chipper suddenly?"

"Sex talk revitalizes me, darling," Eryn replied

seductively. Smitty rolled his eyes, and we all laughed.

I met Eryn on I-95, in the same security line as last time. Anna and Erika turned around as I walked up, both giddy with excitement.

"We heard about the boat drill!" they exclaimed. I smiled as they asked for details, but it was hard to describe over the security officer's loud shouts for everyone to stay quiet. We made it through the security pat-downs, and I handed my crew card to the same grumpy officer as before. He started to ask for my I-95 when my face popped up on his computer screen. He turned to me with his usual nonplussed look.

"The American," he said flatly, handing me back my card. I gave him my biggest smile as I walked past, deciding I would kill him with kindness every time I saw him.

A metal staircase led us down to a platform floating on the water. It was very windy, causing the platform to bob frantically against the smaller boat. Two large men—one on the platform and one in the tender boat—helped everyone board. Eryn hopped on in front of me, and the men made me wait a moment for the waves to calm. Before I knew it, the platform guy grabbed one of my arms while the other man grabbed the other, guiding me onto the boat. I kept my balance as the tender jostled on the waves, making my way to the bench where Eryn was sitting.

"I love getting a manhandling in the morning," she joked as I sat down.

"So, I'm betting physical touch is your love language," I teased as the engine fired up and we pulled away from the cruise ship. Anna leaned forward to mention that Eryn used all the love languages on all types of people, cheekily pinching her leg. Eryn laughed and swatted her hand away.

The boat was mostly filled with guests, identifiable by their ship cards around their necks with "Vivace Vision" printed on lanyards. An elderly couple sat on the bench next to me; the lady, wearing a pink visor, gazed out at the ocean, while her husband, head back and bobbing with the waves, seemed asleep—hopefully, not dead. Across from us sat a younger couple with two teenagers. Both teenagers were heads down, scrolling on their phones. The mother was on her phone, angrily yelling at someone about a shipment not being delivered. The husband, the only one not on a device, instead stared directly at Eryn's chest. Eryn seemed unfazed, shrugging at me when she noticed. Then, catching my eye, the husband and I awkwardly looked away. As the boat lurched from a big wave, alarming many guests, the teenagers and the mother remained unfazed.

"So, what do you girls do onboard? Let me guess...you're the dancers, right?" the husband leaned in, posing the question to all of us. All three girls smiled and nodded. He leaned in further, away from his wife, and continued, "They finally let you girls off the ship, huh? What do you do to blow off steam? Go to the beach?" The girls answered briefly with polite agreement. He pressed on, "Yeah, I can see you work hard on those tans... especially you," he looked directly at Eryn. Anna and Erika shifted uncomfortably, while Eryn got a sly look in her eye, leaning forward and subtly adjusting her chest.

"Well..." she began to reply when the wife abruptly clicked her phone shut.

Cutting Eryn off, she exclaimed, "You ladies must be the dancers! Oh, how could you not be with such beautiful bodies... Honey, don't they have great bodies?" she asked her husband, flipping her hair.

I couldn't tell if she was serious or calling him out. She continued before he could answer, talking about their home and how many cruises they had done. I started to tune her out, and the husband slumped back on the bench. The woman was still talking as the boat reached the dock.

"It was so nice chatting with you girls!" she exclaimed as she stood up and motioned the kids to get off the boat. The husband glanced back at us as he exited.

"So nice talking with you!" Anna mocked in a high-pitched nasal voice.

"You can tell who wears the pants there," Eryn remarked as she hopped off the boat.

As we walked down the pier towards town, they admitted that it happens all the time.

"I mean, they can't help themselves," Eryn said as she pulled her blouse over her head. Her long red locks spilled down her bare shoulders over her bikini top, paired with a sheer sarong around her waist.

"Were you really about to flirt with that guy?" I asked her.

"Oh, I give 'em a quick runaround to raise their spirits... he obviously wasn't getting it from her! Oh! I heard a rumor that the next cruise is a swingers charter!" she said excitedly.

Erika explained that a charter was when a large group bought out all or most of the ship. "Ship Life" never ceased to amaze me.

What would a swingers cruise be like? I asked myself.

As we strolled down the quaint main street of Kona, I could smell the salty tang of the ocean mixed with the sweet aroma of tropical blooms. People were renting paddleboards and paddling out into the ocean from a small beach.

"Are we shopping then eating, or eating then shopping?" Erika asked. Anna and Eryn had different ideas.

Anna said she was starving and wanted to eat first, but Eryn countered, "We will feel fat after and not want to buy anything. Have a bloody mary; that'll fill you up, Your Majesty!" she said jokingly, dragging Anna towards a bar ahead.

Erika and I followed behind. She asked me to recount precisely what Serge had said during the drill and grinned broadly as I told her. Then she told me that Marcello had mentioned Serge asking about me... whether he was going out with the girls and if I might be there. She told me that he hadn't been onboard that long and didn't have a girlfriend yet, so now was the perfect time to "pounce."

We sat at the bar in a cute tiki-themed restaurant on the main path through Kona. The bartender made our bloody marys in front of us, and we all cheered, "Girls Day!" Eryn pulled the appetizers list from the menu and placed it in front of Anna, saying, "That's all you get... remember we have weigh-ins coming up." Anna grimaced and looked at me, explaining that the dancers were weighed several times during a contract to ensure they maintained their starting weight.

"Vivace Cruise Line doesn't support body positivity?" I asked.

"There's a petition to get weigh-ins stopped," Anna said.

"But not by tomorrow, so drink up your meal, babes," Eryn added, picking up Anna's bloody mary and putting the straw to her lips. Anna took a big sip and sighed as she put the drink down.

"Okay, out with it," Eryn said, looking at Anna.

She hesitated for a moment and then admitted that she wanted to break up with her boyfriend onboard, but she couldn't decide whether to do it now or wait until the contract ended to make it less awkward. Eryn said she wasn't surprised since the boyfriend hadn't spent the night in their cabin in ages.

Anna retorted at Eryn, "Well, it's impossible with the revolving door you've created to our cabin and your head repeatedly hitting the bottom of my bunk with each moan."

Eryn cackled loudly. I laughed, glad that Georgette wasn't bringing men back to our cabin. I hadn't considered how the crew who shared rooms sorted out that particular situation. The girls said that the old-fashioned "tie on the door handle" was often used.

Anna put her arm around Erika, saying she didn't want to bring down the mood for Mr. & Mrs. Marcello Barbieri. A big smile appeared on Erika's face, and she playfully shoved Anna off, telling her not to jinx it.

"Oh, come off it! You two act like a newlywed couple already. He's probably perusing one of the jewelry shops as we speak," Eryn said, finishing her bloody mary.

We all finished our drinks and continued down the main street. Kona was so cute and picturesque—right off the postcards in the shops. We passed cozy lanai cafes where ukulele melodies filled the air. Surf shacks adorned the streets with surfboards in vibrant shades of sunset orange and ocean blue. The girls led me off the main road, and soon enough, we were in a fabulous dress boutique. The girls flipped through the racks, holding some dresses up to themselves and others up to me.

"Found it!" Eryn yanked me over to the full-length mirror and held up the tiniest black dress I had ever seen. I made a ridiculous face, and we all started laughing when we heard another voice behind us.

"And whatever might the occasion be?" I looked in the mirror and saw Georgette stepping out from behind the dressing room curtain. The girls began explaining that a crew costume party was coming up when Georgette cut them off.

"Oh, please don't think I haven't seen the Italian fairytale unfolding before my eyes," she said, looking at me.

I blushed and wasn't sure how to respond. Georgette's eyes moved from me to the other dresses the girls were holding and raised a slightly judgmental eyebrow.

"This one," she said, holding up the white dress she had in her hands. She draped it on the cushioned chair beside her, gave us a curt nod, and walked out of the shop. We all inched towards the chair, looking at the dress, and I knew she was right—it was perfect.

"Okay, the hot bitch goddess wins," Eryn said, putting the black dress back on the rack.

I smiled to myself and thought... *Maybe Georgette did care after all.*

X

CHAPTER 10

That night, we had our regular gallery hours. It was the last night of the cruise – the following day, we would dock in Honolulu while the current guests left and the new guests got onboard. We had our final appointments, and Theobold seemed quite pleased with how the cruise had gone. He congratulated all of us for reaching our monetary goal for the cruise as he popped a bottle of the free champagne we gave the guests at the auctions.

Georgette paused for a moment before slowly taking a brief sip – I assumed this brand of champagne was not what they drank at her estate back in England.

Smitty downed his glass quickly as I laughed and looked at Theobold, who smiled back at me with his Hollywood smile and then turned back to his desk. Seated in his chair with Georgette leaning over his shoulder, they discussed the schedule of the following cruise.

Smitty and I started organizing all the supplies for the upcoming auction when a woman in a white uniform walked into the gallery. I recognized her as Ziwe, who helped us get onboard my very first day. She nodded at Smitty and me as she walked towards Theobold's desk.

Georgette straightened from her leaned stance as Theobold looked up from his chair, welcoming Ziwe in, and asked, "To what do I owe the pleasure?"

She explained that management was stepping up their game, increasing customer service during dinner hours, and assigning more departments for "table touching." Smitty chuckled under his breath, and I watched Georgette adopt an icy gaze as she slowly placed a hand on her hip. Theobold sat back in his chair and crossed his legs, a slight smirk on his face.

"What's table touching?" I whispered very quietly to Smitty.

He responded just as quietly, saying it was when the managers meet upstairs in the buffet during dinner and go table to table asking the guests how they were enjoying their cruise.

"It's completely cringe... Art has never been asked to do it," he concluded as he looked on like he was watching a reality television episode.

Theobold placed his fingertips together, "So you want the Art Auctioneer," he paused, acknowledging himself, then continued, "To go and ask the guests how their cruise went when they no doubt will raise a grievance because... let's be frank... it is what they do," he opened his hands, palms outwards like it was apparent and continued.

"And the Art Auctioneer will be able to do...what exactly? Fix the temperature of their steak? Bring them yet another beer? Wipe their mouths when they are done? Fix every little flaw in their dreamland experience?" He stared at Ziwe with a look that I couldn't tell if it was confidence or arrogance as Smitty chuckled quietly again.

Georgette stood still as a statue, as she stared right at the woman.

I saw Ziwe's face darken, and she raised the clipboard in her hand, "It is a new mandate that all heads of department are required to participate," she emphasized "all" as she put the clipboard on Theobold's desk and slid it towards him.

He sat unmoving for a beat, his long arms draped along the armrest of his chair, and then leaned forward slowly. Picking up the clipboard and glancing over it, "My, that does sound like it's a Vivace Cruise Line requirement, and last I checked, we are employees of Landmark Quest."

Ziwe glowered at him and followed his statement with, "Under Vivace Cruise Lines."

Theobold fired back, "Well, this schedule is for dinner times during days at sea," he said as he pushed the clipboard back to her. "And that is precisely when we are all here in the gallery for checkout, making the money that keeps this ship and the cruise line operating and also keeps you employed. But let's just check, shall we?" he asked as he picked up the phone on his desk and dialed.

A short conversation ensued with us only able to hear Theobold's side... "It's no problem at all...

we will certainly keep smashing our goal. Cheers, thank you," Theobold said as he ended the call and placed the phone down.

"Your boss just confirmed that our place is here making money," he said, staring at Ziwe with a look that could kill. With Theobold and Georgette's formidable energy, you could cut the tension in the gallery with a knife. Smitty and I looked at each other in amazement.

Ziwe picked up the clipboard, "Let us see," she said as she turned and walked out of the gallery, not looking our way.

"You do that," Theobold said as he watched her leave. And with that, the two of them went back to their planning on the computer as if the last ten minutes never happened.

In the last hour before we closed, Georgette handed me the stack of our final invoices. "You do remember how I showed you?" she asked, more of a statement than a question.

A few days ago, she showed me how to process invoices and charge the guest's shipboard accounts. I nodded as she started to turn away. I took my chance, "Georgette... I wanted to thank you for the dress today. You were spot on... I was wondering...

Well, it's date night for Smitty, and the girls are busy with the final shows and costume cleaning... So, I wondered if you wanted to get a martini with me after work?"

She turned back slowly, looking almost as if she were examining me, and finally said, "No."

Disappointed, I thought to myself, *I tried*, as I turned to leave.

Then I heard, "But I do appreciate it... greatly... perhaps another time." I looked back and met her gaze as she flashed a quick, small smile my way. Her hair gleamed in the gallery lighting above as her earrings glittered, which made her appear to glow as she smiled.

Now that is progress, I thought as I walked out of the gallery with the invoices.

I was behind guest services at the very end of the long reception desk, where the processing machine was – away from the staff members helping the long line of guests. Almost halfway through the invoice stack, I recalled what Georgette had taught me, but it was difficult to focus with the loud mixture of live music from the atrium, ship announcements from the PA system, and guests complaining at the front desk. I felt terrible for the front desk agents and was astonished at how they kept their cool with the guests, some of whom were becoming increasingly angry. A majority were demanding refunds for all types of reasons – the food overall was terrible, they had gotten sick, they didn't enjoy Hawaii like they thought they would, and closest to home, they felt coerced by the sales departments to spend too much.

Focus, Bree, I told myself.

The machine to process the invoices was an antiquated system that made you do way more math than should be necessary. Math was never my strong suit, so I was saved by the trusty calculator app on my phone. As I continued punching numbers into the system, I felt like I was being watched.

I looked up and briefly locked eyes with a guest trying to get my attention. As he approached me, I explained that I wasn't a guest service agent and could not assist him. He waved me off, annoyed with my response.

Shifting my focus back to punching numbers, I still felt someone looking at me. I looked up to scan the crowd again, past the long line of guests for the front desk and saw Serge at the far end of the atrium. He was leaning against one of the large ornate columns throughout the lobby and talking on his deck phone - he always seemed to be on that thing. As he continued his conversation, he maintained eye contact with his dark eyes. They were soft but intense on me as I held his gaze.

An elderly lady's voice crashed through my entrancement, "Miss! Miss! I need help, please!" I broke our eye contact to look at the woman and was nearly blinded. She was wearing a ton of sparkly costume jewelry – necklaces, pins, rings, and a sequined blouse – she was a walking disco ball. I kept smiling politely while she aired her grievances about the cruise. When she stopped for a breath, I finally told her the same thing as the previous guest – Unfortunately, I wasn't a guest service agent.

She immediately became snippy and asked, "Why in the world are you back there then?!" I didn't have the time or the chance to explain before she walked off, casting reflections of light on the ground around her.

Yikes...I need to get out of here, I thought to

myself. I looked back to where Serge had been, but he wasn't there anymore.

I started on the last invoice, dividing the totals, when Serge's hand suddenly appeared and lightly took mine from the keyboard.

"You handled the scary, shiny lady?" he asked, giving me that "look."

I laughed and agreed that I was fending them off back here and wished there was another place where I could handle the processing away from the guests. He was still holding my hand, and I glanced around to see if anyone noticed. I wasn't great with public displays of affection, especially not in an environment like this, where you were seemingly under a microscope. I apologized and thanked him for his help at the boat drill, explaining that this first cruise had been an overwhelming blur.

"No doubt...but surely there are some high-lights, no?" His accent was highly enchanting.

"Oh, there may have been one or two," I said coyly.

He smiled, said he would be finished working in an hour, and asked when I would be done. When I told him hopefully soon, he asked if I wanted to join him for a drink... Not to be confused with the date I still owed him, he clarified.

I happily nodded, and he said he could pick me up at the gallery. Releasing my hand, he smiled and disappeared into the back office. That giddy feeling was back but was promptly interrupted by yet another guest, "Miss!" I kept my head down and finished processing the last invoice. Gathering the completed stack of papers, I fled guest services, pitying the poor staff members who had to endure that entire line.

Returning to the gallery, only Smitty and Georgette remained. I handed her the invoices, which she filed away, and we finished preparing the gallery for the next day. Smitty said goodnight and floated out of the gallery for his date with Holiday. Georgette and I exchanged a grin. We closed the main entrance doors, and Georgette took a large key out of her purse to lock them. We turned and saw Serge standing in the hallway.

He raised a hand with a "Ciao" towards Georgette. She looked at him and then at me, "This is yours...I have my own," she said, handing me the key while ignoring Serge. She gave me one last glance and walked away.

Serge released a cautionary whistle as she left, "Not very friendly, that one." I told him she wasn't so bad – more of a slow burn. "As you say," he walked towards me and lifted his arm to escort me to the bar.

I thought we were going to the crew bar again, but it turned out there was an officer's bar as well – a bit smaller than the main crew bar, but just as loud – not with music but chatter from the other officers unwinding at the end of a cruise and the rings of their deck phones going off frequently. We sat in a corner booth, and a waiter came over to order our drinks. Serge motioned to me first - I ordered a martini, and he ordered an Aperol Spritz. He sat leisurely with one foot resting on his knee and an arm stretched across the top of the booth towards me – nearly touching my shoulder – and smiled as he looked at me. I was determined not to act so nervous around him.

The drinks came, and as I leaned over to take my martini, I purposely threw my hair over one shoulder and crossed my legs towards him as I settled into the booth. Raising my glass towards him, I said, "To my savior and narrowly escaping captain's court!"

"Prego," he replied as he met my cheers.

I wasn't sure if it was being delirious from the cruise or the enchanting tones of his voice, but our conversation was easy and natural. We talked a bit more about our families, my life in LA, his in Italy, and we inched closer to one another. Soon enough, his hand was on my shoulder, brushing my hair softly to my back. After another round, I was twirling a lock of hair in my hand only to let it fall and rest my hand on his arm. Our chemistry grew stronger as we continued getting closer, and I thought he might try to kiss me.

Did I want him to kiss me? Yes. Was this moving too fast? Maybe, but "Ship Life" did move fast, I thought to myself.

It was becoming clear that it was a sink-or-swim mentality. I was lost in my thoughts at the same time as I was listening to Serge when another sound slowly broke into my bubble. It became louder, and Serge finally asked if I should get that as he looked behind me. I turned and saw it was my deck phone ringing... it was the first time the damn thing rang and didn't make me jump. I supposed having a gorgeous Italian caressing your shoulder had that effect. I grabbed the phone just as it stopped ringing and saw that I had missed several calls from the same number.

"I should probably see what's going on," I said as I dialed the number back. The loud noises of guest chatter and music mixed together blared on the other end, followed by a cold, "Where on earth have you been?"

It was Georgette – not sounding happy at all.

"Oh, I'm just..." I paused, looking at Serge. "What's wrong?" I asked.

"Come to the guest service desk immediately!" Georgette ordered as she hung up the phone.

Serge looked at me like he had heard the other side of the conversation, raising his eyebrows, "She's not that bad?" he asked slowly.

"I should probably get up there," I said begrudgingly. Breaking our physical contact, I apologized for leaving so suddenly. "Call me!" I said as I waved the deck phone at him. He winked as I left the bar – not the ideal ending I had in mind.

Back at the guest service desk, it was like déjà vu, except this time, a glowering Georgette was standing by the processing machine with crossed arms. She pulled me into the back office and held an invoice up, looking at me.

"I have spent the last twenty minutes being dressed down by a guest who is NOT Mr. Richardson!" She pointed to the name Alan Richardson on the invoice. I had entered the wrong cabin number while processing and charged the wrong cabin. "Now his bank has frozen his account, and he cannot settle his shipboard statement," Georgette continued.

I cringed, knowing exactly which invoice it was —the one I was in the middle of when Serge had interrupted me.

"This is outrageous behavior, Miss Bradley! Not only will accounting be up most of the night thanks to your mistake, but I will most certainly be explaining to the Hotel Director tomorrow exactly why a guest's bank account was frozen due to the art department... What do you think this is? The bloody Love Boat?! I've already reversed the transaction and charged the correct cabin, but you had best get your head out of the clouds and focus. This is a serious business... not Love Island, darling!" Her tone grew icier the longer she went on.

I wanted to sink into the floor—again—that was twice in one day. Georgette took a breath.

"You know, I thought I saw a shade of my younger self in you, but now I am simply left with utter disappointment. Get your act together!" she said as she threw the invoice in my hand and promptly left the office, leaving the other crew members staring wide-eyed at their desks.

I felt like a teenager again, as if my mother had grounded me. I wanted to run after her and tell her that I did care about this job and wasn't taking it lightly. However, I realized I had allowed myself to be distracted. This world was so confusing, with many things happening simultaneously and blending personal and professional life all into one chaotic bubble.

The day had drained me emotionally. My limbs felt weighed down by exhaustion as I walked outside to the back of the ship where the white-water trail of the ship's wake extended into darkness. Leaning against the railing, I felt small and insignificant against the dark expanse of the ocean. I could barely see the horizon line as it blended into the starry night sky. I wasn't sure if I was suitable for this job.

I could simply walk off the ship tomorrow in Hono-lulu and fly home, I told myself. My chest felt heavy at the thought. I stood there for a while, the wind whipping around me, as I played out different scenarios of leaving the ship in my head.

When I got back to the cabin, it was pitch black. I could barely make out the silhouette of a sleeping Georgette. I quietly removed my shoes and slipped into bed in my work outfit. I didn't want to risk waking Georgette and suffering a second wave of her wrath. I closed my eyes and thought, *Tomorrow can only go up from here.*

XI

CHAPTER 11

It felt surreal that my first cruise was completed. I honestly thought it would be my last cruise when I woke up. I had barely slept—partly because of the blow-up with Georgette and partly because of the metal luggage trolleys continually banging against the thin wall that separated my cabin and the I-95. On turnaround day, the passenger announcements were piped into the crew areas for some silly reason, and every time a group of passengers was called to leave the ship, another announcement blared into my cabin.

So, I was awake when Georgette turned on the

light and began showering and dressing. I pretended to be asleep—or dead—which may have been preferable to her. Once she left, I crawled out of my bed. I was about to grab my suitcase when the deck phone loudly went off. I was really beginning to hate that thing. I reluctantly answered it and heard Smitty on the other end asking what I was up to, "Because there's no way you could still be sleeping through all this." I let out a big sigh and filled him in on the events after we closed the gallery.

"Damn, girl...I'm sorry. That does suck...But today is a new day, and we get to press the reset button. I mean, she might not even be angry still. Even divas have to blow off steam, and when they do, it's apocalyptic! But it's gorgeous and sunny out..."

I cut him off, "Oh, let me guess, you can see it's sunny from your boyfriend's big porthole in his huge cabin."

Smitty paused for a second. "Okay, I'm going to let that slide because you've had a rough night, but you better check that attitude because I know the perfect thing for us to do. Be ready in fifteen?"

I told him I was still in last night's outfit.

"Okay, thirty then," he said, as he hung up the phone.

I quickly showered, threw on some denim shorts and a tank top, and tied my wet hair up in a bun. I met Smitty by security on the I-95 with the luggage carts still clattering by. As I approached, he made a comical pouty face, and I told him I wasn't in the mood.

I looked around, "Is it just us? Where's the boyfriend?" I asked.

"He is on 'Just Ask' torture this morning, so it's just you and me, lady! And we are going out, and we are thriving!" Smitty proclaimed.

The security officer yelled at Smitty to be quiet.

"After we get past these guys..." he whispered, as he put his bag through the security scanner.

I looked out the window of our Uber as we drove away from the port.

"It is a gorgeous day!" Smitty exclaimed.

I nodded and muttered, "A beautiful backdrop for all my drama on deck." I decided to try and stop feeling bad for myself, be present, and remember where I was. Smitty searched his backpack for something and finally pulled out some sunglasses and popped them on. He turned his head to face me, wearing the most ridiculous sunglasses I had ever seen—hot pink rims with a sparkly palm tree over each mirrored lens that looked like a tropical antennae. He made a face at me, and I burst out laughing.

"See! I knew that would get you!" He took the glasses off, looked at them, and asked, "What? They're cute!"

I couldn't have adored him more—he really knew exactly what I needed to cheer me up. I asked him where we were going, and he said it was a surprise as we turned onto the main drag through Waikiki. In the distance, I could see the silhouette of Diamond Head Crater rising majestically on the horizon. The beach was on our right, filled with activity and families building sandcastles. Surfers rode the waves in the distance while others paddled to the shoreline dotted by colorful umbrellas that contrasted the azure colors of the ocean. I told Smitty I didn't bring my bathing suit, and he said I wouldn't need it. The Uber stopped, and we got out on the corner. I looked around and didn't see anything besides a few touristy shops. I turned to Smitty with a quizzical look, and he pointed up.

I followed his finger and saw the second level of

the building next to us. The railings were wrapped in rainbow garlands, and I could hear pop music playing. As we walked up the stairs, the music grew louder, and I heard people talking excitedly. The sign above the door said *Hulas* and the host welcomed us, throwing a rainbow flower lei over our heads.

"Welcome! Everyone gets laid here!" he joked.

Smitty grinned and responded, "I mean, that already happened this morning, but who's counting?!"

I love a good gay bar, and Smitty was right—it did lift my spirits. We sat at the bar, and Smitty told the bartender that I needed a pick-me-up. He nodded and went to make the drinks. Smitty watched him walk to the other side of the bar. "Oof...If I weren't taken, you would be on your own, girl, because I'd be all over that!"

The bartender brought the drinks over—something light, fruity, and not too strong. We both took a sip, and Smitty swirled around on the barstool to face me.

"So, before all the invoice drama...what happened with Officer Hottie? He took you to the officer's bar?!" Smitty asked.

I told him it went really well and was a total vibe before the phone rang. We talked more about Serge and when I might see him again. He gave me the lowdown on being back with Holiday and how their relationship had picked up right where they left it at the end of his last contract. And, of course, we rehashed the whole table-touching episode.

As we chatted over a few more drinks, more and more gay men showed up. The first few were in sailor hats and outfits with varying lengths of shorts, which I thought was cute. But I soon realized that everyone coming in was dressed like a gay sailor. I turned to Smitty, "Did we miss the memo?"

He popped on the pink palm tree glasses again and explained that every Sunday, this was the meetup point for a gay sunset catamaran trip. Unfortunately, we would have to be back onboard before they returned. The cute bartender rang a giant silver bell over the bar, and everyone cheered in their sailor garb. Shots were being passed out through the whole crowd. As he handed two to us, I said I was fine, but Smitty took his in hand.

"To Guess the Price tonight," he said before he threw it back.

The crew was serious when they said we were hitting the reset button. That afternoon back on the Vision, everything repeated as if it were my first day onboard. We did the required safety drill for the new passengers. I was much more prepared this time for my megaphone speech, which I thought went well. I got dressed for work, and Smitty and I set up our Guess the Price station in the central atrium—same as the last cruise with the same painting. We got the same type of reactions from the new passengers. I found it funny that people guessed—sometimes tens of times— and repeatedly asked when we would announce the winner so they could be sure to be present. However, when we did announce the winner at the auction, the people who guessed closest usually weren't there. The ship had so many activities for the guests happening at once that getting them to attend your event was a battle.

The spa girls had their table set up on the other side of the atrium, advertising all their services and products for sale. Emma and a few of the others from the crew bar, whose names I had forgotten, waved at me. The excitement of their first night onboard was buzzing amongst the new passengers, which was infectious and provided a renewed energy within me. It was excellent motivation to keep the same level of enthusiasm for getting people to guess. It really was just putting on a show—like the dancers—only different. As I thought about the dancer girls, they magically appeared, walking across the atrium toward us.

All three were wearing the bright red "Just Ask" T-shirts. Anna and Erika's shirts fit like a regular T-shirt should; however, Eryn's looked two sizes too small, with the sleeves rolled up so her boobs really popped and the bottom tied in a knot exposing her midriff.

Smitty let out a, "Whoa, ma'am! I cannot begin to imagine what they are 'just asking' you!"

Eryn giggled, "Everything they usually do and maybe a bit more...remember, it is a swingers cruise...I just tell the men I'm a lesbian and the women that I'm straight."

"And the truth is somewhere in the middle," Erika quipped.

Eryn hip-bumped her and played up her Scottish brogue, "Ya havta have fun with it...otherwise, I'll end up looking like you two miserable hags!"

Erika chimed in, saying the swingers charter was half of the passengers.

"Half the ship!" I exclaimed.

"Well, let's hope they appreciate art too," Smitty mused, crossing his fingers.

The girls laughed, prompting Anna to insist I spill details about the officer's bar tonight at our letter-printing party. Realizing the long night ahead, I mentally prepared myself.

Here we go... Reset button, I thought.

The next day was a day at sea. The cruise line marketed it to passengers as a day to relax before the upcoming port tours, but in reality, it was the first major opportunity for all the retail departments to start selling. Each cruise was a competition to outperform the others – on the last cruise, the art department had dominated, so now we were defending champions. Smitty and I were up at 6 a.m., preparing the auction room. Normally, we'd have a break between setup and the auction, but last night's schedule for this cruise, which was prepared by Georgette, gave us an extra shift of Guess the Price in the morning.

"Yeah... she's still mad..." Smitty remarked, standing beside me at our table outside the auction lounge. The ship was quiet, with only a few passengers passing by and fewer taking a guess. "How are we supposed to tell who's a swinger and who's not? Is there something about pineapples in a shopping cart?" Smitty joked, eyeing a passing couple.

I chuckled at his far-fetched idea. "That's a bit obvious, don't you think?" I replied.

He continued brainstorming aloud, speculating on secret codes or signals – perhaps a guidebook or a massive group chat before boarding.

As he spun his theories, a couple approached our table, curious about our activity. I launched into my pitch, explaining the upcoming auction. We engaged in small talk; they mentioned celebrating their anniversary and buying a new house – all the right things for a salesperson to hear. They showed particular interest in the GTP painting by a well-known pop artist, which the husband recognized. He enthusiastically described the artist's career and technique, essentially doing my job for me. Before I could ask, he suggested the painting could

be the centerpiece of their new home's entryway –
a promising lead. Then, turning to me, he asked,
"How would you feel walking into our house and
seeing this? Comfortable? Engaged? Intrigued? We
want our home to feel open and communal for our
guests from the moment they arrive."

Facing them, I nodded along as Smitty silently
gestured behind them, mouthing the word "open"
after the husband mentioned it. I suppressed a
smile and focused on the couple. I agreed with
their vision and began employing my sales techniques to gauge their seriousness.

People often buy art for status, and it seemed
this was a key appeal for the husband. I reassured
him that the painting would create a welcoming
atmosphere reflective of their desired ambiance –
essentially echoing his sentiments to affirm his decision. The wife chimed in, saying she was pleased
to hear this because I reminded her of one of her
close friends. The husband eagerly agreed. Suddenly, I seemed more interesting to them than the
painting itself. Smitty gestured excitedly behind
them – I couldn't tell if he was thrilled or having
a fit.

Stay focused, Bree. Okay, these guys might be

swingers, I thought to myself. *That's fine if they're flirting with me. If I can sell them this painting, they can flirt all they want. If I'm the reason they buy, that's okay.*

Playing along, I said I got a great vibe from them and that this painting was my favorite from our collection – it deserved to be showcased in a beautiful new home with such a lovely couple. It would serve as a wonderful reminder of their anniversary. I pulled out all the stops, impressing even myself. The husband looked at his wife, who nodded at everything I said, while Smitty silently applauded me behind them. Then, the husband put his arm around his wife, drawing closer to me.

He turned on the charm and asked, "So, if I decide to buy it, are you going to whisper the price to me?"

Be flirtatious, Bree, I told myself. I imagined Serge standing there, asking me the same question.

With a coy smile and a toss of my hair, I replied, "Well, I could get into trouble," glancing from the husband to the wife and back again. "But... I really like you both, and this painting belongs with you. Here's what I can do for you..." I grabbed a guessing slip, wrote a price on the back, folded it, and handed it to him. He paused, taking it and brushing against my hand. "That's not the retail price you're guessing, but it's the price I can let it go for," I told him.

Opening the card, he looked at it. "Come to the auction today. You'll find out the retail price, and impress everyone when you make it yours at the price in your hand. Here's my number if you have questions until then... I'm Bree."

Taking the card back, I wrote my deck phone number and returned it to him. The couple looked thrilled – as if I had just agreed to swing with them in that brief exchange. They both smiled, and the husband assured me I'd see him at the auction.

As they walked away, Smitty gave me a look of amazement. "Um... who were you just now?! I'm feeling hot just watching you! He's definitely buying it!"

We both jumped excitedly. "I think so too!" I exclaimed.

XII

CHAPTER 12

I returned to the cabin to shower and get changed for the auction. I was beyond excited but tried not to get too ahead of myself. I quickly grabbed a salad in the crew mess and headed upstairs to the auction lounge. Georgette's announcement sounded over the PA system as I entered the passenger area. Smitty was standing at the registration table where Eryn, Anna, and Erika were seated, organizing the bid cards. Since they were laminated, Erika was wiping them down with a sanitizing cloth.

Smitty gave me an excited smile as I walked up

to them. "I told them something amazing is about to happen, but I haven't told them what because I don't want to jinx it!" He looked at me, then back at the girls, "But I really want to tell you!" He drew out the "really" part.

"Well, if we can't talk about that, can we talk about what we are all wearing tonight?" Erika asked all of us.

I asked what was happening, and all three girls looked at me and said, "The traffic light party!"

Anna took the lead, "Okay, so it's a great mixer for all the different departments. You wear red if you are taken and completely closed off. Yellow means you are in an open relationship, or it's complicated..."

She was about to finish when Eryn chimed in, "And green means you are single and ready to mingle, baby!" I laughed and said that we obviously knew which colors Eryn and Erika represented. Anna said she wasn't sure if she would be yellow or red.

I looked at Smitty, who asked, "Is pink an option? Like red adjacent? Because we are together and not seeing anyone else, but like we aren't married..."

Eryn laughed, "You two are the 'reddest' gay couple I have ever seen, but you..." she looked at me. "You had better be as green as the Scottish highlands in summer!" I told them I didn't think I packed anything green, but the girls said they would find me something. The rest of the planning would have to wait since several passengers were showing up for the auction.

Smitty and I went inside and saw Theobold and Georgette standing on the stage. He motioned for us to come for a quick pre-auction meeting. Apparently, the morning sales events had not gone well for the other departments, but Theobold said that was normal for a charter cruise. It just meant we would have to be at the top of our games today.

"Which means laser-focused," Georgette said to the group but was looking straight at me.

Georgette opened the lounge doors, and the crowd started coming in. It wasn't nearly as large as the crowds we had last cruise – maybe most of the swingers weren't into art. I looked at everyone as they came in, searching for my couple, but I didn't see them. I immediately had several guests around me asking where the free champagne was and received a few annoyed looks when I said it would be served when the auction commenced. I started looking at the bid cards in people's hands; unfortunately, I didn't see any 300 numbers to signal a potential lead. I kept scanning the crowd and saw Georgette talking with a lady but cutting her eyes at me with a "why aren't you talking to people" vibe. My couple wasn't there, which was discouraging, but I made my rounds talking about the paintings and trying to find any decent leads in the crowd.

I quickly found this group was completely different from the last cruise. A few people gasped from sticker shock when I quoted them a price. One lady said, "That is more than we paid for the cruise!" I got a lot of, "We are just here for the free champagne" or "We just want to enjoy the show."

Smitty walked by me, whispering, "Do these people not know how an auction works? I'm about to tell them the 'show' is in the theater tonight at eight, dammit!"

I smiled and felt a bit better that he was also having difficulty finding anything of quality, but then I saw Georgette shake the hand of the lady she had been talking with and place a sales slip on the artwork in front of them.

I have to find something, I thought to myself as I went back into the crowd in search of a lead. I felt the minutes ticking by, and still no luck. I saw Smitty placing a group of four animation cells with a sales slip next to Georgette's sale. Panic was setting in.

I can't be the only one not to sell anything before we even start, I told myself.

But, unfortunately, I was.

I saw Theobold looking unimpressed at the small group of sold art.

"At least do something useful and start clearing room for people to sit," Georgette ordered in an icy tone as she passed me and made her way on stage to announce Theobold.

The auction was underway and not going well. Despite Theobold's charm, the small crowd was unresponsive, and many were haggling with the bartender for more free champagne. It was supposed to be one glass per person, which I soon discovered was my unenviable job to enforce. One man started getting loudly upset when I told him he couldn't have another, which earned me cutting glances from both Theobold and Georgette. My patience was running thin. I went to the bar and told the bartender to stop serving. If anyone else asked me, their answer would be, "I'm so sorry, we ran out." I let out a sigh of exasperation as I looked across the room...People were literally sitting on their bid cards with no intention to bid on anything.

How am I supposed to work with these people if they just want to watch a show? I asked myself.

"Tough crowd, huh?" a voice said behind me.

I turned to see the husband from this morning. I couldn't have been happier to see him, and my smile must have shown it because he matched it with a big smile of his own.

How far am I going to have to take this flirting charade? I asked myself.

He leaned in to whisper in my ear, "We talked it over, and we are going to do it," he said as he put something in my hand. I tried not to look utterly shocked as I opened my hand and saw the card with the sales price I had written down earlier - $38,000.

Stay calm, Bree. Act like this happens every day, I told myself.

He said he couldn't stay for the whole auction but would stay until his wife arrived. I wasn't going to let him get away. I quickly ran and asked Eryn for number 300, giving her a wink as she handed it to me. Handing the bid card to him, I sat him down in the front row and grabbed the Guess the Price painting. I brought it to the assistants who were taking and removing the artworks on stage to be auctioned, telling them this one was next.

Suddenly, Georgette was there in hushed, aggravated tones, saying the guess the price winner was to be announced at the end of the auction as she yanked the painting away and placed it against the wall. She walked off, staring daggers at me.

That is it! I am done being intimidated by this woman, I told myself.

Theobold called for the next artwork, and the assistant was about to take another artwork when I held his arm to stop him. I grabbed the painting where Georgette had placed it, carried it onto the stage myself, and placed it on the easel.

Theobold paused slightly on the microphone, caught off guard. I gave him an affirmative nod as I placed the sales slip on his podium and walked off stage. He continued speaking as he looked at the slip.

"Well, ladies and gentlemen, I believe most

of you were playing a little game last night and this morning. So, it appears that we are going to announce the winner now." He gave a cheeky smile to the crowd, "Now, just to be clear, you do not win the painting." That got a laugh from the crowd. "So, I will tell you the retail price and then open it up for auction. When we are done, I shall announce the lucky winner!" He paused and continued, "The retail price of this original acrylic painting is...$45,000..."

That earned some gasps from the crowd as Georgette walked up to me, looking every inch of an evil queen. She towered over me ominously.

"Just what the hell do you think you are playing at?" she asked angrily but was promptly cut off by Theobold on the microphone.

"I shall open the bidding at $38,000..."

I took a long second to give Georgette a sharply raised eyebrow, then snapped my head hard in the other direction, purposely flipping my hair to nearly smack her.

I locked eyes with my buyer and gave him a nod. He threw bid card 300 high in the air from the front row, earning another gasp from the crowd.

Theobold acknowledged his bid, "Looking for 39... going once, going twice...Sold for $38,000!"

The gavel hit the podium with a loud crack, and the crowd started cheering and clapping in the lounge. The room felt electrified, and I was in awe of what had just happened. I walked away from Georgette, who had a stunned look on her face, and went to shake my buyer's hand. He smiled as our hands met, and then as he stood up to hug me, he said, "That was amazing! I'm Greg, by the way."

The moment went into slow motion. I saw Theobold clapping on stage with his gavel still in hand. Smitty was in the back of the lounge with the dancers jumping up and down like cheerleaders. Georgette stood in the middle of the lounge where I left her, still with that shocked expression, then slowly started clapping her hands.

Theobold continued, announcing the winner who guessed closest and resumed the auction. My big sale seemed to energize the entire room, and more people began bidding on other artworks as the auction continued. The crowd grew more excited and murmurs turned to cheers as Theobold presented the major discounts on offer. My feet were hurting as I ran to people to assist them in their bidding, but I didn't mind since I was still on a high from my big sale.

"That was absolutely fierce!" Smitty exclaimed as the auction ended, and we collected the bid cards from people leaving the lounge. I beamed with happiness and pride. As we shut the doors to the lounge, I heard the loud pop of a champagne bottle being opened. We turned to see Theobold still on stage at his podium and pouring four glasses. Smitty and I excitedly ran over to accept a glass. Georgette was the last on stage to slowly take her glass from Theobold.

"Well, that started as an absolute disaster, but then this little minx saved us all!" Theobold said as he raised his glass.

"She sure as hell did!" Smitty beamed as he took a sip.

"Yes...very surprising indeed..." Georgette trailed off and slowly took a sip, looking me dead in the eyes.

"To Bree!" We all raised our glasses in celebration.

We didn't have nearly as many appointments for checkout as last cruise's first auction. In fact, I only had two framing appointments, and both of them decided to go for it. I was on a hot streak. Since Greg was the top bidder, his appointment was set with Theobold. However, Greg requested that I deal with him when he showed up with his wife. Theobold said I could certainly join them and invited me into his office. I sat on Theobold's side of the desk across from Greg and Cindy, his wife. I was impressed with how smoothly Theobold handled them, using the fact that Cindy had missed the auction to his advantage and going through an abridged version of the auction's highlights.

Greg seemed still high from his winning bid and the crowd's fanfare. As Theobold went on, he was sure to keep referring back to me and capitalizing on the rapport I had built with them this morning. He must have been picking up on the swinger vibes they were giving off. By the end of the appointment, Greg signed an invoice for $52,500, picking up a few more artworks for their new home. Everyone was smiling and shaking hands. Greg and Cindy asked if Theobold and I would join them for dinner and drinks. I looked at Theobold, who said we could set something up and would be in touch as they left the gallery. We walked out of his office, and it seemed Georgette and Smitty had also finished their appointments since I didn't see them anywhere. Theobold walked to the gallery doors and slid them shut behind him as he turned to look at me.

"Well, as a rule, closing early is usually bad business. However, it seems someone has caught a whale," he said.

I smiled and threw my hands up in a playful shrug, "Guess at least one swinger couple likes art!"

He nodded and smiled, "Yes, well, aside from us selling the swingers, it is a good thought they had...we should go for a drink...just you and me...or dinner...if you wanted..." he said, looking at me with a confident grin on that handsome face.

My initial crush on him had faded since I had been flirting with Serge. Theobold was a different type of handsome from Serge. His blonde hair, light skin, and thin, model-like build were almost the opposite of Serge's dark complexion and ath- letic build. Not to mention his British accent and Serge's Italian one – both were lovely but very different.

I was a bit stunned at the words coming out of his mouth. We hadn't really spent any time together - certainly none outside the gallery. Aside from selling art, I didn't have the slightest clue he had any interest in me.

He stood still, looking at me, "I mean, that is, if you aren't busy with your Italian friend."

I also didn't know he had any idea about Serge. This ship was like a high school and word traveled fast.

I stumbled through my words, saying that I had already agreed I would have dinner with Serge, and for some reason, I felt oddly guilty.

Why? I asked myself.

Theobold held up his hands graciously, "Not to worry. But do let me know should the situation change." He walked towards the door to the crew area, "You smashed it today. Have a lovely evening; I'm sure any shade of emerald will look stunning on you." He disappeared through the door.

Emerald? I asked myself, confused. And then I remembered...the traffic light party.

XIII

CHAPTER 13

I had never been to a traffic light party... I had never even heard of it before, but it was a big deal onboard. Although apparently, it could get exceptionally provocative, so only a few Hotel Directors would approve the party. Since I didn't have anything green, Eryn told me to come to her cabin to borrow something.

Her door swung open when I knocked, revealing Eryn in a mermaid tail dress – sparkly green sequins hugged her hips down to her ankles where pink stilettos popped out the bottom, and a silk mermaid fin trailed behind her heels. The look was completed by an aqua-colored lace bra and a sparkly tiara on top of her red curls.

"Wow!" I said in awe. "I know you said people go all out but isn't this a bit overboard?"

She looked down at her outfit, "What? It's green!"

I asked her where she got the mermaid dress, and she said she nicked it from the costume room. I walked into their small cabin, the same as mine, and saw Anna wrapped in yellow caution tape that she fashioned into a dress.

"So, we are still on the fence about the boyfriend?" I asked since she wasn't wearing red.

She held up another roll of tape, saying she would wrap him as well and attach him to her, "So it's complicated," she laughed.

Eryn took a half-empty wine bottle from Anna and took a sip, then pointed to the bed where a green tartan dress was laid out, "That's for you." I picked it up and looked at it, but I said I felt underdressed compared to them.

Eryn grabbed her boobs in the aqua bra, "We can swap if you want... not sure if you'll fit, though!" We laughed, and I told her the tartan dress would be fine. They helped me dress and put some makeup on, and before long, our heels were clicking down the I-95.

We received a fanfare of catcalls and whistles as we headed toward the crew bar. Eryn beamed in satisfaction. We walked into the dark bar decorated with red, yellow, and green balloons and illuminated by flashing party lights. The DJ played loud music that vibrated the dance floor, which was already filled with crew members. The party was well underway, and almost everyone was dressed in traffic light colors. Many people cheered as we walked in, though I suspected most of it was for Eryn and Anna's outfits. We navigated through the crowd, scraping past other crew members, to our usual booth and found Smitty, Holiday, and Erika all dressed in red. Erika let out a shriek of excitement when she saw Eryn and Anna.

Smitty stood up in a red tracksuit and hugged us all, "Excuse me, ladies... but Halloween is two months away," he said with a grin.

"Meow!" Anna responded, kissing him on the cheek. "Where's my other half?" she asked, holding up the extra roll of caution tape.

Smitty pointed at the bar, "Over there with the other white uniforms."

Erika stepped over Holiday in the booth and took Anna's hand. "We are going to fix that now," she said as she held up a red feather boa, which was no doubt borrowed from the costume room as well. The girls went over to their boyfriends and began wrapping the men in their "accessories."

As I watched, I saw Serge standing with the other officers in his white uniform. The girls brought them over to our booth, leading their boyfriends on makeshift boa and caution tape leashes. Serge followed behind, giving me a big smile as he approached me.

"Not in a festive mood?" I asked, looking at his white uniform.

He said he couldn't stay long since he had to work that night. "But I had to make a visit to see what color you would be wearing. I'm thrilled to see I am...how do you say?... Getting the green light?" he asked as he ran a finger lightly down my arm.

"Thanks to the mermaid," I laughed, motioning to Eryn, who was now propped up on her side on top of the table, surrounded by a group of green and yellow crew members. Serge said he was pleased she was distracting the rest of the competition. He pulled me to the side of the booth and seductively leaned in close to me. I felt so attracted to him as he looked at me and said he enjoyed our time in the officer's bar the other night.

I agreed, saying I also had a great time, and it was too bad he had to go to work. The bar was becoming so crowded that his body was pressed against mine, increasing the sexual tension between us. He looked at his watch, saying it was a shame he had to go, but he hoped I was free tomorrow night for dinner. I smiled and rested my hand on his chest, saying I should be able to make that work. He took my hand and gave it one of his signature kisses.

"Have fun tonight... but not too much. Ciao, Bella," he said.

I let out an excited sigh as he left. I wasn't sure if I was warm because it was so crowded or because I was so turned on. I maneuvered through the crowded bar and rejoined the group.

"That looked hot and heavy," Smitty said as I stood beside him, and he handed me a glass of wine.

I did a cheers with him and Holiday, who was wearing a red tailcoat that a circus ringleader might wear. I told Smitty that I had something to tell him later, which piqued his interest. We mingled throughout the bar; this was the first time I noticed that departments weren't huddled together amongst their own. The spa girls were sprinkled around – mostly all of them in green. We passed by Ziwe, who was dressed in yellow. She acknowledged us but still seemed put off by the table-touching drama. One of the guys from the front desk came up to me and offered to buy me another drink.

"Two white wines... Thanks!" Smitty chimed in. To my surprise, the guy bought us both a drink. They were highly discounted for us in the crew bar, but it was still nice. He tried a few flirty lines on me, but nothing that could compete with Serge's Italian accent. I thanked him for the wine and returned to the dancer girls. They congratulated me again for my big sale today and asked how it went with Georgette afterward.

"I have never seen that look on her face before!" Erika said as she played with the red boa around Marcello's neck.

"Is she coming tonight?" Anna asked.

I shrugged, saying I hadn't seen her since I was in the office with Theobold most of the night.

"She can borrow my red 'Just Ask' shirt!" Eryn said.

As we laughed at her response, Georgette walked in, as if on cue. She was with the spa manager, and the two of them made their way to the bar. She was dressed in a gorgeous, gold-fitted pantsuit that attracted stares from everyone as it gleamed in the light while she passed by.

"Who does she think she is? Bloody Elvis?" Eryn asked.

"A super chic Elvis," Erika stated as she watched Georgette take a sip from the martini the bartender handed her. We discussed what the color gold might symbolize at a traffic light party.

Smitty offered up, "Untouchable?"

Eryn said, "Gold like the chastity belt that's no doubt under there…"

I told them I was pretty sure she hated me even more now. We decided I shouldn't let her bother me and just celebrate the day – which we did indeed. After another round of drinks, we danced the night away until red, yellow, and green all blurred together.

The next morning my deck phone went off in my cabin, making me jump out of my sleep and smack my head on the ceiling – again. At this point, it didn't even hurt anymore, but I felt a slight headache from the party as I answered the phone.

Smitty was on the other end, "Good morning," I said groggily.

"Bitch, it is the afternoon," he responded just as tired. "I can't be asked to get off the ship to-day...Wanna go tan on the crew deck?"

I hopped out of my top bunk, landing in front of Georgette's made-up bed with her gold suit from last night laid out with a dry cleaning slip waiting for pickup – she must have gone into port already. I remembered we were back in Kona and would have to take the tender in. Not wanting to be stuck in close quarters with the guests, I agreed, and Smitty said he'd pick me up in ten minutes.

The crew deck was a small outside area at the front of the ship where Leo DiCaprio would scream, "I'm the king of the world!" There was a small pool that the crew called "the bathtub" be-cause it was so small and shallow that the Hawaiian sun heated the little bit of water in it. We grabbed two sun loungers from the stack on the side and laid them out. The sun felt amazing as we discussed the party's highlights last night and everyone's color choices. I decided to tell Smitty about Theobold asking me for drinks or dinner. He sat up and raised his sunglasses, "Shut up!" I told him I had no idea, and it came out of nowhere.

"He's my boss... Isn't that an HR issue?" I asked.

Smitty laughed, "Ha! What HR?" He explained that since Vivace didn't directly employ us, it was a big gray area regarding support from HR or medical coverage and things like that.

"So, the rule is just don't get sick...or pregnant," he said, looking at me when he got to the pregnant part and then laid back down.

I told him there was zero chance I was pregnant, and he laughed, "Maybe not after tonight!"

I squirted some water from my bottle on him in response.

"Well, I was going to say you could get ready for your date with the girls in the dressing room tonight, but after that behavior, ma'am..." he said jokingly.

We tanned for a while as I looked up at the

clouds slowly moving across the blue sky. Even though the ship was anchored away from the island, I could still smell the floral scents in the breeze. Finally, we decided to take, as Smitty called it, a "disco nap" before gallery hours.

That night in the gallery was quiet, with most passengers between dinners and shows. Theobold sat in his office while Georgette sat Smitty and me down to review the upcoming scheduled presentations and which ones we preferred to do. I ended up saying I would do the one called "History of Art." That was the one I would be most comfortable with since I had taken so many art history courses in college. My experience with Greg and Cindy at the last auction had definitely boosted my confidence, so I wasn't as nervous as I used to be, but I still wasn't looking forward to presenting a seminar in front of Georgette Day's judgmental eyes. She was being cordial with me at the moment so there seemed to be a balance of peace.

Ship Life has shifted yet again very quickly, I thought.

I didn't think Smitty realized how close I was to packing up and leaving before he whisked me to the gay bar in Honolulu and allowed me to decompress. I felt slightly embarrassed and a bit guilty that I was going to give up, so I didn't mention it and promised myself I wouldn't let myself get to that mental state again. Luckily, I had a date with a handsome Italian officer to look forward to.

After we closed the gallery, I stopped by the cabin to pick up the white dress Georgette had suggested at the shop in Kona. I was surprised to see her sitting at the desk as I entered. She was so rarely in the cabin when I was, aside from sleeping, that I thought she was purposely avoiding me. As she applied some eye cream, her gaze went from staring at her face in the mirror to mine.

"So...Tonight is the big night, is it?" she asked like she already knew.

I nodded as I grabbed the dress. I smiled and held it up, acknowledging again that I had her to thank for letting me have it.

"I mean, I'll do my best to pull it off like you would," I said to her mirrored reflection, trying to compliment her.

She was putting on lip gloss now and raised her eyebrows at me. I figured this was as good a moment as any, "I hope everything is okay between us...I didn't mean to offend you at the auction...I just really wanted to get the artwork up so he would bid on it before he left, and you know, it got crazy so quickly. I just hope we can move forward..."

She finished with her lip gloss, put the tube on the desk, and turned in her chair to face me.

"Why do you think you could offend me? The goal is to get to - and then exceed - our target...As long as we achieve that, darling, I really couldn't care how we get there. My main priority is to keep the team focused and performing at their highest level, and if I see that focus shifting – I will correct it." She returned to the mirror and continued, "This job requires thick skin, darling... It's not for everyone. If we blew smoke up everyone's rear end when they made a sale, we would never get anywhere. That being said...I am pleased to see another capable woman in the company finally – it was beginning to become too much of a boy's club." She began touching up her mascara, "Now, you best run along before you're late. Enjoy yourself...but do try not to fall too deeply under Italian enchantments."

I told her I appreciated it and left the room. I supposed that meant we were in a decent place –

at least the icy demeanor seemed to have thawed a bit.

As I found my way to the dancer's dressing room just behind the theater, I heard the cruise director on stage wrapping up the show as the audience clapped. The dancer girls filed into the room, fully dressed in rhinestone corsets and feather headdresses. Since I hadn't had time to see any of the shows, it was fun to see them all in costume. Alina, who I only saw with her boyfriend during our letter-printing parties, waved to me. The other girls seemed to keep to themselves. Smitty popped in behind them and promptly began helping everyone undress as he went from each of them, unzipping their corsets from the back. I asked if I should come back after they changed. Eryn turned to me, completely topless, saying that no one cared. It seemed she was correct, and they quickly got out of their costumes and into tracksuits. Smitty popped a bottle of champagne that he had pilfered from the gallery as Alina and the other dancers left the room.

We sat down at the room-length table lined with vanity lights. Smitty sat a glass of champagne down in front of each of us. Eryn began washing off her stage makeup, saying that the swingers were a lively crowd tonight. Anna and Erika chuckled, saying it was probably because of her wardrobe malfunction. During the show, the dancers had a choreography number involving chairs where they quickly sat down and popped back up. Apparently, when Eryn popped back up, her wrapped mini skirt stuck to the chair, and she was parading around the stage in only her dance belt for the rest of the number.

"It became a Las Vegas revue real quick!" she exclaimed as she got up and started brushing my hair. "Are we going sassy or classy?" she asked.

Erika and I said classy at the same time.

"Fine," Eryn rolled her eyes and began putting my hair in an updo. Anna was helping Erika with her hair since she and Marcello also had a dinner date tonight. As I looked at myself in the mirror while Eryn did my hair, she put a piece of paper in front of me with some words written down.

"I took the liberty to research some dirty Italian words that might help tonight."

I laughed, picked up the paper, and read, "Cazzo."

"That means dick," Erika said.

"See, she knows!" Eryn said happily.

"Of course, she does – she has an Italian boy-friend. I'm sure she's very familiar with his 'cazzo'!" Smitty joked.

We all laughed. I read from the paper again, struggling through the pronunciation, "Prenderlo nel culo..."

Erika said she didn't know that one and looked at Eryn, who answered, "In the ass!"

Smitty cackled. I crumpled up the paper, giving Eryn a look in the mirror, "We said classy, right?"

Smitty cut in, "Hey! Classy ladies can be kinky too...Sometimes with more than one person!" he said as he looked at me with a knowing wink.

The girls looked at each other quizzically.

"What does that mean?" Erika asked. Then everyone looked at me.

"Oh, fine!" I said as I told the girls about Theobold asking me out.

"Bloody hell! It's only her second cruise, and she's already got two trophy men on her mantle!" Eryn quipped.

I reassured her that I had no "trophies" on my mantle and didn't intend to date my boss. Anna mentioned that since both Theobold and Georgette were single, she had been waiting for the two of them to get together...or maybe they were already and keeping it secret. I told them that she kept her personal life very private.

"Well, I'm sure she wouldn't keep her thoughts private if you started screwing her boss," Eryn giggled as she opened a lipstick tube and began applying a bright red lip color on me. I turned to look in the mirror and was startled by how bold the color was – especially against the ivory color of my dress. I usually wore more muted tones, but I had to admit, I liked the confidence boost a red lip gave me.

That confidence grew as I walked down the hallway towards the restaurant with Erika next to me. As it happened, she and Marcello were also having a dinner date at the same restaurant. The Vivace Vision had several themed restaurants onboard, and the French bistro was the most popular...and romantic, apparently. We planned to meet our dates at the restaurant since they were coming directly from the bridge, where most crew members weren't allowed.

As we made our way to the restaurant, we

caught several stares from passengers which made us smile at each other and playfully strut down the red patterned carpet of the promenade deck like it was a catwalk. However, my strutting was short-lived when I almost tripped as my deck phone started screeching and startled me. Erika laughed, finding it funny that the deck phone always made me jump.

She is just lucky she doesn't have the burden of carrying one, I thought as I answered the call.

Serge's voice surprised me on the other end—he had never called me before. He apologized and said the meeting on the bridge was running longer than expected and that he and Marcello would be a few minutes late. I said that was no problem and we would wait at the bar in the restaurant. We walked up to the hostess at the desk under the classy French bistro sign. I smiled at her and said we had two Staff reservations. The hostess looked at me, then at Erika, and then back at me.

"Oh, it must be the dancer's night out," she said flippantly. I told her I wasn't a dancer; I was with the art department, to which she responded mockingly, "Same thing, honey...Enjoy your pax access."

The term "pax" was short for passenger, and she

clearly was not thrilled that we could dine among them. She had opened the door for the previous couple to let them in but stood there with her arms crossed, clearly not intending to interact with us any further. Erika rolled her eyes and pulled the door open. As we sat at the bar, she told me that was just another instance of the Staff vs. Crew divide and that there was usually an attitude when Crew had to wait on Staff.

We ordered two glasses of wine. Erika said she usually didn't go to the passenger restaurants because of the awkwardness with the crew, but Marcello had told her tonight would be special. I smiled at her, matching the excited smile growing on her face. I asked her what she thought that meant, but she said she didn't want to assume anything.

"Sensible," I said as I took a sip. Halfway through our wine and chatting more about "Ship Life," I saw Serge and Marcello in their white uniforms walk into the restaurant and make their way to us at the bar. Marcello leaned down and kissed Erika on the lips while Serge did his signature move of taking my hand and kissing it. They both revealed a single red rose from behind their backs, handing them over to us. Erika threw her arms around Marcello and kissed him back on the lips. Serge gave me a hopeful look as if expecting me to do the same to him. I smiled and kissed him on the cheek, leaving a red lipstick stain, which brought a huge grin to his face as I rubbed it away.

The restaurant was almost entirely full of guests who gave the uniformed officers passing glances as we were led to the last two tables on opposite sides of the wood-paneled room. Erika gave me a playful wink as we separated and went to our tables. LED candles flickered in the middle of the table and cast soft, warm reflections across the red table-cloth. Real flames were a big no-no onboard for obvious reasons. I even had to have my curling iron checked by the electrical engineers when I signed on to ensure it wasn't a fire hazard. Even with the restaurant being so full, it still felt intimate. One of the musicians played 'La Vie En Rose" on the piano a few tables away from us, and the lighting dimmed as if on cue after we were seated. Our two plush velvet chairs were positioned intimately close to one another. Their elegant curved backs were comfortable and positioned us in such a way to gaze into each other's eyes.

Serge complimented me on how stunning I looked. As his warm compliment washed over me, a blush rose to my cheeks, and a soft smile graced my lips.

"Thank you," I replied, feeling a flutter of appreciation in my heart. "But let's not forget how handsome you always look in your uniform," I added with a playful wink, allowing my gaze to linger on him for a moment longer.

His eyes sparkled with delight, and a hint of color touched his cheeks as he returned the compliment with a grateful smile. He apologized again for not being able to escort me to dinner, and I said I didn't mind. Before we could order drinks, the waiter brought over a bottle of red wine and said it was compliments of our friends at the other table. We looked over and saw Marcello and Erika raising their glasses at us from the other side of the room. I was pleased that our waiter was much more friendly than the hostess, welcoming us and saying he recognized me from the art department. He told me he was a big fan of art, so he went to watch the auctions when he could. He poured the wine as he went over the specials of the night. Serge told me the coq au vin was stupendous, mimicking a chef's kiss with his fingers as he described it in detail.

"Well, I suppose I have to have that then," I said.

As the evening unfolded, the ambiance of the bistro seemed to amplify our connection, creating an intimate space where time seemed to slow to a blissful crawl. Savoring each sip of wine and every bite, we found ourselves drawn deeper into conversation, sharing stories of our lives on land with an effortless ease. With his hand resting gently atop mine on the table, I felt a flutter spread through me, a silent affirmation of the growing bond between us. Amidst the warm mood lighting and the tantalizing aromas of French cuisine, there was laughter, shared dreams, and stolen glances. It felt like the beginning of something truly special, unlike the several lackluster first dates I had endured in LA.

Across the room, I heard an excited, "Oh my goodness!" I looked over and saw Erika opening a small jewelry box with a sparkly ring inside.

I gasped, looked at Serge, and asked, "Is he proposing?... Did you know he was going to propose?!"

Serge laughed and said it was a present, not an engagement ring. He had gone with Marcello to help him pick it out at the jewelry shop onboard. Erika's smile was so big that it might as well have been an engagement, I thought.

"They do make a beautiful couple...do you think he will ask her soon?" I asked as I looked back into Serge's dark eyes.

He didn't answer but got a look in his eyes that I wasn't sure how to read. He continued telling me about the hypothetical trip to Italy we would take together after the contract and all the places he would take me to. I was heady with the image of me and him rolling around the sunflowers in Tuscany.

For dessert, we indulged in a decadent tiramisu. As the creamy dessert was placed before us, a mischievous grin appeared on Serge's face. He dipped his spoon into the luscious layers of mascarpone and espresso-soaked ladyfingers before reaching across the table, offering me a taste. I couldn't help but smile at his playful gesture, feeling a rush of warmth at the intimate exchange.

After dinner, we went to the martini bar a few decks up with Erika and Marcello. She flashed the ring on her finger excitedly. Marcello joked that it was now Serge's turn, to which he seemed bashful. One of the passengers sitting next to us commented on what gorgeous couples we made. When she said it, Serge's response was instinctive and tender. With a gentle smile, he wrapped his arm around me, drawing me close in a gesture that felt both protective and affectionate.

After we finished a round of martinis, Erika and Serge said they were heading back to Marcello's cabin. I hugged Erika goodnight and watched as they walked away hand in hand. I turned back to see Serge standing with his hand held out. He said our nightcap was waiting in his cabin. I smiled, slowly taking his hand and wondering what his cabin looked like. Smitty and the girls had been speculating for days now. Erika said she knew he had a balcony because Marcello's cabin did, but Serge's cabin was likely even more lush since he was the first officer and Marcello third.

Smitty's mantra of dating the top crew members for their cabins and privileges popped back into my head. Then, I remembered he told me those crew members became exes whose names became login passwords for Smitty's personal accounts.

Boyfriends for passwords, I thought amusingly.

As we made our way back to his cabin, my heart

raced with anticipation, my thoughts consumed by one simple desire: for Serge to finally lean in and kiss me. The size or decor of the cabin didn't matter to me in comparison to the possibility of that moment.

I walked in as Serge held open the door to his cabin and was blown away. His bathroom was larger than my entire cabin - complete with a huge glass shower and a marble bathtub! He had a bedroom connected to a sitting room with floor-to-ceiling glass doors that opened onto a large oval balcony.

"Okay, this is not fair...How do you expect me to return to my tiny broom closet after seeing all this?!" I asked jokingly.

He walked over to the wet bar in the sitting room and started making a martini. "So, don't go back then," he replied with a mischievous grin, his eyes sparkling as he began to expertly mix a martini. His casual suggestion hung in the air, daring me to entertain the possibility of staying in his luxurious cabin for the night.

"Don't tempt me," I said, unable to resist a playful tease, as I took the martini he had just poured. "I could literally hide out in here, and they would never find me! Would you defend me if they came to take me away?" I asked in a flirtatious tone.

He smiled, pouring the rest of the contents from the martini shaker into a glass, and led me outside. As we stood together on Serge's private balcony, enveloped in the darkness of the night, the vast expanse of the starlit sky stretched out before us, the shimmering reflections of the stars danced on the tranquil waters below. As we gazed outward, Serge's words washed over me like a gentle breeze.

"I've been wishing for this moment ever since I saw you," he confessed, his voice soft and sincere.

Though it sounded like a line, I found myself unable to resist the allure of his words, choosing instead to embrace the magic of the moment. I looked up into his dark eyes and saw the reflection of starlight on the water in them. At that moment, everything seemed perfect. And then, with a tenderness that took my breath away, Serge leaned down and captured my lips in a kiss that was both sweet and passionate, igniting a fire within me that burned brighter than the stars above.

XIV

CHAPTER 14

The obnoxious ring of the deck phone woke me up. I reached out to silence the incessant noise.

This thing is going to give me PTSD, I thought. *Who was calling this early?*

I realized it wasn't my phone. My battery was dead, yet the ringing persisted. Then, I remembered where I was. The soft, luxurious sheets brushed against my naked skin as I rolled over and saw Serge answering his phone.

"Ciao," he said and continued speaking in Italian. He leaned over and silently kissed my shoulder as he listened to the person on the other end.

As I glanced around the room, I couldn't help but marvel again at its spaciousness, especially now with the daylight pouring in through the large glass doors. The room seemed to expand before my eyes, bathed in the soft, golden glow of the morning sun. For the last twenty or so days, I had grown accustomed to waking up in a windowless cabin, where darkness enveloped me like a heavy blanket in a tiny bunk bed and the familiar thud of my head colliding with the low ceiling, so this felt surreal. Then I remembered that I had not planned to spend the night, but his king-sized bed was just so comfortable that I must have passed out. It still felt so luxuriously large. With a contented sigh, I closed my eyes and let myself sink deeper into the bed.

I'm usually not the type of girl who goes all the way on a first date, but "Ship Life" really made you feel like you were separated from your "Land Life." I never imagined in my wildest dreams that I would end up on the balcony of a palatial cabin under a starry, Hawaiian night sky with a gorgeous Italian First Officer... It was like right out of a movie. But sometimes being on this ship did feel like a movie...at times, a comedy or horror movie, but right then - a rom-com. I had talked with several crew members who had told me that you have your "Land Life" and then your "Ship Life," and the two were completely separate.

Already, "Ship Life Bree" was looking very different from "Land Life Bree."

Still on his call, Serge got out of bed and walked out on the balcony completely naked. I couldn't help but admire the sight of his bronzed skin bathed in the soft morning sunlight. The contrast of his exposed form against the backdrop of the ocean and sky was beyond enticing, and I found myself momentarily transfixed by the sight.

Finding my dress on the floor and quickly putting it on, I looked in the mirror next to the bed and saw a tousled mess of "bedhead" hair. I frowned, throwing it into a bun, hoping to tame the wildness of my hair into some semblance of order. As I sat on the edge of the bed, putting my heels back on, Serge finished his call and came back into the room. Sitting beside me on the bed, he gave me a big smile and kissed me. Usually, I can't stand kissing with morning breath, but again, "Ship Life Bree" was breaking all the rules. He said he had hoped to order breakfast for us, but there was a situation on the bridge that he had to handle.

"Of course, you can order breakfast in your room," I joked, laying my head on his shoulder. I told him I should get going as well as I finished buckling the tiny strap of my heel. He slipped a new pair of underwear on from his bedside drawer and walked me to the door.

"I shall see you very soon," he said as he kissed my hand. I nodded and gave him an alluring wink as I left, certainly feeling like a "New Bree."

I had done the "walk of shame" before, maybe twice. Both times didn't really bother me much. I just hopped into an Uber the first time...the second time, I was close enough to my place that I walked home on Hollywood Boulevard, and I didn't know anyone I passed – nor did it look like they even noticed. However, doing it on a cruise ship was an entirely different situation. The first thing I realized was that I left my name tag in Serge's cabin, so I was paranoid about being stopped by the safety officer and noticing I was in last night's cocktail dress, which luckily did not happen. However, walking down the I-95 to my cabin, I felt the weight of judgment pressing down on me with every step. Everyone seemed to look me up and down with scrutiny.

Was it all in my head? I asked myself. I tried to convince myself it was just my anxiety, but the longer I walked, the more it happened. With each passing moment, the corridor seemed to stretch out before me like a never-ending metal runway of shame. The saying I heard from Smitty and the spa girl the other night hauntingly flashed through my head, *There's nothing finer than a Diviner, but if you want the best, go Landmark Quest...*

I supposed I wasn't helping disprove that stereotype at the moment.

The faster I tried to walk, the louder the noise of my heels reverberated against the unforgiving metal floor and drew even more attention my way. I tried not to make eye contact with anyone...That is until I heard a loud catcall approaching me, and I knew who it was before even looking – Eryn.

"Well, well, what do we have here? Do we have a strumpet in our midst?" she cackled, really putting her Scottish brogue on the word "strumpet ." I must have looked mortified, and she got a bit more serious, "Girl, no worries! I'm all about sex positivity...and you know I expect all the dirty details!"

I blushed and told her I'd catch up with her later. As we parted ways, I had the feeling that the rest of the cast would know all my business within the hour.

My feeling was confirmed when I no sooner entered my cabin, and the phone on the wall started ringing. As I answered the phone, Smitty's voice greeted me with a mixture of excitement and concern.

"I've been calling you for the past hour, but your deck phone isn't ringing..." His words trailed off as realization dawned on him. "Oh my god, are you just getting in?!"

I couldn't help but smile at the playful accusation in his voice. "None of your business, mother!" I retorted, my tone teasing yet affectionate.

There was a moment of shocked silence on the other end of the line before Smitty burst into laughter. "Girl, you are so busted! I am so jealous!" he exclaimed, his voice filled with genuine amusement. I heard Holiday say something in the background, "Oh, please...You know I'm kidding," Smitty said, away from the phone.

The ship was back in Hilo, one of the last stops before we sailed back to San Diego and finished this cruise. Smitty said he and Holiday and the girls were going to get lunch in town, and I should come along to "spill the tea." I agreed and set the phone down. Georgette's bed was made up as usual, and so was mine. I wondered what she may have thought when she woke up and saw that my bed hadn't been slept in last night. I figured I would deal with that later. I quickly showered as the warm water washed away any lingering traces of sleep, leaving me feeling refreshed and invigorated. I felt a surge of happiness and contentment and realized that "Ship Life" was starting to agree with me. I popped on my sunglasses and walked out the door to go enjoy Hawaii and update the group on last night.

XV

CHAPTER 15

"Ship Life Bree" was in "work hard, play hard" mode. As I reflected on the past two months, I couldn't help but marvel at how far I had come since first stepping foot onboard. With each cruise, I had grown and evolved, transforming into someone who felt truly at home on the high seas. The art department had been exceeding its goals each cruise, and we even got a shout-out in the monthly email blast from the company. The department photo we took for the email looked hilarious. Smitty and I appeared like the poster children of Theobold and Georgette, who came off as a celebrity couple that had consciously uncoupled. Georgette seemed to be content with my performance and work ethic. There hadn't been any more meltdowns behind the guest service desk since the last time. However, the guest service staff still got wide-eyed whenever they saw Georgette, so her reputation remained intact. Our relationship was still very professional. I hardly saw her outside of work since I spent my nights in Serge's cabin now. The decision to spend my nights with Serge had been a natural progression, borne out of a growing connection and mutual affection. While our relationship was still relatively new, it had quickly become a source of comfort and stability amidst the hectic pace of "Ship Life."

I found myself fully embracing Smitty's philosophy of "Boyfriends for Passwords." The perks of dating without the drawbacks of full commitment seemed like the perfect arrangement for someone navigating the complexities of "Ship Life." Serge and I were great. We did our separate jobs most of the day and saw each other in the evenings for quiet movie nights in the cabin, drinks with Smitty and the cast, or double dates with Erika and Marcello. On Serge's insistence, I had moved most of my clothes and things into his cabin... He certainly had the room for it and said all the back and forth between my cabin and his to change and shower was ridiculous. Not to mention, his king-size bed did not make me miss the top bunk or smacking my head on the ceiling.

Now that all my trainings were completed, I had much more time to explore Hawaii. I took advantage of escorting the passenger tours. It was a great way to meet the passengers and find leads for the auctions. I made friends with the shore excursions manager and asked him to put me on the most expensive tours so I could mingle with the more affluent guests, which led me to escort the exploration tour of National Volcanoes Park in Hilo. As we ventured into the park, I couldn't help but feel a sense of awe and wonder at the sheer magnitude of the landscape before me.

At one point, I unexpectedly ran into some fellow crew members who pulled me away from the beaten path, away from the passengers, and led me to a restricted area where the lava flowed freely. With a mischievous gleam in their eyes, I watched as they picked up a large stick from the surrounding brush and dipped it into the glowing mass of molten rock, the intense heat causing it to burst into flames with a mesmerizing crackle.

One time on Maui, I went with Smitty and the gang as they rented convertibles, and we did the famed Road to Hana. As we wound our way along the twisting roads, each turn revealing a new vista more stunning than the last, I couldn't help but marvel at the natural splendor that surrounded us. From verdant valleys to dramatic sea cliffs, Maui seemed to unfold before us like a living tapestry of color and texture. We stopped at the Seven Sacred Pools, known to locals as the Ohe'o Gulch. Nestled amidst the lush greenery of the rainforest, this hidden gem was a paradise of natural crystal-clear plunge pools, beckoning us to dive in and explore. It was a moment of pure bliss—a chance to disconnect from the outside world and connect with the natural world in all its glory. Surrounded by the sights and sounds of Maui's pristine wilderness, I felt a sense of peace and serenity wash over me, a deep appreciation for the beauty of Hawaii.

As evening descended upon Maui, we went to a secluded beach, where locals and visitors alike gathered for a sunset ceremony unlike any other. As the sun dipped below the horizon, casting a warm golden glow across the sand, the gathered crowd began to form a drum circle, the rhythmic beat echoing in the stillness of the evening. Around us, fire dancers twirled and spun, their movements illuminated by the flickering flames as they danced. Meanwhile, children wandered among the revelers, their hands dipped in buckets of brightly colored paint. With joyful abandon, they approached us, leaving vibrant handprints on our bodies as a symbol of connection and unity.

As the sounds of ukuleles filled the air, we gathered around a beach bonfire, the crackling flames casting a warm glow over our faces. Above us, the stars gleamed in the night sky, their brilliance mirrored in the glow of the ocean waves. It was a celebration of life, love, and the beauty of the natural world. As we sat together, surrounded by the sights and sounds of Maui, I felt a deep sense of gratitude for the experiences we shared and the friendships that bound us together.

As I returned to the ship, exhaustion washed over me, and I couldn't wait to crawl into Serge's inviting bed and drift off to sleep. The comfort of his spacious cabin enveloped me as I drifted off to sleep next to him.

I was startled awake when Serge gently shook me at 4 a.m., promising a special surprise as we prepared to disembark from the ship. With my curiosity piqued, I groggily followed Serge's lead as we made our way off the ship. The air was cool and crisp, a hint of anticipation hanging in the pre-dawn stillness. As we ascended a winding switchback road, our car's headlights pierced through the darkness, illuminating the path ahead. The air grew colder with each twist and turn, the altitude increasing as we climbed higher and higher into the night. Finally, Serge parked the car, and we stepped out into the chilly mountain air.

Surrounded by darkness, we made our way to the edge of the lookout point, guided only by the faint glow of dawn on the horizon. The sign ahead confirmed our destination: Haleakalā Crater. With anticipation building in my chest, I followed Serge to a secluded spot among the rocks at the top of the crater. Finding a large flat rock, Serge draped a blanket over it, creating a makeshift seat for us to watch the sunrise. He then wrapped another blanket around us both, pulling me close as we settled in to await the spectacle unfolding before us.

As the first hints of light began to paint the sky in shades of pink and orange, I felt a sense of awe wash over me. We were perched above the clouds, the mist swirling below us like a sea of cotton candy. Through breaks in the fog, glimpses of the crater's rugged terrain emerged, adding to the sense of otherworldly beauty that surrounded us.

And then, in a blaze of neon orange, the sun breached the horizon, casting its warm glow over the landscape. It was a moment of pure magic—a breathtaking panorama unfolding before our eyes as we sat nestled together. I leaned into Serge's embrace, feeling the warmth of his body against mine, I knew that this was a memory I would cherish forever. As we watched the sun rise above Haleakalā, I couldn't help but feel grateful for the simple joy of being alive and the beauty of sharing it with someone special.

Honolulu had become my shopping day, and the Ala Moana mall near Waikiki was proving dangerous for me - or rather, my credit card. "Ship Life Bree" had completely changed her style from the more bohemian styles that "Land Life Bree" favored. After months of witnessing Georgette's runway fashion style and formal nights out with the dancers and spa girls, I had grown to love a more modern, sleek look. "Ship Life" had given me way more confidence in myself, outwardly and inwardly. Georgette even complimented me a few weeks ago on a jumpsuit I had bought, and having her fashion approval felt like a major accomplishment.

Smitty and I met with her to review our seminars before presenting them to the guests. It was like attending an LA audition with me standing in the middle of an empty room and Georgette casting her critical gaze upon me. As I delivered my presentation, her eyes bore into me, dissecting my every word and gesture with a discerning eye. When the critique came, it was delivered with the precision of a seasoned director. Georgette's feedback was concise: work on stage presence, keep the microphone close, minimize hand gestures. It was constructive, but her scrutiny was palpable. She was much more demanding on Smitty.

"No, Smithsonian," Georgette's voice echoed through the room like a broken record each time he turned to look at a slide or spent too much time on a slide or too little. But despite the initial challenges, we persevered. Through practice and dedication, we honed our skills, refining our presentations until they sparkled. And when the time came to host our own seminars, we did so with confidence, earning applause from the guests who attended. We had been transformed, much like the gems in Georgette's dazzling jewelry collection—each facet polished to perfection, every detail meticulously refined until we shone with brilliance.

One morning, Serge and I were woken up for cabin inspection. On each cruise, security came through the crew hallways and checked to ensure you had nothing "illegal" in your cabin. That meant anything from actual illegal drugs to silly things like taping pictures to your wall or having an extension cord to plug in your hair dryer – sometimes they even confiscated your hair dryer. Luckily, since Serge was the First Officer, security barely did anything besides check his cabin off the list.

I found out at breakfast that not everyone was so lucky.

The rule for alcohol in the cabin was that only one bottle of wine was allowed and no hard alcohol. Smitty usually hid all the wine bottles for our printing parties in one of the art lockers, but Eryn forgot she left a half-empty bottle of vodka in her mini-fridge and had an official date in Captain's Court. She laughed as we sat in the crew mess, finding the whole thing ridiculous. Holiday looked unpleased since he was the head of the production cast and had to attend as well. As we left the breakfast table, he asked Eryn to take it more seriously so she didn't get in further trouble.

"It will all be fine, darling. Trust me, I can handle those men," she said as we left the crew mess.

I had a slight issue of my own because I had lost my name badge. I thought I had misplaced it somewhere in Serge's huge cabin, but it wasn't resurfacing. So, I made my way to the crew office just off the I-95. The unkempt crew member sitting on the other side of the window looked like he had not left the office for several days. His greasy hair hung in limp strands around his face, framing a pallid complexion marred by patches of stubble and dark circles that seemed to have taken up permanent residence under his bloodshot eyes.

I explained the situation, and without even looking at me, he told me that replacing a name badge was fifty dollars plus a penalty of losing my pax privileges for an entire cruise.

"That's absolutely ridiculous!" I exclaimed. "Fifty dollars for a cheap piece of plastic? And losing pax privilege... for a first offense?!"

The man finally looked up at me, and a grin appeared on his face as he looked down over my body. I couldn't shake off the icky feeling that settled in the pit of my stomach when he casually suggested waiving the fee as a favor to a "pretty lady." It left a sour taste in my mouth, especially coupled with his dismissive attitude towards my concerns about the privileges.

I reached for my deck phone, dialing Serge's number without hesitation. I held the guy's gaze, determination flashing in my eyes as I recounted the situation to Serge, making sure to empha-size the unfair and inappropriate treatment I was receiving. As I hung up the phone, satisfaction washed over me as I watched the confusion spread across the guy's face.

His own phone rang on the other side of the window, and I couldn't help but smirk as he answered, panic evident in his voice. With a new-found sense of empowerment, I listened as he assured Serge that resolving the issue wouldn't be a problem and promised a replacement by the end of the day. As he hung up, his demeanor shifted, his previous arrogance replaced by a palpable sense of defeat. With a victorious flip of my hair, I turned on my heel and walked away, my head held high.

Dating the First Officer certainly had its perks, and I wasn't afraid to leverage them when it came to standing up for myself.

That night, Smitty and I were doing our usual round of Guess the Price in the atrium, but I felt like something was off. I noticed I was getting severe side-eye from the spa girls across the way.

"Apparently, the acupuncturist was super into Serge, and then you snapped him up," Smitty told me and continued, "I'd be careful... She might have a voodoo doll of you riddled with acupuncture needles!" He made a face, and I looked at him facetiously, "Ha-ha."

This wasn't the first time I had heard of other female staff and crew members not being happy with me for landing Serge so quickly, but I wasn't going to let it bother me too much. Holiday passed by us and delivered his update on Captain's Court earlier that day. He and Eryn had sat down as an officer read the offenses like it was the Supreme Court.

"These guys get off on their power trips up there," he said, "But luckily, Marcello was up there, so we had someone on our side."

The minute they started reading the penalties, Eryn began sobbing uncontrollably to the point that the men said they would mark it down as only a warning.

"That girl deserves an Academy Award because the second that door shut behind us, she was all smiles again. She knew exactly what she was doing!" Holiday laughed.

"Good! A lot of the men on this ship treat women like garbage," I declared, my frustration evident as I recounted the incident with the pervy name badge guy in the crew office. "It's about time we took some of our power back."

"Here, here!" Smitty chimed in, his tone playful as he raised a mock toast. "Power to the women and the homosexuals onboard! Okay now, can we talk about what's really important right now?... Halloween!" he exclaimed, seamlessly transitioning to a lighter topic.

With the holiday just a few days away, there was a buzz of anticipation for the large crew party planned on the outer deck at the back of the ship. When I mentioned to Smitty that I hadn't decided on a costume yet, he made it clear that I couldn't just throw on a corset and some ears and call it a day.

"That's what the spa girls do," he quipped, the implication clear. He stressed that as part of the entertainment department, we were responsible for setting the bar high with our costumes.

I found it intriguing how the categorization of the art department shifted depending on the situation. If someone needed us to co-host bingo, suddenly, we were part of the entertainment department. Yet, when it came to helping with the weekly cabin inspections, we were conveniently considered part of the hotel department. Georgette had finally had enough one day when a hotel staff member approached the auction lounge to schedule one of us for cabin inspection rounds. He regretted it as she shut him down quickly. She stood tall at the podium, exuding authority as she addressed the confused staff member.

"Now, see here, darling. I find it rather perplexing that we are part of the hotel department this week when, just last week, we were firmly told we belonged to the entertainment department.

So, which is it to be?" she paused, not allowing him a chance to interject.

"Shall I make the decision myself since it appears everyone else is rather befuddled? Very well. As members of the entertainment department, we shall not be participating in your little inspection raids." With that, she dismissed him, "Now do run along." Witnessing an angry Georgette in action when I wasn't the one on the receiving end was quite the spectacle.

Returning to the present, I agreed with Smitty and assured him I would try to construct a Halloween costume worthy of his approval.

Little did Smitty know, I already had my costume planned out down to the last detail. When I saw the yellow plaid jacket and miniskirt in a costume shop in Honolulu, I knew exactly who I wanted to be – Cher Horowitz from Clueless. Even more perfect, my deck phone was perfect to double as a huge '90s cell phone prop. Serge seemed particularly excited as I got dressed in his cabin on Halloween night, slipping into the character's knee-high white schoolgirl stockings. I couldn't help but notice the way his gaze lingered on my legs. Unfortunately, the Captain frowned upon his officers dressing up, so Serge was relegated to his standard white officer's uniform. He gave me a very handsy hug as I left his cabin and said he would attend the party later. There was an unmistakable hint of desire in his embrace that left me excited as I made my way to the dressing room, and the dancers greeted me with squeals of delight. They were all in high spirits, finishing up their makeup and blasting songs by the Spice Girls – which were their chosen costumes for the evening. With her red hair, Eryn had taken on the role of Ginger Spice, while Anna rocked the Baby Spice look with her blonde hair styled in two high ponytails. Meanwhile, Erika embodied Posh Spice in an iconic "Little Gucci Dress."

After toasting to the '90s divas, we headed to the open deck where the party was in full swing. Staff and crew members, along with a few adventurous guests who had managed to sneak past the "Private Event" signs, were already in attendance. The deck was transformed into a vibrant spectacle of party lights and music, the sound of laughter and chatter filling the air as people danced and socialized under the starry night sky. The effort put into the costumes varied, but it was clear that everyone had given it their all.

We spotted Holiday and Smitty on the dance floor, with Holiday dressed as the Phantom of the Opera and Smitty bedazzled in a silvery jumpsuit adorned with crystals and a candelabra headpiece featuring flickering LED candles. We all asked him what he was supposed to be, and he said he was the iconic chandelier from Phantom.

Eryn cackled while Anna cracked a dirty joke, "So, is the chandelier going down tonight?" She teased, a playful glint in her eye. Smitty, never one to back down from a challenge, fired back with a retort of his own.

"The same way you'll be polishing that lollipop you're holding, Baby Spice!" he quipped, earning a round of laughter and applause from the group.

I channeled my best Alicia Silverstone/Cher impression, "As if!"

Smitty had predicted correctly that most of the spa girls were dressed as sexy kittens or bunnies, with a few nurses and police officers mixed in. There were several stormtroopers taking pictures with people. When they finally took their helmets off to have a drink, I saw it was the guest services staff. I was impressed...They rivaled the stormtroopers I used to see out on Hollywood Boulevard posing with the tourists.

As the night wore on, we danced to the live band, led by the jazz singer dressed as a zombie bride twirling on stage. After a while, we grabbed another drink – this was one of the few crew parties where alcohol was free. We leaned against the ship's railing to catch a breath of fresh ocean air.

Suddenly, Smitty's head whipped around, his eyes widening in awe, "Holy shit! She looks amazing!!"

Following his gaze, we spotted Georgette making a grand entrance onto the deck through the sliding glass doors. The crowd parted as she moved forward like she was royalty. Then I realized she was... Dressed in a form-fitting, off-the-shoulder black silk dress paired with sheer black stockings and heels, she exuded the elegance of Princess Diana in her famous "Revenge Dress." A multistringed white pearl choker necklace adorned with a colossal gemstone shimmered as she made her way to us.

"I'm dead...absolutely dead and gone!" Smitty was beside himself with excitement, bowing down to Georgette in adoration. It was no secret that Smitty was obsessed with British royalty and all the movies and TV shows that featured them but was especially enamored with the former Princess of Wales.

She laughed slightly, "Oh, do get up, and let's have a picture, shall we?" Selfies and group photos ensued, and I was surprised to see Revenge Diana and the Spice Girls standing together, happily laughing about something.

"Look at Halloween bringing everyone together!" Smitty cheered as he kissed the Phantom.

I commented, "We really covered the '90s tonight between Clueless, Diana, the Spice Girls, and Phantom."

Then Holiday quickly corrected me, Phantom was 1986, babe."

"Close enough!" I said as we headed back to the dance floor.

XVI

CHAPTER 16

We wrapped up the cruise with a successful final auction. I was finally allowed to handle other clients besides just framing, which felt like an accomplishment. Georgette trusted me to process the invoices again after I had successfully completed it for several cruises. As we closed the gallery, Theobold summoned us all into his office and informed us that we would have a ship visit from one of Landmark Quest's managers the next day when we arrived back in San Diego. It was a standard meeting the company held to meet the team, inspect the gallery, and ensure everyone was performing up to standard. Slightly annoyed that this meant we couldn't get off the ship, we agreed to meet back in the gallery the following morning.

I woke up as Serge's breakfast order was wheeled into the room – a major perk of living with the First Officer was having a silver service breakfast. It certainly was an upgrade from the crew mess. We ate in the sitting area, and I expressed my disappointment that we never had enough time to drive up to LA so I could show him around.

Now that I was almost halfway through my contract, my previous life in Hollywood was starting to become a bit blurry. We showered together and got ready to go to work. I was really getting comfortable with this daily routine in the lap of luxury. We kissed each other and walked out the door.

As I slid open the doors to the gallery, everyone was already seated.

"How was your breakfast, Madam?" Smitty asked facetiously since I told him Serge always ordered in for us. I made a face at him as I sat down, and we waited. It was silent as we sat there, Theobold reading a newspaper, and Georgette touching up her manicure and periodically checking her watch.

"Where is this bloody woman?!" she finally exclaimed in a frustrated tone as she turned to Theobold. "What was her name again?"

Theobold said he didn't know.

Georgette prickled, "What do you mean you don't know? You added it to the security guest list last night... You did add the name, did you not?" she demanded.

He gave her a look over his newspaper.

"For goodness sake, Theobold! I asked you to do one thing – one bloody thing, and it doesn't get done. Well, it's no wonder she's not here since she's most likely stuck at security with the rest of the rabble." She took a breath as she stood up and smoothed her dress out, "No matter...I will handle this... As I always have to..." she said under her breath as she walked out.

Smitty watched her leave, then looked at me and whispered, "Mom and Dad are fighting!" Theobold put his paper down and confessed that it was his fault and had slipped his mind. Then he pulled out his Mont Blanc pen, which he had each client sign their invoice with, and started on the crossword on the back of the newspaper, enlisting Smitty and me to help him complete it.

After a while, I heard Georgette's voice from the hallway, "I am so sorry, it seems it was a clerical error with the system... You know the computers they give us are from the Stone Age." She blamed Theobold's mistake on technology as they entered the gallery. The woman was dressed like she might be walking on the French Riviera, in a flowy full-length blue caftan that she had belted around her large waist and a matching silk scarf wrapped around her head like a hood with her frizzy blonde hair popping out one side and down her shoulder.

"Hi there, I'm Monica," she introduced herself to Smitty and me. She must have noticed us looking at her outfit, "Oh, I figured I'd dress up for those hot Italian officers that are always roaming around!" she said excitedly as Smitty gave me a look. Then Monica turned to Theobold, "Oh my, but maybe I just dressed up for you, handsome," she smiled at him as she took her scarf off. It was all I could do not to burst out laughing, and I looked over to Smitty, holding his head, trying not to as well.

Theobold stood up, "And welcome, Monica, to the Vivace Vision." She held her hand out like she wanted Theobold to kiss it, but he quickly shook it awkwardly. She giggled as I watched the awkward scenario.

How is this odd woman a manager at Landmark Quest? I asked myself. It was as if they were sending a decoy actor to see how we would react to a crazy person.

"Right, well, shall we get started?" Georgette asked as Monica was still smiling at Theobold.

"Oh, alright," she said as she sat down. "I usually start with inspecting the lockers because they are usually shit holes, but I know you guys clean them right up when I come onboard... Plus, it's a lot of stairs to deal with," she admitted. The four of us sat across from her as she opened a folder of papers and began reading out our sales numbers from the previous cruises.

Theobold chimed in, "And I am happy to report that we smashed it this cruise as well."

She looked up, gave him another big smile that lingered awkwardly, and finally said, "Oh, that must be because of you two handsome gentlemen."

This woman is clearly not a girl's girl, I thought silently.

Monica looked at Smitty sitting next to

Theobold, "Although that pretty hair is a bit long, I'm surprised the Captain hasn't had you cut it yet."

Poor Smitty, I thought, listening as he reassured her that it wasn't an issue. And so far, it hadn't been. Plenty of people brought it up when he joined the ship, and he quickly shut down the inquiries, saying that if the Captain wanted him to cut it, he would have to come and tell him in person.

Our Captain was nonexistent. Aside from his two announcements at the start and end of a cruise and his photo posted on the officer board, I never heard from or saw him. Serge told me that he did very little but still collected a pretty paycheck. Smitty told me that most captains were divas and sent their first officers to enforce the grooming policy rules. Since I had brought Serge onto our side, he figured he was in the clear.

There was that idea of "sides" and "alliances" again... After a few months, I saw how having the "right" people in your corner was beneficial.

Monica began asking each of us what our duties were and how we performed in the auctions and asked us to rate our sales skills from 1 to 10. We were a great team since we were number one in the fleet so I thought our answers would be obvious to her, but perhaps these were just standard questions. She told us that the company's CFO, who was also her cousin, was looking to start increasing our targets.

Now it makes sense how she's a manager, I thought.

Theobold shifted in his chair, "I'm sure you can agree, Monica, that our target is already extremely high."

She nodded, then shrugged, "Well, you know, he does what he wants to do. I'm just passing on the message. You'll just have to train them up more!" she said, motioning to the rest of us.

Theobold put his fingertips together, "Yes, well, Bree and Smitty here have been improving with each cruise and doing extremely well. And Georgette is most certainly the glue that holds this whole department together. She truly is invaluable."

Georgette nodded in thanks.

Monica got a twitch in her eye, then looked at Georgette, "Well, she can't be that great if she can't even remember to put a name on a list. I just have a feeling that it was your fault, a 'clerical error,' or whatever you want to call it. Oh, I know how long you've been with the company, and they hold you on a pedestal for some reason, but I don't see it," the woman sneered, her tone dripping with disdain as she directed her venomous words at Georgette. "If I told my cousin about your mistake, he wouldn't be happy that I had to wait to get on-board..." she continued, her voice laced with thinly veiled threat.

I was stunned by the woman's unhinged behavior, her unwarranted attack catching me off guard.

What is her problem? Is she on medication? Or perhaps she is jealous of Georgette's position and authority? I questioned myself.

Whatever the reason, her blatant hostility was both bewildering and infuriating. As the tension in the air thickened, I felt a surge of protective instinct wash over me. This was not her ship—it was ours. And I was not about to let her bully Georgette without repercussions. I interjected before the woman could launch another verbal assault.

"Actually, it was my mistake," I asserted, my voice steady despite the turmoil swirling within me. "Georgette asked me, and I said I would take care of it, but it just completely slipped my mind," I confessed, playing the ditz card.

Georgette turned her eyes to look at me but kept completely still as if she was about to pounce.

Monica's demeanor suddenly shifted as she smiled and said, "Oh! Well, I guess it's not a big deal then... Hey! So, how's the food upstairs?!" she asked excitedly as if she hadn't just tried to rip Georgette to shreds.

Smitty's eyes almost popped out of his head at the complete 180 from the woman.

"Oh, and I have to meet with the Hotel Director as well... Is he attractive? I really don't want this outfit to go to waste!" she said as Theobold offered to escort her to the HD's office. "Bye, everyone!" she yelled from the hallway.

Smitty gave a slow, confused wave as we watched her disappear around the corner.

"Ummmm... I'm sorry...What just happened?" Smitty asked, looking at Georgette and me.

"An imbalance of medication would be my guess," Georgette answered and looked at me.

I apologized for my abrupt interjection, but the woman's erratic behavior had pushed me to speak up. Georgette paused for a moment, her expression unreadable as she considered my words. Then she delivered a response.

"If you think I couldn't have handled that frizzy, neurotic, thirsty product of nepotism," she said, each adjective dripping with disdain as she smoothed her hair with deliberate precision.

"Then you gravely underestimate me... Bree."

Her use of my name caught me off guard. A short, but genuine grin graced her lips before she turned and left the gallery, leaving me and Smitty in a state of disbelief.

"Never, not once, has she called you Bree!" Smitty exclaimed, his excitement palpable as he rushed to give me a big hug. "I don't know what the fuck happened these last forty minutes, but I feel the need to celebrate it... We still have time to find a happy hour in San Diego!" he declared with infectious enthusiasm.

XVII

CHAPTER 17

Two more weeks passed as we finished another cruise, and this time, I outsold Smitty, to which he said that I was buying the wine for the printing parties from now on. I supposed I should buy a few rounds, but it was a pain to keep running to the crew bar every day at 3 p.m. for "Wine O'Clock" to buy a bottle of wine. Many days, I wasn't even back on the ship by 3, and I couldn't bring alcohol onboard. Maybe Serge could make some magic happen. He was becoming my secret weapon around many rules and red tape onboard.

That is until we received an email in the gallery inbox with the subject line: Code Red.

No matter how different the crowd could be on each cruise, they all had one thing in common... Many people refused to wash their hands. It was gross, but no one in our department had gotten ill so far, so it hadn't affected us... until now.

Code Red was an emergency medical situation in which a certain percentage of the passengers reported being ill during the cruise. Over 30% had reported ill with a stomach virus on the current cruise, so they declared us officially in Code Red. Which meant ship management was required to limit passenger touchpoints to slow the spread.

Theobold read the email aloud, saying they required 75% of each department to assign themselves to a schedule for serving the passengers upstairs on Lido Deck at the buffet – no exceptions.

Theobold let out a low whistle, "Well, unfortunately, 75% is you three, I'm afraid."

None of us were too thrilled with this mandate, but there seemed no way around it. Begrudgingly, the next day, Georgette, Smitty, and I went up to the buffet and reported to the Food & Beverage Manager, who handed us an apron, long rubber gloves, and a paper hat with a hair net. He told Georgette since she had short hair, she didn't need to wear the hair net.

"Well, thank goodness for small miracles," she said unimpressed.

Smitty and I looked so ridiculous in the hair nets and paper hats that we couldn't help but laugh at one another as we pulled the rubber gloves on. Georgette, however, did not find anything humorous as she placed the paper hat on her head as if she was being physically forced.

"Honestly, it just looks like you're doing a quirky fashion shoot," I told her as we walked out behind the buffet counters. All kinds of food options were displayed in large metal pans with steam rising from below. I could feel the steam waft over me as we walked by. The clattering sounds of trays echoed as crew members took them from their towering stacks to serve the guests. They assigned Georgette and me to the salad bar.

"Well, at least this can't be too traumatic, can it?" Georgette asked herself as the first guest in a long line approached her. "Yes, Madam, what would you like?" she asked in a strained tone. She placed all the ingredients the woman requested in a salad bowl, "Ah see, it's not that difficult," she said under her breath. Then the woman asked for ranch dressing; however, when Georgette reached for the dressing bottles, none of them were labeled.

She looked at me, "Darling, which one do you think?" she asked with the most vulnerability I had ever seen from her.

This was clearly way out of Georgette's wheelhouse. To be fair, Smitty and I were in the same boat. They assigned Smitty to the burger bar, where you had to cook the burgers in front of the passengers.

Smitty turned around, "I'm sorry, there's been a mistake...I...I don't cook...I mean, I don't know how. He placed an uncooked patty on the grill, and flames leaped up suddenly, making him jump. He silently voiced, "Help!" to me across the bar, but I was stuck trying to figure out which bottle was ranch.

There were two bottles with white dressing, so I pointed to one that Georgette grabbed and put a dab on the salad. The woman got annoyed and said that it wasn't ranch. Georgette tried the other bottle, which was ranch this time, but she had to remake the whole salad for the woman and finally squeezed out the ranch dressing. The woman said she wanted more, and Georgette squeezed again.

"Just go until I say stop," the woman said disgustedly. The salad was drowning in ranch dressing when she finally said stop and grabbed the bowl from Georgette.

"Bloody hell, this is torture," she said to me as two people came up and barked their orders. It became clear that the way I made my salads, trying to stay healthy, was not how these passengers wanted their salad made. Everyone wanted hardly any lettuce or vegetables, but all the fatty meats and piles of croutons drowned in all types of dressing, and they wanted it right away.

"Damn Theobold Thorne for this! Of course, he couldn't get off his bloody throne to come and endure this!" Georgette muttered angrily.

I couldn't help but giggle, and then I heard someone yelling at Smitty about burning a hamburger patty.

"I told you! I don't know how to cook..." Smitty protested. "I always date someone who cooks...or I order in," he added with a feeble attempt at humor, but the manager's stern expression made it clear that this was no laughing matter. The manager's patience seemed to be wearing thin as he snatched the grilling tongs out of Smitty's hand, his lips pressed into a thin line of disapproval. As the manager ushered Smitty over to us at the salad bar, Georgette's relief was palpable.

"Oh, thank goodness, darling, we are drowning here!" she exclaimed, thrusting a salad bowl into Smitty's hands. It was chaos—a whirlwind of tossed lettuce, scattered toppings, and frantic attempts to keep up with the lunch rush. Yet, amidst the madness, there was a strange sense of camaraderie. Our ineptitude had inadvertently brought us together, forging a bond in the chaos. And strangely enough, being so bad at our jobs seemed to work in our favor—we were all banished from the buffet for good. Afterward, in the elevator, Georgette's stern gaze met ours.

"We shall not talk of this again," she declared, her voice carrying a note of finality. The elevator doors opened and she strutted out, regaining her impeccable composure as if the last hour up in the buffet had never happened. Smitty and I exchanged a knowing glance, silently acknowledging the unspoken pact. Whatever happened in the buffet line stayed in the buffet line.

The next day at the auction, Eryn and Anna roared with laughter at Smitty's recounting of the Code Red buffet story.

"Oh, I would have paid good money to see that!" Eryn cackled on, but the laughter diminished quickly. Something was off with them. I asked them where Erika was, and they became very silent.

Smitty also sensed it, "What's going on, ladies?"

The two girls looked at each other and nodded. They said Erika had come to their cabin in hysterics the night before. Marcello had revealed to her that he married a woman in Italy and had a child with her.

I gasped in shock.

They continued saying, to make it worse, that the wife and kid were coming onboard for the next cruise.

"The asshole told her that he can't acknowledge her, and she can't talk to him or be in the cabin because that's where they are staying," Eryn said, looking at the ground.

"She's still inconsolable, but she asked to be alone, so we let her stay in our cabin," Anna said.

"And the wife has no idea either?" I asked, still in shock.

They shook their heads. The sheer audacity of Marcello's actions left me speechless, the weight of his betrayal bearing down on me like a crushing weight.

What the hell? They seemed like such a solid couple, I thought to myself. I knew how strongly Erika felt for Marcello, and I really thought he felt the same way – he sure acted like it. I thought back to that night at dinner when I assumed he proposed to her, but then I also remembered that odd look Serge got when I asked him if Marcello was proposing.

Had he known something then? I asked myself.

The auction did not go well. It was another crowd full of people wanting the freebies. I stopped the bartender from serving again and felt terrible for Theobold as he went through the entire auction with hardly any bids.

The cruise was quickly unraveling into a string of disasters—the Code Red, the drama between Erika and Marcello, and now this dismal auction crowd. It felt like the universe was conspiring against us, throwing one obstacle after another in our path. Theobold finished the auction and walked offstage behind the curtains. Georgette signaled the art movers. She hadn't sold anything either, so she didn't come down hard on Smitty and me. During my break, I went to find Serge. I called him, and he told me where to find him.

I descended the crew staircases to the lower decks below my cabin. I hadn't been down below the water line yet, and I could hear the water rush against the ship's hull. As I ventured further below the water line, the corridors grew dimmer, illuminated only by the occasional light bulb overhead. It was a stark contrast to the polished veneer of the upper decks, a reminder of the gritty reality that lay beneath the surface of the glamorous cruise ship.

After walking down several narrow hallways, I found Serge in an office, sitting at a desk beside a large, barred cell. It was the "brig," which was ship slang for jail. It was freezing that far down inside the ship, and I asked what he was doing there. He said that he enjoyed the sound of the water, which helped him focus on getting paperwork done. I looked around, noticing the walls behind the bars were painted pink.

I joked that I didn't think pink was his color.

He explained that pink was calming for rowdy inmates, but they didn't have to arrest passengers often. Occasionally, they would put someone down there to sleep off their drunkenness. There was a big metal door on the far side of the brig that looked ominous to me. I asked where it led, and Serge said it was the morgue. That surprised me. I had not thought about it, but, of course, this "floating city" would need a morgue. He said they used it a lot more than the brig. I asked if anyone was in there now, and he shook his head. He told me I would know if I heard an announcement saying "Operation Rising Star." A shiver went down my spine. Dying at sea was not the way I wanted to go. I told him about Marcello and Erika and asked if he knew Marcello was married. He threw his hands up, and I gasped.

"I knew he had been seeing a woman in Naples... I didn't know it was his wife or about the baby," he said. I must have appeared shocked by what he had just told me. He explained that it wasn't unheard of in this line of work, and gossiping about such things was considered bad form. "Erika is a sweet girl. She will move past this," he said as he got up to hug me.

"Yeah, but she shouldn't have to move past a huge lie like this. I'm upset that you didn't tell me all this time," I said as I pulled away from him.

"Tell you, and then what?... Put you in an awkward position? I didn't want to do that to you," he said as he hugged me again.

I felt weird, and it was the first time I didn't want him to touch me. Our relationship had been going so smoothly that we hardly fought at all. I never imagined anything like this would bring on our first big fight. I told him I had to return to work. The sound of the rushing water seemed to have gotten louder as I left the brig feeling very conflicted.

The gallery was empty that night. We had so few appointments that Theobold didn't even come in. Smitty and I sat at our checkout stations while Georgette leaned on the glass display case in the middle of the gallery.

"Oh, how the mighty have fallen," she mused aloud, her voice tinged with resignation.

I couldn't help but agree with her assessment, though I added that it wasn't just us—the entire cruise seemed to be plagued by a peculiar energy. I started thinking about Erika, how bad I felt for her, and how angry I was at Marcello, which led me back to Serge. I could see why he thought saying something would put me in an awkward position, but if I was the one with the secret, there was no way I could keep it from my...

Then I paused.

What did I call Serge? I asked myself.

We hadn't labeled our relationship. I didn't call him my boyfriend, but he was certainly more than a friend.

How mad could I really be? I asked myself, but then told myself I was allowed to feel what I was feeling. Maybe I had deeper feelings for Serge than I knew. It was only meant to be a fun fling with a cute guy in his nice cabin. I started to get a headache. "Ship Life" was beginning to drive me a bit crazy as my thoughts continued going around in circles. I looked up from my desk and caught Georgette's eyes analyzing me.

"Smithsonian, would you please fetch a box of invoice paper from the locker downstairs?" Georgette asked Smitty, who popped up and said he'd be back. I watched him leave, still deep in my thoughts.

Suddenly, I heard her voice, "Trouble in paradise?" Georgette was across from me, where a client would usually sit. "You look a million miles away. Penny for your thoughts?" she asked as she lightly ran a finger over the black tablecloth.

I looked at her and said, "Well, I am sure you have heard by now."

"Darling, everyone has heard about the dirty dog," she answered.

I told her I was just angry at Marcello and upset for Erika.

"Did I not advise you to be cautious of Italian enchantments not that very long ago?" Georgette queried. I agreed but said that Erika and Marcello seemed like a much more solid couple than Serge and I.

"Did they indeed?" she said, raising her eyebrows at me. My alarm grew as I processed Georgette's words.

"Wait, did you also know he had a wife?!" I exclaimed, the shock evident in my voice. She rose from the table with a solemn expression, pacing slowly around the desk as she spoke.

"I didn't have to know," she replied, her tone tinged with resignation. "With these officers, it's always a different version of the same old story. When it feels too good to be true, that is precisely when it all comes crashing down." Her words hit me like a cold wave, sending a shiver down my spine.

Was Serge hiding something from me? The thought filled me with a sense of dread, a nagging suspicion that I had been blind to the warning signs all along.

"Look, darling," she continued, her voice tinged with concern. "I'm not saying your First Officer also has a wife and child somewhere, but if you are seeing red flags, perhaps now is the time to... rethink things."

Her words echoed in my mind as I grappled with the implications of what she was saying.

Can I trust Serge, or am I simply setting myself up for heartbreak? I asked myself cautiously.

She looked at me, "And don't misunderstand me, I am loving having the cabin all to myself. I've turned your bed into a fabulous shoe display... However, it is always there should you need it," she finished.

I couldn't help but chuckle at her remark, the tension of the moment dissipating with her light-heartedness.

"The bed? Or the shoes?" I quipped, a playful smile tugging at the corners of my lips.

Smitty returned with the box, a bit out of breath, saying something about that being his car-dio for the night since the storage lockers were located several decks below. He put the box in one of the gallery cabinets and sat at his desk. Another hour passed, and not a single person had walked through the gallery when Georgette said she was putting us out of our misery – the gallery was closing early. Smitty jumped up from his chair and hastily broke down his folding table. I began doing the same to my checkout table as Georgette set out signs advertising the upcoming event, Smitty's seminar. It was the first time since I came onboard that the gallery had closed early, and I wasn't sure what to do with myself. I didn't feel like seeing Serge.

"Come on," Smitty grabbed my hand and led me from the gallery and through the atrium. I was about to ask where we were going when I heard the Cruise Director's voice over the PA system announcing that the production show was about to start. I had wanted to see my friends perform on stage for a while now. So far, I had only heard Holiday's one song on the crew night out months ago. I felt a streak of excitement as we approached the theater, and I saw the dancers standing outside the entrance, welcoming the guests.

The girls had matching rhinestone corsets and vast plumes of feathers rising from their glittering headdresses. Anna saw us in the line and pulled me aside. I told her I was excited to see her in action finally. She smiled and thanked me but said Erika was still not doing well. They had revised the dance numbers to accommodate for her absence. Her headdress and earrings glittered in the light as she shook her head in concern. She and Eryn had left Erika in their room, and she asked if I would check on her. I agreed in a second, and Anna handed me her room key.

"And don't worry... You'll be able to see the show another night when it's better because we aren't down a dancer," she said, walking into the theater behind the last guests.

XVIII

CHAPTER 18

I made my way down the crew staircase to the I-95 and headed towards the dancers' hallway. I was a bit nervous.

What should I say? I asked myself. *Just be there for her,* I thought as I knocked on Anna and Eryn's cabin door. My memory flashed back to when I knocked on this door, and Eryn opened it in her racy mermaid outfit. This time, the door didn't open, and I knocked again... Still no answer. I hesitated, then put the room key in the slot under the handle and opened the door as I heard the lock click. It was pitch black inside – the same as my cabin.

I called for Erika in the dark and heard a rustling of bedsheets and some slight movement in the darkness.

"Who's there?" Erika's voice sounded low and tired. A night light popped on by the bottom bunk bed, illuminating Erika's head from under the covers.

"It's Bree. I came to check on you and keep you company... If you want?" I asked as I stepped closer to the bed. She pulled her knees up under the covers and made space for me to sit. I sat down and laid over her body to hug her, telling her I was there for her.

Several wadded-up tissues were scattered around the bed as she pulled her arm out from under the covers and grabbed my hand. She said that nothing made sense anymore, and she felt so lost. I reassured her that it was perfectly fine to feel that way, but she was strong, and she would get past it. She stared at the ring Marcello had given her. It sparkled in the light on the nightstand.

"I thought that he loved me..." She started sobbing, and I squeezed her hand. "Why doesn't he love me?" she asked me through her sobs. I told her he didn't deserve her and that there was a great guy out there waiting for her. I knew it sounded cliché as I said it, but it seemed to help. She looked at the clock next to the night light, "Aren't you supposed to be working?"

I sat up and attempted to make a joke, "Oh, didn't you hear about how glorious the auction was today?... Yeah, it was a glorious shitshow!"

To my delight, Erika let out a tiny giggle. I laughed and continued, "Yeah, if anyone should be crying, it's me, so I don't know what your problem is..."

Erika giggled a bit louder.

"Damn, this cruise sucks!" I said.

Erika rolled over to look at me, "You can say that again." I laid down beside her in the tiny bunk bed and put my arm around her. She closed her eyes and let out a sigh. We laid there for about an hour or so as she went through their relationship and how she never saw any red flags, crying intermittently throughout.

Eventually, the cabin door opened, and Anna and Eryn walked in wearing their post-show tracksuits and full-stage makeup. Smitty popped his head in as well.

"And how are we doing in here?" Eryn asked.

I looked at Erika as she sat up in bed, "A bit better, I guess," she said with puffy eyes and dried mascara running down her face.

"Well, good because you have us all night, babes. What do you feel like doing?" Eryn asked, and Erika gave a small shrug.

Anna said, "Let's have a girl's night in – no boys allowed!"

"Hey!" Smitty interjected, and Anna giggled.

"No straight boys, you daft thing!" Eryn quipped, playing up her accent to get a laugh from us. She motioned for Smitty to come in.

"I know exactly what we need to feel better – it helps every time," I said as the girls looked at me. I turned to look at Smitty, who knew exactly what I was talking about.

"Right there with you!" he said as he pulled his hard drive out of his pocket. He plugged it into the TV, and Eryn pulled some wine bottles out of her suitcase, which she had been hiding from the cabin inspectors. Before long, all five of us were hud-dled in the bunk beds and began binging Golden

Girls episodes. In that tiny cabin, surrounded by the warmth of friendship and the familiar antics of Blanche, Rose, Dorothy, and Sophia, it felt as though the negative energy from the cruise had been lifted from our shoulders, if only for a fleeting moment.

I didn't sleep in Serge's cabin that night. I was so tired after leaving the dancers' cabin, and since my cabin was much closer, I opted to return there. I also felt like I needed more time before we continued the conversation from the brig. My absence would hopefully give him a better understanding of my feelings.

In the darkness of my cabin, I climbed over a sleeping Georgette and passed out in my top bunk, which had been cleared of her shoes. When I woke up, she was gone. I showered and started to get dressed, which proved a bit more challenging since the room was lurching one way and then the other. The ship had begun its string of sea days back to San Diego, and the sea was rough. Several of Georgette's perfume bottles clinked as they fell over on the desk.

I met Smitty in the lounge on deck 6 to help

him set up for his seminar. As I walked in, he was doing a mic test, looking a bit tired from our Golden Girls night. When he saw me, he started talking in his best southern accent to emulate Blanche Deveraux, his favorite Golden Girl. He said he related to her racy ways. Eryn had also tried to claim Blanche last night, but Smitty had told her she was definitely a Dorothy, which we all laughed at. I happily claimed Rose for myself.

"I'm not setting the art up with this weather," Smitty said. "All I need is a frame falling on someone and getting sued... If anyone is suing, it's going to be me."

I raised an eyebrow at him.

"What? I gotta get rich somehow!" he quipped. I said that his boyfriend might become famous, and he could be a kept man.

"A girl can dream..." he said as he pulled the projection screen up.

Smitty had done this seminar multiple times now and expressed his boredom at having to do it. The projector fired up, and the first slide appeared on the screen, featuring the artist next to the rustic nature landscapes he was famous for. It wasn't my art style, but people went nuts for his work, making him one of our top sellers. The artist's entire brand was built upon this wholesome family mentality, so I laughed when Smitty said, "I decided to remove the slide where I say that he is now a raging alcoholic after his kids disowned him and his wife took his company after finding out about all of his affairs... like someone else we know..."

He meant Marcello. I agreed and mentioned that Erika seemed to be a bit better after our binge session.

"She's picking up the pieces, girl. I will be shading him so hard the next time I see him. What does Serge say about the whole thing? Isn't Marcello like his best friend?" he asked. I sighed and told him about the Serge drama and that I slept in my own cabin last night.

"Yikes... This cruise really is cursed," he said as he looked at his phone for the time. "T minus five." We arranged the chairs in rows in front of the screen and sat in the front row as the ship continued to crash against the big waves.

We were still the only two people in the lounge ten minutes later. Smitty looked around the empty lounge. "I mean, I guess we were doing so well

before that it's about time we had a bad cruise."
He shrugged at me as he said it. I told him that I
thought a lot of the passengers were seasick. Walking around the ship, I noticed paper puke bags had
been placed out for the guests, and there were several hazard signs on the ground in different areas,
signaling where someone had vomited. An elderly
lady with a cane slowly walked into the lounge.
Smitty turned and greeted her.

"Hi there, ma'am. Are you here for the seminar?
There are plenty of seats!"

She looked confused and asked if this was
where Bridge was taking place.

"Nope, this isn't Bridge, but it is where you can
listen to a wonderful art seminar hosted by me!"
Smitty said with a cheeky grin.

The lady looked even more confused. "No,
thank you," she said as she turned around and
walked out.

Smitty turned back to me. "This is what we
are dealing with... bridge bitches." I giggled as
he continued, "Should I jump overboard now or
later when the next auction is empty as well, and
we get blamed for it?" I told him that Theobold
and Georgette knew it was a dud of a group on

this cruise. He started collapsing the projection screen and said that every auctioneer became very grumpy when they turned in a low sales number at the end of the cruise.

Smitty wasn't wrong. The next day at the auction, we stood next to the registration table, waiting for the guests to show up. I asked Anna and Eryn how Erika was doing, and they said that she had moved out of Marcello's cabin and back into the cabin she was assigned to with Alina.

Georgette's announcement sounded over the PA system. We listened as it ended with the usual bing-bong noise, and by the time she made it up to the lounge, only a handful of people had registered.

"Wow... Even the free booze can't motivate this crowd," Eryn stated.

The weather had worsened, and the ship was rocking even more than yesterday. Ship management told us it was affecting all the departments onboard. Theobold mentioned that Landmark Quest didn't accept bad weather as an excuse for not hitting our target, and I had tried to reassure him that the next cruise would be better. Now that I think about it, I was probably trying to reassure myself as well. By the time the auction was meant to start, we had fewer than ten people. Theobold summoned Georgette over to the side of the stage and whispered something to her before he disappeared backstage. Georgette took the microphone and announced that, unfortunately, due to the weather, the auction had been canceled, but everyone would be awarded a free work of art. I frowned at the last part because I knew what the rest of my night looked like... Listening to more excuses why they wouldn't be framing.

I was spot on as I heard all the same objections and how many family members had a frame store. Nonetheless, I still used my sales tactics to try to convince them, but it was a lost battle with this cheap crowd.

I walked towards the finance office to turn in the smallest stack of invoices ever. The line at the front desk was so disorderly it was almost frightening. Not only were the passengers screaming at the front desk staff with complaints, mostly about the weather, but they were also fighting with each other over things like line-cutting. I felt bad...I was annoyed at the guests for telling me they wouldn't frame their free art when these poor staff members were being shouted at about circumstances they couldn't control. I really couldn't imagine how the staff members didn't snap. As I quickly ducked into the back office, I heard a woman shouting and demanding a full refund on the cruise because of the rough seas. I handed the invoices to the accountant, who told me not to feel bad because none of the retail departments had done well on this cruise.

"At least we can boot them off tomorrow and press the restart button," he said, trying to cheer me up. He had always been nice to me when I saw him. He was the one who bought me a drink at the traffic light party.

"Maybe we can commiserate over a drink in the crew bar tonight?" he suggested. As I left, I gave him a quick smile and said maybe I would see him there. I felt like there was enough happening at the moment, and I didn't need to complicate things any further. I walked back to the gallery to help Georgette and Smitty close. Theobold had not shown up all night. We closed the gallery early again and agreed to try and forget this cruise.

Smitty said he was exhausted and mentioned

having a movie night with Holiday. The production show had also been canceled due to the weather, so the cast had the night off. I was on my own, it seemed. I walked through the atrium, and the noise of the guests' complaints blended into a dull drone as I continued down the hallway. I was tired, but I hadn't decided where I wanted to sleep. It had been two days since I slept over with Serge. Due to the bad weather, all the officers were stuck working overtime on the Bridge for most of the day and night, so there hadn't been time to talk about things yet.

I walked past the martini bar, so lost in my thoughts that I almost didn't see him.

I stopped to look closer and saw Theobold sitting in the very corner of the bar. I was about to move on but decided to see how he was doing. As I approached him, I saw several empty beer bottles in front of him. He was still in his suit but had removed his tie, leaving the first few buttons on his shirt open. His hair was a bit disheveled, and he didn't seem to notice me approaching.

"Here you are," I said as I reached the table.

His glassy eyes looked up at me, and a grin spread on his face. He opened his arms wide like he was presenting on stage. "Well, if it isn't Breanne Bradley," he slurred his words a bit. I had never seen him in this state before.

I hesitated, "I just wanted to say hi... I should probably go." I started to back away.

"Nonsense! Sit... Please!" he motioned to the chair next to him with his beer bottle. "Have a drink... What would you like? It's on me. Even if I didn't make any money this time around, I've got you," he said, looking at me.

"How many of those have you had?" I asked jokingly.

He smiled and said, "As many as it takes to forget this crime scene of a cruise."

I laughed. Even drunk, he was still eloquent. I repeated what the accountant had told me about everyone doing horribly on this cruise, so we shouldn't blame ourselves too much.

"But I agree... this cruise has been a nightmare and can end like yesterday," I said.

"Yes, I did hear something about a meltdown within your circle..." he trailed off, waiting for a response from me.

"Yeah, it's a bit of a situation, but we are working on it," I tried to keep it pretty vague.

He put his hands up, "Not meaning to pry. I don't usually pay any mind to the ship gossip, but I am trying not to think about the lashing I will get about this tragedy tomorrow."

I had never seen this side of Theobold. He was always so sophisticated and suave. I started to feel bad – yes, we all failed as a team, but as the auctioneer, I supposed the company may hold him more responsible.

"Well, we have Georgette," I said. "Isn't she like a big deal at the company? Maybe she could help soften the blow," I suggested. Theobold started roaring with laughter.

"Don't be fooled by the shiny veneer of Georgette Day," he said as he finished his beer and picked up another from the table. "Her family is very close with mine, so I am privy to her dirty laundry..."

I wasn't sure if I wanted to hear what Theobold was about to say.

He continued, "She is the black sheep of the family... They practically paid the company to take her off their hands. Her name isn't even Day – it's Covingard. The family was so embarrassed by their darling daughter that Lord Covingard donated a considerable sum to Landmark Quest. Thus, the legend of Georgette Day was born," he said with a flourish of his hand.

I was stunned.

Georgette was an embarrassment? I thought to myself. I couldn't imagine a universe where that could be a possibility. She was always so confident and elegant, which I admired.

Theobold took another drink, "Have I ruined the façade? I will admit it does work in her favor out here on the high seas...Far away from the drama with mummy and daddy. Oh look, I know she has not been easy on you, but you shouldn't let her intimidate you...You have been giving her a run for the title lately...You are... quite spectacular," he said, and before I realized what was happening, he leaned in and kissed me.

I froze.

Everything went into slow motion. It was so sudden and out of nowhere. I thought we had moved past that time he had low-key asked me out months ago. I pulled away, and he almost fell over.

"Apologies," he said, putting his head in his hands.

"I should go," I said as I leaped out of my chair. I looked around to see if anyone had seen it.

How long did I let that go on? I asked myself, nervously.

It was such a shock that I had no idea. Maybe I was overthinking it, and it had been only a second. Then my stomach sank.

Across the bar, in the open hallway, I saw Georgette.

She was frozen in place; her eyes were wide with surprise, but in a flash, turned to a dark glower. Then she snapped her head the other way and stormed down the hallway.

I rushed away from the bar, leaving Theobold, head in hands. I called for Georgette, trying to tell her it meant nothing, but I couldn't see her down the hallway. I ran to the end and smashed through the crew entrance, but there was still no sign of her. I was spinning – this was an absolute disaster. The ship lurched as it hit a large wave, knocking me into the wall.

My world was literally and metaphorically crashing around me.

I wasn't sure what to do... Go back to the cabin and face Georgette, or go to Serge and tell him about the kiss or not? Either way, I felt incredibly guilty.

I decided to go to Serge's cabin. I didn't know if I had the energy to face Georgette...I wasn't even sure what had happened, how it happened, or how I felt about it. I knocked on Serge's door...He had made me a copy of his key card, but it felt wrong just to go in right now. The door opened, and he smiled when he saw me.

"I was hoping I would see you tonight," he said. I hugged him as the door shut behind me.

"Today has been insane," I said, feeling like I was almost going to cry. He held me in his arms and assured me that everything would be okay, sharing that he had a crazy day as well. He picked me up while still holding me and carried me to the bed. Cupping my face in his hands, he kissed my forehead and apologized for not considering my feelings and for not telling me about Marcello earlier.

I also apologized, acknowledging the complexity of his situation and expressing my understanding that he didn't want to involve me in it. He gave me a long kiss on the lips as he ran his fingers through my hair. Feeling relieved we were moving past our issues, I decided not to mention Theobold's kiss. It's not like I wanted it, and I shut it down immediately, so I opted not to bring it up. Being back in Serge's arms and bed felt great, and I realized how exhausted I was. It really had been the worst and most stressful cruise, so I allowed myself to melt into him.

XIX

CHAPTER 19

I woke up to the sunlight pouring into Serge's cabin. I had missed this for the last two days. It was so much easier to wake up and start your day in natural light than a pitch-black box. The chaos of the previous night and the whole cruise came crashing back to me, and I could not wait to press the "reset button" and start the new cruise.

Embark Day was a long day for Serge, starting early in the morning on the Bridge. I barely heard him leave the cabin at 6 a.m. The ship announcements woke me at 8 a.m., which still felt too early. I sat up and saw the breakfast trolley Serge had ordered, which had a big bouquet of flowers with my name on them. I smiled and had my breakfast out on the balcony. I felt like Serge and I had gotten back on the same page, but the rest of my "Ship Life" was a complete mess. I needed a break... I needed to reconnect with "Land Life Bree" for a minute.

I decided to take a personal morning as I walked down the gangway alone and took a walk in San Diego. I found a cute park, laid my beach towel out on the grass, and called my parents. I had been updating them occasionally, but this was an unload. I held my phone up to my face as I vented on our video call. I told them mostly everything but left out the part about my boss kissing me.

I was pretty sure if they heard that, my father would have been on the first plane out to California. Mom was as upset as I was for Erika. I had mentioned her and Marcello quite a bit while recounting some of my double dates with Serge. My dad asked if this cruise had been "a bunch of swingers" again... He was still a bit uncomfortable about the chartered cruise from months ago.

I laughed, "No, Dad... the swingers actually purchased a lot!" They reassured me that the next cruise had to be better than the last and just to stay focused and be the strong woman that they raised. Even in my mid-20s, that still felt good to hear. It felt safe. For a minute, I thought back to how much simpler life was in Savannah compared to the literal and emotional tumultuousness of the last cruise. I almost wished I could go back in time, but then decided against it. I had grown up so much from that girl in Savannah. If I had told that girl that she would be presenting seminars and selling thousands of dollars of artwork to strangers on a cruise ship, she wouldn't have believed it. Then I thought about the good things onboard: Smitty and my friends in the cast, the confidence I had gained in speaking and selling, and Serge...

Yes, we had a stumble, but I did feel safe with him... And I did have feelings for him - aside from all the advantages that accompanied him. As much as Smitty preached about dating solely for the perks, I knew he and Holiday had something special and he knew it as well.

Then my dad started asking all the detailed safety questions, almost like I was at boat drill. I had been through numerous drills now, and though they were still annoying, they went much more smoothly than my first. I actually got applause from my megaphone speech now, and luckily, I hadn't been interrogated by any more officers with safety questions. I had thought about it since; I was pretty sure Serge did that on purpose to get me to go out with him. He confirmed it when I asked him weeks ago.

Was that slightly problematic?... Especially if it had been someone I wouldn't have wanted to go out with? Yes. But a lot of that happened on ships. Eryn told me I was one of the lucky ones – being hit on by someone you are attracted to. Anna had also said that when she went to HR on another ship about a crew member being inappropriate, she was told, "It's just part of ship culture." The "Me Too" movement was so recognized on land. However, it hadn't seemed to have made the jump into "Ship Life."

My mom brought me back to the conversation, asking if I would be done by Christmas, and I could see her disappointment when I told her I didn't think so. I always went home for Christmas throughout college and even my first year in LA, so I knew this would be hard for her. I wrapped up the call with my parents. I told them I loved them as I ended the video call. I felt lighter - more grounded. I put my sunglasses back on and popped my ear pods in, putting on my favorite playlist as I lay in the sunlight.

I woke up as some people playing frisbee ran past me. I hadn't planned to fall asleep but could tell my body needed it. A memory from the training back in Miami came to me where they had told us exhaustion was a part of the gig from time to time, so they certainly weren't lying. I walked around a bit more, found a cute little bar near the ship, and had a glass of wine... I felt like I would need it for the night to come.

Back on the ship, I got ready for work in Serge's cabin. I looked in the mirror at the cream-colored pantsuit I was wearing. I felt really good about it, but it didn't help my anxiety about going to the gallery tonight. I hadn't seen Georgette since the awkward kiss last night.

Is she going to tell what she saw? Has she already told people? I nervously asked myself.

If she had told Lauren, the spa manager, she would have told the spa girls, and then the entire ship would know by now. As I walked down the

I-95, I tried to make eye contact with everyone to see their reaction. To my relief, I wasn't getting any dirty looks or knowing glances. As I stepped into the gallery to grab the Guess the Price box, I looked around for Georgette but didn't see her. I was holding the box when Smitty's hands appeared behind me and grabbed the box, startling me.

"I got it, girl," he said as I jumped... I didn't see him come in. "Are you good?" he asked.

I told him I was fine, and as we walked out of the gallery, I took one last look for Georgette... Nothing but an empty gallery. The suspense was killing me.

We set up GTP at our usual spot in the atrium. Despite my great day in San Diego as "Land Life Bree," now I was back to "Ship Life Bree," and my thoughts were scattered.

"Are you sure everything is okay?" Smitty asked, looking at me with his hand extended out, holding guessing slips towards passing guests. I told him everything was fine, and I was just tired.

"I feel you on that. You know you look tired when you run into Georgette Day in the streets of San Diego, and she confirms it," he said, smoothing his long hair back.

"You saw Georgette?!" I asked, way too neurotically.

He raised an eyebrow and said in a confused tone, "Yeah...why?"

I broke eye contact. "Oh, no reason...How did she seem?" I asked.

Smitty clocked me again, "She seemed fine; why?"

I can't tell him...If she hadn't said anything, that meant it probably wasn't out, and if I said anything, it would spread like wildfire. That wasn't good for any of us in the Art Department, I thought.

Smitty was about to press me again when Eryn walked up. She was back in her "modified," as she called it, "Just Ask" T-shirt.

"I swear they get bigger every time you wear that shirt, babe," Smitty said, looking at Eryn's boobs.

She blew him an air kiss, "Thanks, doll, but focus, please...I saw her!" She seemed nervous, which was very odd for Eryn. Smitty and I must have looked confused. "The bloody wife!" she whispered loudly...and the kid!"

I gasped lightly.

How could I have forgotten Marcello's wife and

baby were onboard this cruise?!" I scolded myself. Theobold's kiss had me very off my game.

"OMG...Did Erika see?!" Smitty asked, looking around the atrium.

Eryn said they were covering Erika's shift tonight, but it was just a matter of time.

Smitty took a breath, "It's like Dynasty meets The Love Boat!"

Eryn squinted slightly, "I dunno what the bloody hell that means, but this is serious!"

Smitty reacted, "That's exactly what I am saying!"

Eryn suddenly turned, "Heads up," she said as she walked back into the atrium to her. "Just Ask" duties. Smitty and I looked at each other when we heard a voice behind us.

"If you would rather be participating in 'Just Ask," I am sure I could make that happen," Georgette said. We both turned simultaneously to meet her cold demeanor, tight-lipped with arms crossed.

Smitty smiled, "Oh, we were just giving out pointers..."

Georgette raised a sharp eyebrow, "Nice try, Smithsonian," she said as she turned to look at me with the iciest gaze I have ever seen... "And you,

Miss Bradley, get back to work," she said, as she grabbed the few guesses we had collected already and marched off.

"Okay, what is going on?" Smitty asked. I shrugged and jumped back into asking people to guess the price. I actually got a lot of guesses throughout the night because I kept trying to avoid Smitty asking me any more questions. Back in the gallery, Georgette finalized the mailing list from the slips we had brought her. It was dead silent as we stood in front of her, aside from the clicking of her keyboard. She didn't make eye contact with either of us. I could feel the tension building as Smitty's eyes turned sideways to look at me.

"Go get a box of appraisal forms," Georgette ordered.

We looked at each other, and Smitty turned to go when Georgette stopped him, "Not you, Smithsonian." She cut her eyes to me.

My mouth was dry, "Okay, where would I..."

Georgette cut me off, "Don't ask questions, Miss Bradley, just do it."

Our letter-printing party in Holiday's cabin that night was the most serious one we had ever had. Anna and Eryn told us Erika was hysterical after seeing Marcello's wife and child. Holiday was growing concerned as this was Erika's third day in a row "signed off." That meant the doctor had medically cleared you not to work for whatever reason; however, it was a ship rule that if a staff or crew member was signed off for too many consecutive days, they were sent home. Erika had to return to work tomorrow, or she would be booted. Anna assured Holiday that she would make sure Erika would return to work the next day.

Smitty kept looking at me as we passed the printed letters on, waiting for me to say something. Holiday could sense the tension.

"Is something else going on?" he asked.

"Yes...Is something else going on?" Smitty repeated the question directly to me.

I had to say something.

Think, Bree, I steadied myself.

I made up an excuse, saying I was so mad at Serge that I was sleeping in my own cabin again. As I was coming down from my bunk, I accidentally knocked over a bunch of Georgette's perfume bottles and broke them.

"Broken perfume bottles got you back to 'Miss

Bradley'?" Smitty asked, not looking convinced. I shrugged. I knew it was a weak excuse but needed to think of something fast. I took a big sip of wine and tried to change the subject. I asked Holiday about his new show. He had been putting together a solo cabaret-type show for a few cruises and said he would debut it this cruise. The bad weather had prevented one of the guest entertainers from getting to the ship, so there was an open slot to fill. Smitty clapped excitedly and said that it was also not on an auction day, so we would finally be able to go.

"This cruise is already going better!" I said, with a pit in my stomach.

The next day was our first auction of the new cruise. We did our usual 6 a.m. set up in the lounge, and I wasn't shocked to see that we didn't have our break this time – no doubt a part of my punishment since Georgette handled all the scheduling. The crowd seemed much more receptive towards the art than the last cruise, which was a good sign. Smitty and I stood outside the lounge with the dancers at the registration table, and I was relieved to see that Anna had convinced Erika to come back to work. She looked tired with puffy eyes and no makeup and wasn't talking very much, but we were just glad to see her getting out. I asked her if there was anything I could do. She smiled and thanked me, saying she just needed to sleep. She said the ship doctor had given her some medication and was looking forward to sleeping through the night. Anna and Eryn were debating with Smitty about the Thanksgiving dinner for the crew that was scheduled for the upcoming cruise.

"Why are they even doing it when you two and Holiday are the only Americans on the crew?" Anna asked.

Smitty said it was an easy way to get rid of all the uneaten excess food from the passengers, and he wasn't mad about it. Plus, it was an excuse to have a party. He said that he never went home for Thanksgiving on land and that he and his friends just went and got drunk at the West Hollywood bars, so this wouldn't be that far off.

"Well, it's a big deal in my family, and I know Holiday is excited about it as well," I said.

Eryn laughed, "What a shocker...Dan Holiday is excited about a holiday!"

Even Erika laughed at that as we heard Georgette's standard announcement come on the PA system. Eryn and Anna had it memorized at this point and put on an over-the-top impression of Georgette's posh accent, as they followed along with her script.

Before long, we saw Georgette on her way from the back office, where she made the announcement. She walked right past the desk without a word to anyone and went into the lounge.

"What is up her arse?" Eryn asked. But before we could say anything, Erika gasped.

We all turned to see Marcello – He was walking down the long hallway with a woman pushing a baby in a stroller. We couldn't help but stare. It was such an odd sight. I knew the wife was onboard, but actually seeing her and the baby together with Marcello made it real. She was chatting to him in Italian as they walked past us, and Marcello gave us the quickest glance – primarily to Erika – and they walked on.

We all let out a collective sigh as if we had been holding our breath the entire time they were passing us. Except for Erika, who put her hand over her mouth and ran to the bathroom.

Is she sick? Or is she crying again? Probably both, I thought.

"Poor thing," Eryn said.

"The bastard has some damn nerve," Anna said. We didn't have time to discuss it more as passengers were showing up for the auction. Smitty and I went into the lounge.

My stomach was in knots when I saw both Theobold and Georgette standing on opposite ends of the stage. He was going through his notes at his podium, and she stood as still as a statue. The room was dead silent. Smitty asked if we should start the music, and Theobold looked up, motioning for us to come to the stage. As I approached, I looked at him to see if there was any reaction, seeing me for the first time since the kiss... there wasn't. It was as if nothing had happened. I was dumbfounded as he started to give us all a short motivational speech on how we could only "rise from the ashes of the last cruise" or something like that. As he finished, he looked at me and told me I would do his introduction speech today.

"What?" I asked, looking at Georgette, who wore a blank expression, then at Smitty, with a quizzical look, and finally back at Theobold, who wore a confident smile.

"You'll do splendidly," he said, handing me the microphone.

How is this happening? Now I have to get up in front of all these people and introduce my boss, who has just thrown a massive bomb into my life and walked away acting like it never happened, I thought to myself, annoyed.

I didn't have time to think about it further as the music started playing, and Georgette opened the doors to the lounge. The crowd was much larger and more inclined to buy this cruise. I ended up making six sales, feeling good about myself as I filled out the sales slips and placed them on the frames. Georgette and Smitty were also selling a lot. Before I knew it, we were already over $25,000. Selling really did give me a high, buzzy feeling, which helped with the speech I had been assigned to deliver. Georgette lowered the music, and I stepped on stage with the microphone. It was a much larger crowd than at any of the seminars I had hosted. The butterflies were frantic in my stomach.

What was I going to say? I asked myself, frantically. I barely knew Theobold, and after our last interaction, it seemed so bizarre.

I had an out-of-body experience where I became Georgette and just mimicked the introduction she used to give. I didn't even realize I had it memorized until the words started coming out of my mouth. Before I knew it, the crowd was clapping, and Theobold was taking the mic from my hand. As I left the stage, I passed Georgette, staring daggers at me as she clapped.

Had she told Theobold what she saw? Did they have a fight, and that's why I was suddenly giving his intro speech? I wondered to myself.

I went through the usual motions of the auction, congratulating people as they bid, encouraging them to go higher when they got outbid, and keeping the energy moving in the room. Theobold was his usual engaging self on stage... It was as if the last cruise had not happened.

"Well, that was a complete turnaround from the last cruise. I might need a massage from the whiplash," Smitty said as he stacked all the returned bid cards. I laughed at his comment while looking over the appointment list. We had a busy night ahead of us, but I needed to talk to Georgette and clear the air before I could focus on anything else. I couldn't take another day with this anxiety, so I showed up early at the gallery that evening. I pulled my keys out to unlock the sliding doors but noticed they were already unlocked and slightly open. I quietly entered and saw Georgette organizing and updating the display signs for our next event. She looked up as I walked in and then looked away, continuing to shuffle through signs as if I wasn't there.

I approached her, "Georgette, I need to explain what happened..."

She cut me off, "I think it would be appropriate if at least one of us kept it strictly professional and left the personal things alone, Miss Bradley."

I walked closer.

"I totally get that, but I want you to know I was keeping it professional...I just went over to see if he was okay. He is the one who kissed me. I was just as surprised as you were!" I pleaded with her. I left out the part where Theobold had told me about her family. I had a feeling that wouldn't be beneficial to the situation at the moment.

She put the signs down, looked as if she was contemplating the situation, and finally said, "Look, it's clear that we aren't going to be fast friends... I did not want to see what I saw but cannot 'unsee' it. Perhaps it was a mistake to offer you personal advice because I certainly was not trying to steer you in the direction it appeared you were taking. I can appreciate you saying it wasn't what it looked like because I don't have to tell you what kind of situation that would create. I think it's probably best for us both to stay in our own lanes from now on and focus on selling."

I nodded hesitantly, not entirely sure if she believed me or not. "Alright, I get that... I'm sure it looked awful. Again, I shut it down immediately, so I hope that maybe after some time, we could get back to where we were..." I said.

Did that make sense? I asked myself. I wasn't totally sure that I knew exactly "where" we had been before... Our relationship seemingly was one step forward then two back.

"I've said my peace," Georgette said as she walked away from me and began placing the signs around the gallery. Theobold and Smitty arrived at the gallery, effectively ending our conversation. I needed to talk with Theobold as well. I was hoping that maybe after the auction, he would have tried to speak with me, but he disappeared as usual. My anxiety over the whole situation was turning to frustration. Theobold was the one who caused this, and I was the one taking all the heat. I doubt he even noticed that Georgette had seen us. And it seemed she hadn't let him know.

Am I going to be able to pretend like nothing happened? I asked myself. My head was spinning again, and I found it hard to concentrate during my appointments with the clients. I eventually powered through and accomplished some decent upsells. We were on track to meet our sales target, so I felt accomplished as I gathered all the invoices for accounting. Smitty was putting the printers away in the cabinets as I walked over.

"Should we hit up the martini bar tonight?" I asked.

He stood up as he locked the cabinet and said, "That's a great idea! Yeah, you can buy us a round and finally tell me what the hell is going on... Sound like a plan?" he asked with a sassy tone. I was about to say I told him already, but before I could, he followed up with, "And do not try to tell me that some broken perfume bottles caused you to be acting like a total spaz and Georgette to go full boss bitch mode on you, which, by the way, is also falling onto me. And then all of a sudden, Theobold springs his intro on you out of nowhere?" He crossed his arms and waited for my response.

I wanted to tell him, but it was just becoming more involved, and I really didn't want to complicate things anymore. I tried my best to smile and tell him that everyone was just a bit off after the craziness of the last cruise and that things were returning to normal.

He sighed with exasperation, "Fine, girl. You tell yourself that. Enjoy your martini," he said in an unimpressed tone.

I left to go turn the invoices into accounting, and when I returned, Smitty was gone, and so was Georgette. Only Theobold was there in the middle of the gallery, leaning against the display case. I asked him where the others went, and he said he let them go for the night.

"Oh, so we are done for the night then?" I asked as I went to grab my purse.

"Yes, well, not exactly... that is, I feel like... No, I am certain that I owe you an apology," he said as he ran a hand through his hair and looked at me with a furrowed brow. "Last night, I was feeling poorly and not handling my thoughts particularly well, as I'm sure you picked up on. And when I...kissed you...I immediately regretted it. No, that's right. I didn't regret it, but what I meant to say is that it was very inappropriate on my part. I was trying to compliment you and then mucked it all up. I won't use being drunk as an excuse. I just want to say I am extremely sorry, and I sincerely hope I haven't wrecked our working relationship... Hopefully not?" he finished with a hopeful look in his eyes.

It honestly was adorable. I had never seen Theobold act humble before. I took a pause and then said, "Well, thank you. I appreciate it because I've been a nervous wreck since it happened. Do you know that Georgette saw it?" I asked.

He nodded, "Yes, I was getting a sense that she may have... Hence why I had you do the introduction today. I apologize for that as well... If I sprung it on you."

"Um... Just a little bit," I responded in a slightly lighter tone.

"Right, Of course... Bad Theo!" he said as he reprimanded himself.

I felt a slight smile form on my face. This was a completely different Theobold Thorne from the over-confident, handsome showman I had seen before. Well, he was still handsome... maybe even more so now that he was showing a bit of vulnerability.

I caught myself, adjusted my train of thought, and said, "Look, we make a great team, and we have been killing it, aside from the last cruise, and I can tell you are sorry."

He grinned and nodded, "Yes, exactly." After a thoughtful pause, he continued, "It's just I find that you make me slightly nervous, which doesn't happen very often, and I wasn't sure how to handle it... so naturally, I handled it in the worst way possible. I promise you that I will do better," he said as he put his hands together.

"It's all good. I feel much better about it now that we talked, and I think Georgette and I can move on as well," I assured him.

"Wunderbar! I feel lighter already!" he beamed. "Well then, I shall leave you to your evening," he said as he turned and left the gallery.

I breathed a massive sigh of relief and fell into the chair beside me. I replayed the conversation in my mind, processing it once more. The idea that I made Theobold nervous was a revelation. "Ship Life" was accelerating my growth, pushing me to mature in unexpected ways. A year ago, I couldn't have imagined being so assertive about such matters. "Ship Life Bree" was proving to be quite impressive.

I inserted the key copy that Serge made for me and walked into his cabin. Thinking he would still be at work, I was surprised to see him in the sitting room. He was laid out on the couch in his underwear, holding a glass of wine. He smiled as I walked in.

"Well, someone is home early," I said, smiling back at him.

"Si... Too much work lately for both of us," he said as he motioned towards the table next to him, where an empty wine glass stood next to the wine bottle, chilling in a decanter.

"I won't disagree with that," I said as I walked over and picked up the wine bottle. I glanced at the label and remarked on how expensive the bottle was. Serge mentioned it was a gift from the Captain and took a generous sip.

"That overtime is really paying off," I joked as I poured myself a glass.

"Si," he replied, rising from the couch and stepping behind me.

As I continued pouring, he trailed his hands up my arms, gently pushing my hair aside before planting a kiss on my neck. Setting the bottle down, I took a sip of wine, feeling the tension rise as he unzipped my dress from behind. I felt a rush as it fell to the floor. Turning to face him, our lips met in a passionate embrace. It seemed we were back on the same page once more.

CHAPTER 20

We had another sea day on our crossing from San Diego back to Hawaii. The sea day in between auction days was usually calm. Smitty did his seminar, this time with a good-sized crowd in attendance. He was still distancing himself from me. I decided to tell him what happened since it seemed to be sorted out now - I just needed to find the right time to tell him.

It was formal night and the debut of Holiday's cabaret show, so it seemed like the perfect opportunity. Smitty would undoubtedly be in a good mood after, and I was sure we would go out for drinks after where I could pull him aside.

I got ready in Serge's cabin and was excited to debut a new dress I bought at a Honolulu boutique. It was a floor-length black gown that resembled the one Georgette had worn on our first formal night out months ago. I knew I had to have it the minute I saw it. It was pricey, but I had some money to burn since we had been doing so well on our previous cruises.

It really is fantastic when you don't have rent due every month, I thought.

I stepped into the dress, pulled it up, and looked in the mirror as I held it on. It was probably the most elegant thing I had ever worn. I zipped it up at the side as Serge came out of the shower and saw me.

"Splendida Signora," he murmured as he approached, his eyes admiring my reflection in the mirror before he softly kissed my shoulder and playfully unzipped the dress again. Returning his affection with a smile, I pressed a kiss to his cheek and zipped the dress back up. Serge regretfully explained that he wouldn't be able to accompany me to the show as he had Bridge duty. I reassured him that I would be fine and that I had the girls to keep me company. I put on my makeup as Serge got dressed in his uniform. He slicked back his dark hair and began buttoning up his shirt.

"At least I can escort you to meet the girls, no?" he asked.

I finished putting on a red lip and turned to say, "I would love that."

I felt like I was going to the prom as Serge escorted me down the neon-lit hallway towards the martini bar. I saw the girls as I got closer; Anna was in a lace champagne-colored gown, standing next to Eryn in a dark burgundy cocktail dress. Erika was seated next to them at the bar in a pink jumpsuit.

"Hot damn!" Eryn exclaimed as we walked up. "Not even one contract done yet, and our little girl is all grown up," she said as she hugged me. Serge kissed me and said he would see me later as he left for the Bridge. As he left, I turned back to the girls and saw a pained look in Erika's eyes.

"Oh Erika, I'm sorry. I didn't even think..." I said, realizing it must remind her of Marcello. She smiled and hugged me.

"Don't even worry about it, babe. I don't want people walking on eggshells around me. We are going to have a good night!" she said, picking up her glass. Anna poured me a glass of champagne from the bottle on the bar, and we all cheered to a good night.

After the three of us finished the bottle of champagne, we walked toward the theater. Holiday's show was in the cabaret theater, which was smaller and more intimate, with a dance floor in the middle. It was located on the far side of the casino. As we walked through cigarette smoke and the sounds of slot machines, we saw Smitty sitting at the casino bar.

"So, is our superstar ready to shine?!" Eryn asked playfully, snagging Smitty's martini for a sip. Smitty arched an eyebrow at her, reclaiming his drink.

"Well, he better be, because he's been on vocal rest all day, driving me nuts with his notepad scribbling. It's like watching a movie with sub-titles," he remarked dryly.

Anna chuckled, noting that at least he'd be prepared.

"I certainly hope so," Smitty replied, "because if

his voice cracks, the night's going to hell before it even starts." Smitty said and explained that Holiday was an absolute diva after a show if his voice cracked during it.

"Then let's think positive," I said, but he didn't respond.

If anyone is being a diva, it's him, I thought.

Smitty had been my closest ally the entire time, and the distance between us felt so uncomfortable, but I was confident we would be able to squash it after the show.

We walked into the theater and saw that Holiday had reserved five seats in the front row on the right side. The seats circled the dance floor, and we crossed to sit down. Smitty sat on the far end, away from me, next to Erika, as I sat by Eryn. The guests were dressed up much more than people on previous cruises, and it felt like a very special affair.

A waiter came over and took our drink order as Anna opened the newly printed program to the front page with Holiday's headshot.

"That's the 'distinguished' shot... He also has 'sexy,' 'playful,' and 'serious'," Smitty said as he made faces for each. The lights dimmed as our drinks arrived just in time. We cheered like fangirls as the curtain rose and revealed Holiday standing there. He winked at us and began singing, opening with a few Broadway numbers and then transitioning into more contemporary ballads. He really was extraordinary on stage. As he sang, a few couples would get up, dance to a few songs, and sit back down while everyone else seemed entranced by Smitty's boyfriend. Holiday's next song was a slow ballad.

"I bloody love this song!" Eryn whispered to me as she danced in her seat to the music, purposely swaying into me and trying to get me to join in. I giggled as she pushed me harder, but my amusement faded abruptly when I heard a gasp.

Eryn froze as we turned and saw Erika's face – even in the dark lighting of the theater, I could tell she had gone white. I followed her gaze to the dance floor and saw Marcello...His wife was guiding him by the hand onto the dance floor.

When did they come in? They must have been late, I told myself.

We had thought there would be no chance of seeing him since he knew Erika and the rest of us would be here to support Holiday. He seemed hesitant as his wife pulled him to the middle of the dance floor. She put her arms around his neck, and he put his hands around her waist.

Holiday looked over at us with a concerned look as he continued singing. Anna grabbed Erika's hand tightly as she stared at the dancing couple.

"What do we do?" I whispered to Eryn.

"I'm about to go shove my stiletto up his bloody arse," she whispered angrily to me. I looked back to the dance floor and saw the wife move her hands from Marcello's neck to hold his face as she kissed him. Erika ripped her hand from Anna's to cover a sob and suddenly shot up from her seat and rushed out of the theater.

Eryn patted my leg, "You stay here; we'll go find her," she said as she and Anna slowly rose from their seats, gave Holiday a reassuring wave, and walked out of the theater. I looked over at Smitty, sitting three empty seats away from me now. He looked at me and patted the seat next to him. I switched seats, adjusting my dress as I sat, and asked if we should follow them.

"I'm sure they'll find her... It's probably best there's not a bunch of people around her while she's that upset," he whispered. I looked back to the stage as Marcello was still dancing and felt a surge of indignation. He was shameless, and poor Erika was suffering. I tried to enjoy the rest of the show, but it wasn't easy, despite Holiday's lovely voice. I could tell Smitty was having a hard time focusing as well. The show came to an end as Holiday took a bow to a standing ovation.

Smitty and I cheered him on, and as the lights came up, I saw Marcello leave with his wife. Smitty grabbed my hand, and we ran backstage. The curtain dropped, and Holiday rushed over to us. Smitty gave him a big hug and whispered something in his ear. He kissed Smitty and said thank you, then put his arms around both of us.

"That wasn't good," he said, talking about Erika. "We should go find her...She was just starting to make some progress, and I don't want her going backward." We walked to the dressing room backstage, and Holiday picked up the phone from the vanity table and dialed a number.

"How is she?" he asked. After a few moments, he put the phone down and looked at us, "The girls are in their cabin... She's not there or in her own..."

The three of us walked out of the theater and

made our way over to the casino bar to wait. Eryn and Anna emerged from the crew door with Alina, Erika's roommate. It was one of the few times I had seen her outside of our printing parties.

"She's not in the dancer's corridor, and we checked the women's washrooms around here," Anna said in a worried tone.

"What in the hell was that asshole thinking?!" Holiday exclaimed heatedly. The growing concern on their faces left me unsettled.

We quickly devised a plan: Holiday and Smitty would head to the security office to review the ship's cameras for any sign of her. Alina and Anna would comb the promenade deck, checking the shops and restaurants, while Eryn and I would search the passenger bars, hoping she sought solace alone with a drink. With our roles defined, we split up and proceeded to our designated areas.

Eryn and I walked as fast as we could in our heels; my dress was making swishing sounds as I moved swiftly. We checked the martini bar, then the Explorer's Lounge, and finally the Irish Pub but found no sign of Erika. Even though we were on a ship, and there were only so many places she could be, the Vision was a huge ship. We had walked the entire length of three decks with no sign of her, and Eryn finally said she needed to stop. We sat down in the nearest lounge, and she removed one of her heels.

"These were not made to power walk in," she said, rubbing her foot. I nodded since my feet were killing me as well.

"It's been over an hour. Where in the bloody hell would she have gone?" Eryn asked, looking at me. I shook my head without an answer.

"This is all that bloody officer's fault," she said.

And suddenly it clicked in my head... My heart skipped a beat as I looked at Eryn, who had also figured it out with a wild look in her eyes. We clasped each other's hands as the PA system chimed overhead.

I heard Serge's voice, "Code Rising Star... repeat... Code Rising Star."

My mind raced back to that day I found Serge in the brig, and he had told me what that code meant. I saw fear come over Eryn's face, and I knew she also recognized it. She ripped her other heel off as I threw off both of mine, and we ran toward the officer's hallway.

XXI

CHAPTER 21

I held my heels in one hand as I lifted my dress with the other, running down the hallway with Eryn. My bare feet softly pounded on the plush carpet. I knew where Marcello's cabin was since we had walked back with him and Erika several times after a double date.

I heard the sound of crying echoing down the hallway as we flew past cabin doors. As we neared the cabin, I saw a group of crew members gathered outside the open door. Marcello stood holding his wife, who was hysterically crying and yelling in

Italian. The emergency medical team was rolling a stretcher into the room, and my heart sank.

Eryn started crying at the sight of the stretcher, and I put my arms around her as the scene unfolded before us. Serge walked out of the cabin with an unsettled look on his face as he glanced at Marcello. He must have heard Eryn crying and turned to look at us. His face went from unsettled to pained as he walked over to us. He shook his head as he hugged me.

"Oh my god," I said in disbelief as I looked over his shoulder. Serge hugged Eryn as well, then released her to face both of us and explained what he knew.

Marcello and his wife had left the theater, headed to the piano bar for a drink, and danced for maybe forty minutes or more. Then, they went to the shops to look at some jewelry before finally returning to Marcello's cabin. That was about an hour after Holiday's show. Marcello had received a call on his deck phone and stayed in the hallway to answer it, and his wife had gone inside the cabin. He had heard his wife scream, ran in to see what was wrong, and found Erika unconscious on his bed. That's when they called the emergency line.

Serge held up a bottle of pills and shook it to show it was empty.

Eryn struggled to speak, "Those are the pills the doctor gave her to help her sleep."

Serge sighed. I hesitated to ask the question, scared that I already knew the answer.

"I heard Operation Rising Star...Is she dead?" I asked. I thought back to seeing the door of the morgue, remembered how cold it was down there, and pictured Erika's body lying there. I felt tears running down my face as the tension threatened to suffocate me with its unbearable weight.

Serge held up his hand to wipe my tears away, "We thought so at first – that's why you heard the code announced. But they brought her back...She is alive. They are taking her to medical for monitoring."

Eryn's gasp was a sharp intake of breath, as if she had been holding it in for far too long. As tears streamed down her cheeks, her cries intensified, each sob carrying with it a tidal wave of raw emotion. It was as though every ounce of fear, worry, and anguish she had been harboring finally broke free, cascading over her. In that moment, I could see the weight of uncertainty lifting from her shoulders, replaced by a flood of relief so palpable it seemed to fill the air around us. Yet, mingled with that relief was a profound sense of sadness, the realization of just how close we had come to losing someone dear to us.

As Smitty and Holiday came racing up the hallway behind us, their footsteps echoing with urgency, it was evident that they too were gripped by the same overwhelming fear and anxiety that had consumed us moments before. Their expressions mirrored our own, etched with lines of worry and dread. When Holiday caught sight of Eryn and her tear-streaked face, his own composure crumbled. Tears welled up in his eyes and poured down his face as he struggled to contain the surge of emotion threatening to engulf him. Without a second thought, I rushed over to Holiday, my own emotions still raw and unsteady.

I reached out to him, offering whatever comfort I could as I whispered the words, "She's still alive." In that moment, he threw his arms around me, clinging to me with a desperate intensity that spoke volumes of his gratitude and relief. And as we stood there, locked in a tight embrace amidst the chaos and uncertainty, I couldn't help but feel a profound sense of solidarity in our shared vulnerability.

As Smitty rushed over to Eryn, they embraced in a silent exchange of shared sorrow and relief.

The medical team wheeled the stretcher out of the cabin with Erika on it, the hushed silence that enveloped the scene spoke volumes of the gravity of the situation and the collective weight of our shared concern. Serge said there wasn't anything for us to do at the moment and that he would keep us informed. He hugged me and kissed me on the head before he walked away with the rest of the medical team, leaving Marcello in the hallway, still consoling his wife.

"This is all your fault! Look what you have done to her!" Holiday's voice reverberated with accusation, his words laced with a searing pain.

But Marcello remained silent, his impassive facade offering no solace or explanation. As Holiday's anger boiled over, his gaze was a fiery intensity that spoke volumes of the depth of his anguish. And in that moment, it was as though the weight of Marcello's actions, the consequences of his choices, had finally come crashing down upon him. His wife looked at us and the anger that was in Holiday's eyes. She seemed to realize what was happening. She pushed Marcello away and stormed into the cabin. He looked at us in despair and slowly followed her, shutting the door.

We found ourselves huddled together in the girls' dressing room, the air heavy with a mix of sorrow and disbelief. With Anna and Alina joining our circle on the floor, we recounted the harrowing events that had unfolded. Holiday reached for a bottle of wine, taking a long, deep swig before passing it to Eryn. Without a word, she followed suit. As the bottle made its rounds, our eyes were drawn inexorably to the empty seat in front of Erika's vanity mirror. In the dim light of the dressing room, we grappled with the enormity of what had transpired, each of us haunted by the unspoken question of whether there was more we could have done to prevent it. We sat there somberly for hours, drinking wine, crying, and consoling each other. And yet, amid our shared sorrow, there was also a profound sense of unity in the simple act of being together and offering whatever comfort we could in the face of an almost unimaginable loss.

As I entered Serge's cabin, I found him sitting on the edge of the bed, his gaze fixed on the distant horizon beyond the balcony. Without a word, I joined him, the weight of the night's events hanging heavy in the air as we sat in silence. Eventually, Serge spoke, his voice steady as he relayed the latest update on Erika's condition. There had been no change, he explained, but she was stable, and plans were underway to transfer her to the hospital once we reached Maui. The Captain had been notified and had issued orders to expedite our journey, ensuring we would arrive by midday. We lay down together and Serge held me in his arms, comforting me. And as exhaustion washed over me like a tidal wave, I found refuge in his embrace, and drifted to sleep.

The next day, the auction was postponed since we would be reaching land about the same time it was scheduled. As the announcement reverberated throughout the ship, alerting passengers to the emergency and our impending early arrival, the rumor mill started spinning. I heard all kinds of whispers amongst the passengers as I walked to the gallery—someone had died, the ship was broken, someone had jumped overboard, there was a terrorist threat... Amongst the swirling theories, I felt adrift, lost in a sea of uncertainty. The thought of Erika trying to take her own life made me ill. Theobold had told me I didn't need to be in the gallery considering everything that had happened —the entire crew had heard by now. I told him I didn't want to be alone sitting in the cabin, and he nodded. He looked genuinely concerned as he sat at his desk.

Georgette was swapping out some of the art on the walls. It was the first time I had ever seen her do that... She had always paid the assistant movers extra to swap out the art in the gallery, but it seemed like she needed something to keep herself busy. I hadn't seen Smitty yet; I assumed he was still in the cabin consoling Holiday. Eryn had called me and said that Holiday went to HR in the morning and demanded that something be done. I thought Theobold's kiss felt like a bomb going off, but all of this made it feel so insignificant in comparison.

I saw Smitty pop his head out of the crew door. He looked tired. His hair, usually smooth and neatly tied back, was loose and a bit wild. He looked at the ground as he walked over to me, seated at my desk. As he sat down in front of me, he had a growing look of concern, and my thoughts went straight to the worst thing I could think of.

He must have sensed my energy, "Oh, it's nothing like that... She is still stable. They are preparing to transfer her off the ship."

I was a bit upset they were not allowing anyone to see her before they took her off. The only person who was permitted to see her was Holiday since he was the head of the entertainment department. Smitty still had a very nervous energy about him as I asked him what was wrong. He paused momentarily, then told me that Holiday had returned to the cabin crying uncontrollably.

"He went to see how she was doing before they took her, and the medical team pulled him aside," he paused and then continued, "They confirmed that she had overdosed on pills, and they were able to pump her stomach and bring her back, but... apparently... she was also pregnant... and she lost the baby..." he said in a low, somber tone.

I heard a loud crash from the other side of the gallery. A shattered frame lay in pieces on the floor before Georgette, her expression one of utter horror. As her gaze shifted between Smitty, who had just disclosed the devastating news, and the broken frame, a palpable sense of distress hung in the air.

"Are you okay?" Theobold asked with a look of concern as he came out of his office.

Georgette did not say a word as she rushed to the crew door and disappeared. We all looked at each other in bewilderment. I slowly rose from my chair, looking at the broken frame lying there.

"I got it... You should go," Smitty said, looking at me and then to the door Georgette had just passed through. I gave him a tight, supportive hug before I left. It was clear that Erika's suicide attempt had deeply affected him, as it had the rest of our group. He, like the rest of us, was struggling to come to terms with the gravity of the situation. Anna and Eryn had retreated to their cabin to help each other get through it.

I walked down the crew staircase to the I-95 and toward our cabin. I assumed that was where she had gone. Everything was a blur... I was in shock from what Smitty had just told me. I had no idea, and neither did the girls, I didn't think. She had seemed so happy before she found out about Marcello, and I wondered if she had told him.

Then I remembered her looking sick and running to the bathroom that day before the auction... I hadn't put it together then. I felt like crying, but I also felt too numb to do so. I reached the cabin door, slowly put my key card in, and pushed the door open as it clicked unlocked.

Georgette was on the ground, seated against her bed, holding her knees to her chest. She had her head down but looked up as I slowly came into the cabin. Mascara mingled with tears, painting a portrait of devastation and heartbreak. She looked utterly crushed. I was about to ask her if she wanted me to go, but I decided against it and went to sit next to her.

I slowly reached over to rub her back as she rocked back and forth. We sat there for several minutes when she finally began speaking.

"Oh, it's all completely horrid! That poor, poor girl. I didn't think it could get any worse, but then when I heard she had lost her child..." Her words trailed off, the depth of her sorrow evident in every syllable. But as her tone shifted from sorrow to righteous indignation, a fire ignited within her.

"These men... these men who think they are so powerful on these bloody boats! They think they can do whatever they want and use whoever they want, and then they just throw you away when they get bored, or you become an inconvenience to them. It has to stop! They can't keep getting away with it. I refuse to let it keep happening... Just ruining a life and walking away like they had no part in it and leaving you to pick up the pieces and figure out how to survive," she trailed off.

As I continued to rub Georgette's back softly, a question lingered in my mind.

"When did it happen to you?" I finally ventured, the words heavy with empathy and understanding.

For a moment, she simply stared at me with her large, watery eyes, as though searching for the right words to convey the depth of her experience. Slowly, she wiped away the mascara streaks from her cheeks.

"It was many years ago now, on my first con-tract," she began, her voice tinged with a hint of sadness. "I was brand new and naive... I escaped onto a ship because being around Mother and Papa with their constant fighting was unbearable. I told myself I would do this just long enough until they worked it out and things settled down... which never happened." She looked directly at me.

"That's when I met him... the Italian First Officer," she continued, her voice filled with a mixture of bitterness and resignation. "I told myself I wasn't there for a romance and just to focus, but he was persistent... and very charming... and when I fell, I fell hard. It seemed like a fairy tale until the day I found out I was expecting..."

My mind exploded. I tried not to let the shock show on my face. I didn't think I was doing a very good job, but Georgette continued her story.

"He wanted nothing to do with me then," she recounted, her tone tinged with bitterness. "Told me he already had a girlfriend expecting a child back on land. So that was it, and I was out... Left alone to go home to my dysfunctional family and tell them. I had hoped they would support me in having the child and keeping it, but Mother was furious and demanded I have it aborted. When I refused, she threatened to disinherit me. Papa did take some pity on me but still agreed there was no way I could keep it and have scandal fall upon the family. I was sent abroad to have my child, and when I finally did, they demanded that I give it up. I couldn't imagine giving my child away to some stranger, so I convinced my father to allow me to give the baby to a friend—a woman who worked for Landmark Quest. He set up a trust for the baby and enough money to care for it, but he covered it up as a donation to Landmark Quest. I provided credibility to the charade by promoting our artists' work through my social media following and singing the praises of Landmark Quest, which brought them many sponsorships and donations to the artists' campaigns... all of which boosted the company's bottom line. It had to be that way so no one would find out. I was heralded as the darling of Landmark Quest, all while my heart was ripped apart having to give my child away."

I had no words. Theobold's entire story about Georgette had been a lie... granted he thought it was the truth, but how awful that Georgette had to go on all this time carrying that secret. I couldn't imagine being in that position and having my parents dictate my choices in such a way. It seemed that we actually had a lot in common at the start of her story—both of us escaping to a life at sea that carried us away.

"Georgette, I am so sorry; I had no idea," I said as I leaned in to hug her.

She laughed a bit through her tears, "Yes, well,

that is rather the point, isn't it, darling? No one does know—apart from Mother and Papa, the solicitors, and my friend who is now raising my child... on Maui..."

Her story kept unfolding more and more. That was where she disappeared every time the ship docked in Maui, and none of the crew saw her. She didn't have a secret lover—She had been going to visit her child.

"I suppose that's the tiniest bit of a silver lining in this tragedy... We will be in much earlier, so I will get a whole extra day to spend with him," she remarked, a faint smile tugging at the corners of her lips despite the tears that still glistened in her eyes.

Everything made so much more sense now. At first, I thought she might have been jealous, and then I thought she was just a bitch—when really, she was trying to look out for me... in her own unique way. Experiencing "Ship Life" through the eyes of Georgette and Erika offered me a profound shift in perspective. What had once seemed like a distant and glamorous world suddenly revealed its harsh realities. Before, I had viewed "Ship Life" as a separate entity, almost like a fantasy world detached from the struggles of everyday life. But now, I understood that it was anything but. It was real and brutal.

Through Georgette and Erika's stories, I came to realize that "Ship Life" could have far-reaching consequences, impacting not only one's time at sea but also reverberating into every aspect of "Land Life." It was a world where love and heartbreak, joy and sorrow, coexisted in equal measure, where the line between fantasy and reality blurred with each passing day. In the wake of their experiences, I couldn't help but feel a newfound appreciation for the resilience of those who called the ship home.

For them, "Ship Life" wasn't just a job—it was a way of life.

And as I reflected on the lessons learned from Georgette and Erika's journeys, I realized that "Ship Life" was not merely a temporary escape from reality, but a mirror reflecting back the complexities of a raw and unfiltered human experience.

I handed Georgette some clean tissues and told her I appreciated her telling me and that her secret was safe. She nodded and said it felt good to be able to tell someone else. As the announcement sounded over the PA system that we were docking in Maui, I got up from the floor and told Georgette to go and have the best day with her little boy.

I watched as the biggest smile I had ever seen from her appeared on her face as she said, "Thank you, Bree."

XXII

CHAPTER 22

I needed to clear my head and get off the ship. So much drama had happened, and I still had another piece of drama that I needed to squash. I called Smitty and told him to meet me on the beach next to the port. A lot of the crew members went there, so he knew where to find me.

As I laid out on my beach towel, I watched as the sun began its descent towards the horizon, casting a warm, golden glow across the Hawaiian sky. "Golden Hour" was one of my favorite times in Hawaii. For a moment, all the chaos and drama of the past few days seemed to fade away. The beauty of the scene before me was breathtaking, the vibrant hues of orange and pink painting the sky. The golden rays of the setting sun washed over me like a blanket of warmth and contentment. I took a sip from one of the mini wine bottles I had bought at The ABC store on my way to the beach.

"Is one of those for me?" Smitty asked as he walked up to me. I smiled and handed him one after he laid his towel beside mine and sat down.

"So, I'm going to tell you the truth," I said. "And when I tell you, hopefully, you'll understand why I am telling you now and not when you asked before." I told him I had meant to tell him after Holiday's show, but obviously, that didn't happen.

"OMG!" Smitty exclaimed after I finished the whole story. "Okay... I can see now why you were showcasing unhinged behavior."

I laughed and playfully hit him on the shoulder as he continued, "Geez, that is heavy... I mean, it's not as heavy as the Erika situation, but still. I'm proud of you that you confronted both of them and put a bitch in place!"

We both laughed and then he tipped his sunglasses lower so I could see his eyes, "You left out one detail, though.... Was the kiss good?" he asked.

I told him I barely remembered it due to the shock it gave me, and he cackled.

"Girl, we are all good. Truth be told, after last night and everything that happened, I realized I was being a petty bitch. You are like my sister, and I won't let stupid things get in the way of that." We hugged each other, and in that moment, any lingering tension melted away, replaced by a sense of understanding and forgiveness. Smitty broke out his speaker to put some music on. We were having so much fun reconnecting that we didn't see the other woman who had appeared on the beach for the sunset.

She finally interrupted us, in a cloud of irritation, and said that we had ruined her sunset meditation. As she turned to leave, her parting word, a venomous and angry "Aloha," hung in the air. We exchanged sheepish glances, realizing that perhaps we had been a bit too loud in our enjoyment of the evening. But rather than feeling chastised, Smitty couldn't help but find humor in the situation.

"I don't think I have ever been cussed out with an 'Aloha'... I kind of liked it!" he remarked with a cheeky grin as we both started laughing again.

The last two cruises had left me feeling emotionally drained and exhausted. With each new twist and turn, I felt like I had been thrust onto an emotional rollercoaster, the highs and lows coming at breakneck speed, leaving me reeling in their wake. I was done assuming it couldn't get worse. The constant barrage of challenges had left me feeling like I had whiplash from the recent upheaval. It really had me questioning whether "Ship Life" was for me.

Am I really cut out for the unpredictable nature of this job? I wondered.

Luckily, the cruise ended on a high note. We were able to recover and have another successful auction. With the air cleared between Smitty, Georgette, and me, our team had undergone a transformation, evolving from a fractured group into a cohesive unit. The tension that had plagued us during the last two cruises had dissipated, replaced by a newfound sense of unity and solidarity. Holiday had received an encouraging update on Erika's condition, and it was a relief to hear that she was on the mend. Her parents had flown to Maui to be by her side. Knowing that she was in good hands brought a sense of peace to the group.

As for Marcello and his wife, their strained relationship had become increasingly apparent, even to those of us who didn't speak Italian. It was evident that she was deeply unhappy as she departed at the end of the cruise. Despite the lingering echoes of turmoil, there was a sense that things were slowly returning to normalcy, just in time for Thanksgiving.

We had planned to go to the crew mess, where they had prepared a special dinner for the crew, but to my surprise, Theobold said he had reserved a table in the passenger dining room – one large enough for the art department and our friends from the cast. So, as the seven of us sat down at the large, lavishly decorated table, it felt like a different version of Thanksgiving with my ship family – dysfunctional as it may be at times. The room was alive with laughter and conversation, the clinking of glasses and the aroma of delicious food filling the air. After the waiters poured wine and brought the cocktails, Theobold rose from his seat, holding his glass of wine.

"I appreciate you all accepting my invitation on this day of thanks. It may be an American holiday they created after they fled us Brits," he said with a grin. "However, I thought this might be a perfect opportunity to fashion it into our own little celebration... To give thanks to my team... and to the staff members who support us. With all the chaos that has surrounded us of late, I hope that we may take this opportunity to come together and heal. So, cheers, and thank you again."

We all held our glasses up to his toast. Theobold took his seat, his words of gratitude lingering in the air like a warm embrace. But before the moment could fade, Holiday rose to his feet, smiling at all of us. He had become more than just a colleague or friend—he had become the father figure and protector of our group. There was a quiet reverence in the air as we turned our gaze towards him, curious to hear what he had to say.

"And thank you to Theobold Thorne for including us in this lovely feast," Holiday said, his voice carrying a warmth and sincerity that touched each of us. "Many of you know this is one of my favorite holidays," he paused as the girls chuckled. Then he continued, "Yes, I know...Dan Holiday loves a holiday. Laugh if you must, but I am thrilled to be able to celebrate with my boyfriend, my girls, and the rest of my ship family. I would just like to raise a glass to Erika and hope she finds the peace and support she needs." We all raised our glasses again. The first course was served, and we all dug in.

It felt good to see us all in one spot, everyone getting along and embracing the spirit of the holiday. I looked across the table at Theobold sitting next to Anna, asking more about where she was from in Australia and seeking tips for his next visit there. Holiday was seated next to Georgette, who asked when his next solo show was so she could come and see it. Eryn sat to my right, taking full advantage of the free wine Theobold was providing as she downed her glass.

I gave her a look, to which she responded, "What? It's free... and it's a holiday!"

Smitty leaned in on my left to ask Eryn, "So, how's the new girl?"

Vivace Cruise Line had rushed out a replacement for Erika. She had joined the ship in Honolulu, and the cast had been in rehearsals to integrate her into the shows.

"She is a total hottie! She's from London, quite fashionable, and very tall! She's like a Black Georgette, really," Eryn said.

Smitty took a sip of wine and commented that

it sounded like she would definitely be "on the market."

"Not if I take her off it," Eryn joked.

As we giggled over the last bites of our first course, a bittersweet realization washed over me. With the arrival of the holiday season, I was reminded that my time on the ship was drawing to a close. In just two short months, my contract would come to an end, and I would have to bid farewell to the people who had become like family to me. As I looked around the table at the familiar faces of my shipmates, I couldn't help but feel a pang of sadness. These were the people I had spent countless hours with, sharing laughter, tears, and everything in between. They had been my constant companions, my confidants, and my support system during my time at sea. But now, as the end of my contract loomed on the horizon, I realized that this moment may never happen again. It was a reminder of the transient nature of "Ship Life."

We jumped straight back into work mode after Thanksgiving passed, going through our usual cycle of Guess the Price, letter-printing parties, and finding our potential "heavy hitters" for that cruise. On auction day, I debuted a brand-new "power suit" I had bought in Honolulu. It was perfectly tailored, and the material had a gorgeous sheen that made it pop as I walked. Over the past few months, I had undergone a remarkable transformation—one that had not only shaped my outward appearance but had also profoundly impacted my inner confidence and self-esteem.

Inwardly, my confidence had soared thanks to the challenges and triumphs I had faced in my role onboard the ship. Each curveball thrown my way had been an opportunity to prove my resilience and determination, to overcome obstacles and make successful sales. Even better, I finally didn't have a panic attack when I looked at my bank account.

Outwardly, my transformation was thanks in large part to the inspiration and guidance of Georgette, whose impeccable sense of style had inspired me to up my fashion game. I had embraced bold new looks and experimented with daring trends, discovering a newfound sense of confidence and self-expression through fashion. But it wasn't just my wardrobe that had undergone a makeover. The spa girls had worked wonders on my hair and skin, helping me to look and feel my best both on and off the ship. I felt like a boss bitch as I walked up to the registration table. Anna and Eryn sat there, along with the new dancer. Eryn was right; she was very beautiful. I introduced myself, and she said her name was Brooke and was obsessed with my suit.

Eryn agreed and said, "Yeah, I thought this was supposed to be an art auction—not bloody Project Runway. Between all four of you gorgeous art folk, how are the guests meant to focus on the paintings?"

I smiled as I walked into the lounge. Smitty was cleaning a few frames as Georgette was organizing the champagne bottles. She turned as she saw me walk in.

"Oh, you do look quite chic," she said. I smiled at her and went to see if Smitty needed help. We adjusted some of the lighting to hit the art just right, and everything looked ready to go. Theobold was on stage going through his notes and quietly motioned for me to come to the stage. I walked over, and he guided me off the side of the stage near the curtain.

"The room looks great, and I know we are

going to smash it today," he said confidently. "I just wanted to check in with you and make sure you are doing alright... I know the last month has been a bit mad, and I want you to know I am here if you need anything."

I smiled and thought that he really seemed to have turned over a new leaf. The confident and charismatic showman was still there, but this genuine, softer side had appeared lately and was a lovely blend. I thanked him for looking out for me and told him I was doing much better and was ready to kill it during the auction.

"Brilliant," he replied, giving my arm a confident squeeze. I walked off stage as Smitty looked at me with a suspicious eyebrow raised. I waved him down, indicating nothing odd had happened.

The auction started, and Theobold was right— we absolutely killed it. It was our most successful auction yet. All three of us had found our big buyer and ended up with invoices from each of them over $50,000. I strutted to the accounting office to drop off a thick stack of invoices. The accounting officer glanced through them and smiled as he told me he had never seen such a successful dream team in the art department.

"You know it!" I exclaimed, and I gave him a confident wink as I left.

That success continued throughout the cruise, and we turned in a final number that broke company records. We took an updated team picture for the company feature, and this time, we embodied a power team and not the dysfunctional family depicted in the previous photo.

Georgette and I treated ourselves to a celebratory shopping spree in Honolulu. I was blown away that she had her own private concierge at Saks, who had an entire rack of outfits she held specifically for Georgette. As we sat down at happy hour amongst all our shopping bags, she snapped a selfie of us and posted it on her Instagram. I felt honored to be featured on her popular account. We sipped our champagne as Georgette scrolled through her phone and leaned in to show me a picture of her son. He was so cute – he looked like a child model, which wasn't surprising being Georgette's child. She lamented at how fast he was growing up.

"Nope, no time to be sad, darling," I playfully mimicked her signature 'darling.' "We have another stop to make after this!" I said as I grabbed the check.

I didn't tell Georgette where we were going as we drove along Waikiki Beach. We got out of our Uber, and I led her up the stairs to Hula's. As she walked in, Smitty threw a lei around her neck, pronouncing her "leid," and she smiled. We sat her down at the bar, and the bartender asked if she was "the fabulous Georgette."

"But of course, darling," she answered and batted her eyes playfully.

Needless to say, Georgette was a big hit with the gays. The usual catamaran tour group had already started the party. I watched as she wore a glittered sailor's hat that one of the catamaran boys had given her and took a shot with the entire tour group – a sight I never thought I would see. After the group emptied out of the bar and left on their tour, Georgette pulled out her laptop. I told her to stop working, but she said she was downloading new movies and TV episodes to appease her network of crew members who assisted the art department around the ship.

True to her role as Gallery Director, she never

did lose her focus on keeping the art department running smoothly.

XXIII

CHAPTER 23

As we started a new cruise, our team felt stronger than ever. We were operating like a well-oiled machine, and it felt great. One of the perks of the turnaround from Honolulu was that the Hawaii ports were at the beginning, allowing us more free time at the start of the cruise. Unlike the hectic pace of auctions and events towards the end of the voyage, we had a bit of breathing room to relax and enjoy ourselves before diving into the busy schedule ahead.

So, Serge said he was taking me on a celebratory date. We had been seeing one another for almost four months now, which seemed a bit crazy to think how fast that time had flown by. I supposed this could count as an anniversary date, as well. With Serge having to work a bit later than usual, he had arranged for a late dinner, which suited me just fine. It would give me enough time to slip into one of the new dresses I had purchased during the shopping spree with Georgette.

After I closed the gallery for the night, I made my way up to Serge's cabin, unlocked the door, and walked in. I was surprised to see Serge already back, but I was even more surprised to see Marcello. They were sitting on the couch with glasses of wine, and both turned their heads as I walked in.

The situation with Marcello was still very tense. After Holiday had demanded HR take action about what happened with Erika, they had opened an investigation. Ultimately, they found there wasn't enough concrete evidence to do anything, which most of us found ridiculous, and had made it clear we wanted nothing to do with Marcello. He had not made an effort to talk with any of Erika's friends—his former friends—to try and explain, apologize, or anything. Serge had told me he was keeping it strictly professional with Marcello since he had to work with him. I respected his decision, understanding the necessity of maintaining professionalism in such situations. After all, Georgette and I had operated under similar principles in the past.

However, the scene in front of me did not look "strictly professional" in the least.

I paused, taking in the scene for a moment.

"Oh, I thought you said you were working late?" I asked Serge, not acknowledging Marcello. He explained that the schedules had changed, and they figured it would be nice to have some wine and catch up.

"I see..." I said as I walked over to the vanity to put my purse down. Serge asked me to sit and join them as he started pouring a glass of wine for me. "No, I am fine... You know what, I'll go, and you just call me when you are done," I said as I picked my purse back up. I didn't want to cause a scene, but I could feel anger building in me. Just the sight of Marcello angered me as my mind flashed back to the sight of Erika being wheeled out on the stretcher.

Marcello stood up and said that he should be

going anyway. He finished his glass of wine, shook hands with Serge, and gave me a wink as he left the cabin. The wink enraged me; it was like he knew something I didn't.

As the door closed, I threw my purse back down and gave Serge a cold stare, arching my eyebrow at him.

"What happened to keeping it professional?" I asked coldly.

Serge's attempt to downplay the situation struck a nerve. He raised his hands in a placating gesture from his position on the couch, insisting that their impromptu gathering was harmless—a mere opportunity to pass the time with some wine.

"He's still my friend, you know," Serge added, his tone attempting to rationalize his actions.

His words ignited a fierce reaction in me.

How could he continue to maintain a friendship with someone like Marcello, especially after everything that had transpired? I thought to myself.

I felt a surge of frustration and incredulity at Serge's apparent disregard for the gravity of the situation.

"How can you still be friends with someone like that after everything he's done?!" I exclaimed, my voice rising with indignation. "He's been acting like nothing's happened since Erika left, and now you're doing the same!"

Serge's attempt to defend Marcello only served to incite my anger further. He stood from the couch, his demeanor tense as he insisted that Marcello was remorseful and that we had unfairly ostracized him without giving him a chance to explain. But his words fell on deaf ears, my frustration reaching its peak as I struggled to comprehend Serge's stance in the face of Marcello's actions.

"Oh, I'm sorry... We should be going to him? When he is the one that led our good friend on for months and months and caused her to nearly kill herself? But we should be the ones going to him?" I asked, laughing at the absurdity of it.

Serge continued, saying that Marcello was heartbroken over the situation. He tried to put his arms around me, but I blocked his hands and said, "Well, I am sure his wife and baby back in Naples can comfort him soon enough."

His expression darkened, "I think you and your friends are being completely unreasonable... Everything has two sides... That girl was obsessed with him and created a fairy tale in her head and craved the attention! She would not have believed it even if he had told her the truth!"

The air crackled with tension as Serge's words hung between us. I couldn't contain my outrage at his callousness, firing back with a ferocity fueled by disbelief and anger.

"That girl has a name—Erika. She was my friend... and yours! How dare you say she craved attention! Are you saying her overdose was a cry for attention?!" My voice trembled with emotion.

"Yes!" Serge's response was immediate and infuriating, his words laced with contempt. "She knew exactly what she was doing—taking those pills in his cabin so his wife would find her and cause chaos—which she did. She needs help, and maybe now she can get it..."

I stared at him, incredulous, unable to fathom his accusations.

"Even if there's any truth to that - which I don't believe - she wouldn't have had to do any of it if 'your friend' had just been honest from the start!" I countered, my voice rising with each word.

But Serge's frustration only seemed to escalate, his words a bitter indictment of our entire group. "It's the same with all of you... Nobody can win.

Your whole group thrives on the drama and the gossip. The whole contract is a soap opera for you all, and you are always in the right. Especially you... There's always something with you... She is mad, or she is tired, or she is sad, and I am the one who is constantly bringing you back up!"

He cut deep, but I refused to back down. "Yeah... It's called a relationship!" I retorted, my voice dripping with sarcasm. Serge's frustration boiled over as he loudly clapped his hands together.

"But we are not in a relationship... Have I asked you to be my girlfriend? No, but I allow you to stay in my cabin, bring all your things here, shower, and do your makeup here..."

The rage inside me reached its peak, fueled by his hypocrisy and betrayal.

"I brought all my shit up here because you insisted on it!... But you're right; you never asked me to be your girlfriend, and we are not in a relationship," I spat, my voice filled with venom. I grabbed my purse off the table.

"And for the record... I would have said no. We are done."

With those final words, I stormed to the door, my heart heavy with disappointment and betrayal.

As I flung open the door, I shot him a steely glare, telling him I would retrieve my belongings later, before slamming the door shut behind me.

The sound of the door slamming shut echoed down the hallway, as I locked eyes with a house-keeping crew member. Her stunned eyes cut away as she saw me, and she went back to folding sheets at her cleaning trolley. I stormed down the hallway, knowing our fight would be the latest gossip spreading throughout the crew tonight. My head was a chaotic storm of emotions. Betrayed by someone I had trusted, angry at the callousness of his words, sad for the loss of what I had thought was a meaningful connection, and numb to the reality of it all sinking in.

How could I have been so wrong about Serge? Was I blinded by his good looks, big bed, and fancy cabin? Had he always seen me as nothing more than a needy girl, incapable of standing on my own and draining his energy? I asked myself.

I thought our conversations had been mutual, a sharing of burdens and frustrations. It had always felt like a balanced exchange of support. Yet, his callous words and dismissive attitude now painted a starkly different picture. My mind was reeling as I sat down in the far corner of the martini bar and ordered a drink.

After that one, I ordered another. Then, after that one, another. I was going through our fight over and over—replaying it in my head. After a while, the replay began to get foggy. I had no idea how long I had been sitting there. I was about to order another martini when I heard a voice beside me.

"Is it one of those nights?" I looked over to see Theobold. I blinked, thinking he was the last person I had expected to see. He put his hands up, "I promise I wasn't spying. I was in the cigar lounge across the way and noticed you...having...a drink," he said, looking at the several empty martini glasses.

It hit me then that we were in the same spot as the night he had kissed me—except now I was the drunk one. I rolled my eyes, "Well, if 'one of those nights' means thinking you're on top of the world, only to be told you're a needy narcissist by someone you should have known better than to date for four fucking months...then yes, it is one of those nights..." I trailed off.

Theobold let out a breath, "My, my...Well, as much as I do love the alliteration...I can confidently confirm that you are most certainly not a needy narcissist." He held up his hand as if he were swearing to a jury. The bartender brought me another martini and a beer for Theobold. I held up my glass, clinking it to his beer bottle, and thanked him.

"You are so right...I mean, I'm nowhere near perfect, but what he said up there was ridiculous...I should have listened to Georgette when she warned me months ago..." I took a sip and looked at Theobold, "You're wrong about her, you know."

Even in my drunken state, I wasn't going to tell him anymore and give away Georgette's secret.

"Well, she is very wise when it comes to keeping order onboard and dodging bullets and things of that sort," he said.

"I bet she's turned my bed back into her shoe rack..." I said flatly, thinking about how I would be sleeping back in my old cabin now. Theobold laughed and said he could imagine the cabin looking like her own personal boudoir. I laughed as well, telling him that he wasn't far off.

"Well, at least we have you laughing again," he said.

That was the interesting thing about "Ship Life" ...It could turn on a dime. He took another sip from his beer and then looked at me with a grin.

"I think I know just the thing to snap you out of it," he said as he stood up and told me to follow him and bring my martini.

We ended up in the arcade a few decks up. I had never been there before. It was after midnight, so it was empty as we walked through. It had every type of pinball and theme park game you could think of – the colored lights from each game illuminated and danced around the room. Theobold swiped his crew card in a machine, and tokens started falling out of the bottom and piled into the collection bowl.

With a big smile, he gathered them all up and asked me, "Which do you want to try first?!"

We played Whack-A-Mole, Roll-and-Score, and the water gun horse race before we finally ended up at the air hockey table. I hadn't played in years, and I was surprising myself with how good I was at it—even while drunk. Theobold would bring rounds of drinks back from the casino bar, which was still open, and I lost count of how many rounds we played.

I was roaring with laughter as I continually beat Theobold, and he would demand a rematch "for his honor." After he finally admitted defeat, we left the air hockey table. I ended up in the bowling alley, picking up a ball.

"Should we bowl?" I asked, looking down the lanes illuminated in black lighting. When the lanes started spinning, I decided against it. Theobold laughed as I stumbled to put the ball back.

"I think it's time I walked you back to your cabin." He held out his arm, his grey suit and blonde hair glowing in the black light. I had forgotten how handsome he was since I had been wrapped up with Serge all this time. I remembered how I felt the first time I saw him walk out on stage – so confident and dapper. I placed my hand on his arm, and without thinking about it, I leaned up and kissed him.

He paused as I did, then put his hands on my face and kissed me back.

We stood there, illuminated in the black light, kissing for a while - He was an amazing kisser. I wasn't sure if I was spinning from euphoria or the alcohol or both, but it felt good. I just wanted to feel good in that moment. And "Ship Life Bree" was definitely enjoying the moment.

XXIV

CHAPTER 24

My deck phone started ringing and jolted me awake. My head pounded as I looked for the phone and realized I had no idea where I was... This wasn't Serge's cabin... and it wasn't my cabin. I answered the phone confusedly.

"Hello?"

Smitty was on the other end, "Um, are you okay?" he asked.

I looked around the strange cabin with a large porthole for a window and answered, "Yeah, I'm fine... why?"

Smitty said that Eryn had heard that Serge and I had a big fight and had broken up.

"Oh yeah, that did happen," I said as it all came crashing back to me. I looked over on the other side of the bed and saw Theobold. He had taken off his dress shirt and lay on top of the covers in a tank top and suit pants.

Smitty continued, "Why didn't you call me? What the hell happened? You know what? I'm just going to come over to your cabin," he said as I panicked.

"No!" I said frantically... "I'm still in bed, I have a headache...and I'm not dressed," I said as I looked down and saw that I was still in my dress from the night before. I started to remember us coming back to Theobold's cabin after our early morning game night.

"Okay, well then, do you want to grab lunch? Everyone is in rehearsal for hours, so I'm just here by myself," Smitty said.

"Sure, but it has to be a late lunch...I need to take care of this headache," I said, not untruthfully.

"Wow, it sounds like someone had a wild night!" Smitty joked. I ended the call and dropped the phone on the bed.

You have no idea, I thought to myself.

Theobold stirred on his side of the bed and opened his eyes.

"Good morning," he said as he rubbed his forehead like he also had a headache.

"Hi..." I awkwardly said, looking at us in bed.

"Last night was fun, eh?" He grinned at me.

I slowly sat up, smoothing my hair, "Yeah...um... Did we?"

He laughed. "Do not worry, nothing happened... well, except for rather exceptional kissing," he added as he kept smiling. I did remember how well he kissed me and how much fun we had. I completely forgot about Serge for the night.

Then I came to my senses, "No! This is not good... for either of us! Do you know what will happen if people think we slept together?!"

Theobold shrugged, "But we didn't sleep together."

I stood up in my wrinkled dress, "You know as well as I do that when two crew members are seen leaving together or coming out of a cabin... they are having sex, whether it's true or not." I placed my hands on my hips, and he started laughing. "It's not funny! You are my boss!" I exclaimed.

He raised his hands as if to calm me down, "Look, no one saw us – I'm sure of it. I was a bit more sober than you last night. So, no one needs to know. We just kissed...and it's not like it was the first time..."

"That doesn't make it better," I said as I sat down to put my heels on. "Look, I appreciate you cheering me up last night, and it was fun..."

Theobold cut me off, "Yes, it was fun...and we could keep having fun. I do like you, Bree."

I sighed, "You hardly know me!"

He responded that "hardly" was a bit harsh, and what he knew about he liked immensely – my attitude, humor, style, work ethic, and compassion for people... He went on, "If you wanted to, we could make this work and keep everyone happy."

I told him that Georgette had dropped me immediately when she saw us kiss, and Smitty knew something was up and got very cold toward me. And it had not been easy to get them back to a normal space.

"That's because we didn't tell them... It was shocking," Theobold responded.

"Exactly!" I said as I grabbed my purse.

"Okay, look," Theobold said as he stood up from

the bed, "I like you... a lot...and I think you may like me as well. I thought I sensed it when you first came onboard, but I missed my chance when you took up with the first officer. So now that you ended things with him, would you be willing to take it slow and see how things could go with us... dinner perhaps?"

Just when I thought things had settled down, everything had turned upside down, but Theobold wasn't wrong. I did have a crush on him when I came on, but I never thought he would be interested in me.

"This has happened very suddenly, and I just need some time to process all of... this," I said, motioning to the unkempt bed.

"Of course, it is completely up to you. I leave the ball in your court," Theobold said and flashed me that cheeky grin. Despite my shock over the situation, I couldn't help but grin back.

I made Theobold look out into the hallway to ensure no one was around. He gave me a thumbs-up, and I dashed out. I panicked, realizing I didn't remember how we got to his cabin last night, but luckily, I found the I-95 quickly and discovered I wasn't far from my cabin. At least I knew the cast was in rehearsal so that I couldn't run into Eryn like last time. I made it back to my cabin, and let out a sigh of relief when I saw Georgette was not there. I didn't know if she had heard of the breakup already and wondered where I slept, if not in our cabin. I popped some headache pills, showered, and met Smitty at the buffet on the Lido Deck.

"So... Tell me everything," Smitty said as we sat in a corner away from the passengers.

I told him about the fight and all the awful things Serge had said about Erika. I was still angry as I replayed the whole altercation for Smitty.

He rolled his eyes and let out an exasperated sigh, "He is ridiculous if he is going to side with Marcello on this... This man deserves no more of your time or energy. You know what this means," he said as he cut his salad.

I wasn't sure what he meant as I gave him a quizzical look.

"It means it's time for a password change," Smitty declared with a mischievous glint in his eye, his lips curling into a playful grin. "Something fun, something memorable... like 'Italian Stallion'? Or perhaps a more direct approach... 'Purge Serge'?!"

He chuckled at his own suggestion, offering a lighthearted solution to my troubles.

"That way, you won't forget. It's what I do with all my ex-boyfriends," he added with a wink, punctuating his advice with a bite of his salad.

"What if I want to forget?" I mused aloud, a hint of vulnerability seeping into my voice. "Forget that I let myself be with someone who thinks like that."

Smitty said that was precisely the reason – so I wouldn't forget and repeat the same mistake again. "You'll change it again, eventually, with another name," he joked as he took another bite. I looked at him and grinned.

"Exactly how many ex-boyfriends do you think I'm going to have this contract?" I quipped playfully, though I felt a subtle nervousness. Joking about future romantic entanglements felt odd, especially given the night spent in our boss's cabin. Yet, I refused to feel too guilty; I had made a silent vow to myself that things wouldn't escalate any further.

The next few days went by quickly as we finished our visits to the Hawaiian ports, and the ship began its run of sea days back to San Diego. Surprisingly, Theobold acted completely normal when I saw him during the auctions and gallery hours.

I asked myself if it had really happened, *Did I dream about making out with my boss?*

He did say he was leaving the ball in my court, and I was determined to leave it there before it messed everything up. The last day of the cruise arrived, and I was setting up the registration table for the final auction. The ship was rocking as the weather worsened, but I hoped it wouldn't get too bad before we finished the event. Anna and Eryn walked up and helped me open the folding table and put the tablecloth on. Both of them had been very supportive since hearing about my breakup with Serge. They told me that Holiday had just received an email from the Captain saying that the weather was supposed to get even worse the next day. Therefore, the ship would overnight in San Diego to wait out the storm before heading back to Hawaii. I asked if they were going to go out, and Eryn said it was her turn to clean all the costumes.

"I shall be the laundry wench all night long," she joked.

Anna said that Holiday had asked her and her boyfriend to double-date with him and Smitty.

"You can be assistant laundry wench with me!" Eryn exclaimed.

I laughed and said I would take a pass. I told them that a bit of time by myself would be good after all the Serge drama.

"Speaking of the devil," Eryn remarked as she glanced down the hallway. Following her gaze, I caught sight of Serge and Marcello strolling along with a group of officers, their crisp white uniforms contrasting sharply against the backdrop of the ship's corridors. My stomach churned at the sight of Serge's stern stare, but what caught my attention even more were the knowing grins and stifled laughter from his companions, as though they were in on some inside joke I was not. As the group passed by, leaving a lingering sense of unease in their wake, I turned to the girls.

"What do you think that was all about?" I asked, hoping for some insight into the encounter.

Eryn and Anna exchanged a meaningful glance before Eryn spoke up, her expression tinged with discomfort. "Apparently, Serge is spreading rumors that he broke things off because you were 'needy' and... lacking in certain areas," she hesitated, her words hanging heavy in the air.

"He's an absolute jerk," Anna interjected. I couldn't help but roll my eyes at the predictable display of wounded male ego.

"Typical," I muttered under my breath, the bitterness of betrayal and humiliation mingling within me. It was a classic tactic—deflecting blame and salvaging one's pride at the expense of another's reputation. But I refused to let his baseless accusations tarnish my self-worth.

"Don't worry, girl. It's not worth it to give him another thought. Now you can get with someone even hotter and stick it to him. A bunch of new crew members are joining the ship tomorrow – maybe your future boyfriend will be there!" Eryn speculated excitedly.

Anna asked me if there was anyone else onboard that I was interested in. I paused and flashed back to making out with Theobold in the black light.

"Oh! She hesitated! That means yes... Who is it?!" Eryn asked excitedly.

I laughed and told her there wasn't anyone and I planned to focus on work, which was true.

The cruise ended without any more drama,

thankfully, and as I walked down the gangway into the night air of San Diego, I let out a contented sigh. My plan was to find a dive bar, have a glass of wine, and chill out for a bit. I stepped into the security line to exit the port terminal, and as I was waiting, I heard Theobold's voice behind me.

"It seems that she's a lone wolf tonight... Where is the rest of your entourage?" he asked.

I turned and looked up at him, "Well, hello. Everyone is busy doing other things, so yes, I am indeed a lone wolf. Which is good because I could use some time to clear my head," I said as I gave him a look that said he was a big reason for it.

He grinned, "Very sensible," he said as he put his bag on the security belt behind mine.

I exited the security building and turned to him, asking what his plan was. He said he was going to his "secret spot" as he kept grinning at me. I rolled my eyes and playfully said, "Should I even bother asking?"

"Oh, of course, you should inquire...but I'm not sure you are worthy," he pondered as his grin grew wider.

"Yeah, you are probably right," I said as I began walking away.

Theobold followed me, "Okay, okay. It's actually nothing that special, really...just an English pub a few blocks away. None of the crew know about it, so it's a bit of an escape. But the fish and chips are amazing, and the Wi-Fi is lightning-fast. It's the closest you can get to the UK here, in my opinion. If you didn't have any plans, I could take you," he said. Then he threw up his hands defensively. "Not as a date... It would most certainly not be a 'date'...it's not a 'date place,' really," he said sheepishly.

I couldn't help but smile, and I had to admit it did sound more tempting than walking around aimlessly and seeing what I could find.

"Well, I have never been to the UK," I said.

His grin turned into a smile, "Brilliant! You're going tonight," he said as he started to lead the way.

He was right; the food was delicious, and it had a dive bar feel with wood-paneled walls and Union Jack flags hanging everywhere from the ceiling. As we sat in the cozy corner of the English pub, the conversation flowed effortlessly between Theobold and me. We exchanged stories of our respective upbringings, sharing glimpses into the worlds we had left behind to embark on this journey at sea. Theobold spoke fondly of his family's illustrious lineage, regaling me with tales of ancestral estates and storied traditions, yet there was an underlying sense of restlessness in his voice as he confessed his yearning to escape the weight of familial expectations.

In turn, I opened up about my own experiences, sharing anecdotes of my humble beginnings and the winding path that had led me to the cruise ship. There was a shared understanding between us, a mutual recognition of the desire to carve out our own paths and forge our destinies on our own terms. The waiter brought us a slice of cake on the house, and we split it as he asked about growing up in the South and my transition to Hollywood. I told him that I also came to ships to get away and travel. Not too far from his reasons, just "without the noble lineage," I quipped.

"Well, you know how Americans are, always looking to marry into a title," Theobold teased, giving me a cheeky wink that made my cheeks flush.

"Will you stop it!" I exclaimed, feeling a playful surge of annoyance as I reached for a fry and flung it across the table at him. Feigning shock, Theobold raised his hands in mock defense.

"Stop what?" he protested innocently, his eyes dancing with mischief. I gestured between us, irritatingly amused.

"All of this... the flirting, the marriage talk, and this so-called 'non-date'," I quipped, gesturing my hands with air quotes with a wry grin. Theobold laughed, the sound filling the air with infectious warmth.

"You're absolutely right," he conceded, his smile widening as he leaned in closer. "It's definitely not a date... and I'm definitely not enjoying it," he declared with a playful twinkle in his eye as he threw the fry back at me.

An hour later, we were on our way back to the ship. His hand brushed against mine as we walked, eliciting a flirtatious look that passed between us.

What am I doing? I questioned myself as we strolled along.

I had just ended things with Serge, and I had already decided I wasn't going to entertain another romance, especially with someone as complicated as my boss. I could feel "Ship Life Bree" coming out again. It was as if she loved the thrill of the unknown - and changing all of "Land Life Bree's" decisions. I found myself teetering on the precipice between past and present, torn between hopeful contentment and the excitement of what could be.

As we returned to the port, we walked into the ship terminal. Theobold held the door open for me. I smiled as I walked through, but it quickly faded when I saw Smitty, Holiday, and Anna walking through the door across from me.

"Oh, well, hello you!" Smitty exclaimed with genuine enthusiasm as he caught sight of me. But as his gaze shifted to Theobold standing behind me, his tone took on a more dubious edge. "And you..." Smitty's voice trailed off. I was busted. I tried to act like everything was normal, but the awkward tension was palpable.

Why am I feeling so guilty? I asked myself. We had just gone for dinner – it wasn't a date – even though it pretty much turned into a date."

"Hi, Guys!" I said way too excitedly.

Theobold held up a hand acknowledging every-one and smiled – also way too excitedly – and began explaining, in too much detail, how we had just run into each other and decided to grab a bite.

"Oh right," Holiday said as we all started moving through the security line.

"Right..." Smitty drew out the word, giving me a skeptical look before going through the body scanner.

I turned to Theobold behind me, rolled my eyes, and whispered, "Real smooth."

We made it through ship security and stepped onto the I-95. The group was still with us as Theobold turned and, with a not-so-subtle look, wished me a good night as he started walking back to his cabin. I did feel a rush of excitement as he had given me the look, but I tried to act nonchalant. I asked how the double date went, and Anna cheekily said, "Not as good as yours did by the looks of it, babes."

I attempted to brush the comment off, but Smitty was not going to let it go so easily. He pulled me into one of the smaller hallways off the corridor.

"Um... what was that?" he asked pointedly. "I thought you said nothing was going on with you two?" I could feel the weight of his question bearing down on me.

Just tell the truth, Bree, I told myself.

I explained to him that it was completely platonic. We just had some fish and chips, and that was it. Smitty looked intently at me for a few moments.

"Okay, you shady lady," he quipped as he ended his interrogation and left with Holiday toward their cabin. Anna headed towards her cabin, and she gave me a wink and put a single finger to her lips. I couldn't help but roll my eyes in response, a half-hearted attempt to mask my slight annoyance. It was one thing for complete strangers to make assumptions about my relationship with Theobold, but for my own friends to do so after I had assured them that nothing was going on felt like a betrayal of trust. The insinuations, however playful they may have been, felt off-putting.

As I made my way back to my cabin, the events of the past few hours weighed heavily on my mind. "Ship Life," with its ever-shifting currents and unpredictable twists and turns, seemed determined to take me on yet another bumpy ride, and I couldn't help but wonder if my seatbelt was tight enough.

XXV

CHAPTER 25

I was coming to enjoy pressing the reset button on a new cruise. The anticipation of what could happen with a whole new crowd of passengers was exciting. The weather had cleared, and the ship set sail for Hawaii. The first night went as usual, with Smitty and me running Guess the Price in the atrium, looking for our big leads for the upcoming auction. The crowd seemed enthusiastic, so we were pleased as we finished and returned to the gallery with our final guesses. Georgette took the final stack and began inputting the cabin numbers into the system. Theobold stepped out of his office, clad in a new suit that hugged his frame with precision. The fabric of his suit shimmered under the light, tailored to perfection and accentuating every contour of his physique. He said he was getting ready to do the Welcome Aboard Champagne Reception as Georgette stood up to accompany him.

"I thought we might mix it up a bit tonight," he said, looking at Georgette and then to me, "Bree, would you like to join me?" Georgette paused, and Smitty blinked hard at the question. I looked at Georgette, who had always done the reception with Theobold, as she waved her hand and said it wasn't a problem and would give her more time to finish the mailing list. I took a second and then said that would be fun.

"Brilliant! Meet me in the atrium in fifteen minutes," he said as he walked out.

Georgette slowly sat back down at the desk, "I wasn't feeling this outfit anyways," she remarked in a playful but slightly suspicious tone. I told her she could wear a garbage bag and still get a standing ovation, to which she grinned as she stared at her computer screen. Smitty, however, urgently motioned for me to join him out in the hallway.

"Okay, seriously?!" he asked as we walked a few feet from the gallery entrance. "He gives you an unwanted kiss and causes all this chaos, but you still go to dinner with him on a 'non-date,' and now he is having you do the reception with him?" I sighed and told him that everything was fine.

So what if he asked me to do the welcome reception? It was a work function, not a scandalous activity for the two of us to engage in, I thought.

"You are just jealous because you don't get a free glass of champagne," I said jokingly.

Smitty almost laughed but composed himself, saying, "Okay, that's only half true and also beside the point. The point is that now that you aren't with Serge anymore, and he's being all flirty again... And you aren't doing much to shut it down this time."

He raised his eyebrows at me triumphantly. I rolled my eyes and told him I was getting tired of telling him nothing was happening. I blew him an air kiss as I turned to go meet Theobold.

I heard Smitty's voice echo as I walked down the hallway, "Deflection doesn't look good on you, ma'am."

The next morning, Smitty and I were doing our early setup for the auction while several other crew members were putting up all the Christmas decorations around the ship. The Vision was a gorgeous ship but already quite flashy with the glitz and neon lighting, so I wondered how adding a ton of Christmas lights into the mix would look.

Returning later for the auction, I passed a towering Christmas tree that stood proudly in the central atrium, its branches adorned with an array of sparkling baubles and colorful lights. As I approached the registration table, I found the girls excitedly greeting and registering the growing line of passengers waiting to enter the lounge. It was a promising sign of a successful auction ahead. Before long, the lounge was open and filled with passengers looking at the art. After finishing our pre-auction sales, I stood up on the stage to do Theobold's introduction. Now that I knew more about him, I switched it up and made it more personal, attempting to endear him to the crowd a bit more. I even said something about him "running away from the aristocracy to come and entertain them today on the Vivace Vision."

As I finished, the crowd began clapping, and

Theobold walked out on stage with that showman smile and took the mic from me, "Thank you, my darling."

I tripped on the step down from the stage when I heard him say it. He had never called me "darling," and certainly not on a microphone for everyone to hear. I regained my composure as I walked away from the stage, and I caught Smitty's expression. It was as if that had confirmed all his suspicions, and he was ready to convict me, lock me up, and throw away the key. Georgette also gave me a very judgmental arched eyebrow.

The following hours felt uneasy as the auction went on, and finally, Theobold ended it after several successful bidding wars. He disappeared backstage as the passengers filed out of the lounge. We closed the doors as Georgette handed the breakdown crew a flash drive – most likely with whatever entertainment they had requested. I couldn't help but marvel at the subtle power she wielded behind the scenes. I found it so interesting that Georgette's flash drives were the extra currency that kept our auxiliary staff happy to help out. After she finished sorting the helpers out, she told us she would be in the gallery as she exited the lounge.

The second she was gone, Smitty pounced.

"Enough with the charade already... If it wasn't obvious before, then it is bitch-slapping me in the face now!" he exclaimed and continued. "Since when is he calling you 'darling'? That is Georgette's whole thing! I mean, have you learned nothing? You just ended things with Serge, and now you are jumping straight into his bed and lying to me about it!"

I cut him off there, "I am not lying! We are not sleeping together! ...We just made out one night last cruise, and it wasn't a big deal..." As I spoke the words aloud, I could see the shock register in Smitty's eyes, his expression morphing from anger to disbelief in an instant. I went on to explain that it was the night Serge and I had the big fight, and I was upset and drunk, and it had just happened, but that was all. Smitty went on a tirade after my explanation.

"Oh! So, let me get this straight..." he began, his voice dripping with sarcasm and frustration. "Our boss kisses you when he's drunk, and you said it meant nothing... Then you kiss our boss when you're drunk and end up in his cabin, but it's not a big deal. Now you are going to dinner and making champagne toasts together, and he's calling you 'my darling'... Who even are you anymore? Soon enough, you'll be saying it's not a big deal, and it means nothing when you are fucking our boss in his cabin!"

Georgette let out a gasp, startling the both of us as we turned to face her. She stood there stunned, holding her handbag, which she had forgotten in the lounge and returned to collect. My stomach sank, and I knew she had heard the last part of Smitty's tirade. Before I could say anything, her stunned look turned to scorn as she stormed out of the lounge. Smitty watched as she left, then turned back to me and crossed his arms defensively. I could tell he hadn't meant for her to hear, but the damage was done.

I lost it.

"What the hell is wrong with you?! Can you imagine how awful she will be to me now, thanks to you? You have built this whole situation up in your mind to the point that I might as well have slept with him because that's already what you think... and now Georgette does as well!" I yelled at Smitty.

He responded, "Well, she has a right to know! Maybe you guys haven't slept together, but this affects me and her. Theobold is our head of department, and if you two are making out and doing whatever else, that is not cool."

Frustration poured over me as I told him nothing had changed work-wise and nothing would change in the future. "We have one month left and have had so much fun. I would hate for this to wreck all that," I pleaded with him.

I could tell he was just as frustrated as he said he wasn't sure how to handle the situation and needed to think about it. I felt awful, but I understood his point about the problematic issues of dating the boss. I tried to avoid all this drama by not pursuing things with Theobold, and it all had blown up anyway.

That night in the gallery only got worse.

"You'll be handling all of the free artwork clients tonight, Miss Bradley," was all Georgette said to me as she handed me a clipboard with my appointment schedule. I couldn't focus during my appointments, and my frustration grew with everyone's ridiculous excuses about why they wouldn't frame.

When I heard the response, "We have a friend at home who does our frames," for the third time, I couldn't handle it any longer. I sarcastically came back with, "Wow! You know, it's just so funny that every single person on this ship has a friend who does framing!" My clients didn't appreciate that and got up and left the gallery. I sighed as I watched them leave and saw Georgette approach, hands on hips.

"Are we just yelling at our clients and chasing them away from the gallery now?" she asked sternly. Theobold had popped his head out of his office during the commotion. He had finished his appointment, quietly walking his clients out of the gallery and said goodbye as he slid the gallery doors shut and turned to the three of us.

"Alright, it seems a team meeting is in order... I am sensing a multitude of tension...What is going on?" he asked cautiously.

I blurted out that Smitty assumed we were sleeping together – which wasn't true, but Georgette had overheard, and now she thought it as well. And they were being awful because they thought he was going to favor me over them. I couldn't stop it from coming out, and even Georgette seemed taken aback that I just laid it all out in the open. Theobold took a long pause, appearing deep in thought. The silence was deafening before he finally addressed all three of us.

"Ah... Alright, as we all know, this ship we live and work on can sometimes not be the most...salubrious setting...and can create an environment where situations can be misinterpreted or blown out of proportion...So, let's just remedy that situation right now...No, Bree and I have not had sex," he stated calmly and pointedly as he looked at Georgette and Smitty and then continued. "We also know that living and working in such close quarters can blur the line between personal and professional. Now, to clear the air...Have we become closer? Yes. However, I don't want either of you to think this should change how we have been running things because it most certainly will not. I did leave it up to Bree if she wanted to pursue things further, and I believe we are ...still finding our way through that," he paused and looked at me.

"Georgette, you certainly know that, in this

company, team members have started dating and become couples...some even married. So, it is not an uncommon occurrence, and those teams were wildly successful... Because the team kept it strictly professional during working hours, and that is exactly what shall happen here. Now, I hope you both can respect that because she and I have been completely candid and put everything out in the open," he finished his monologue, his gaze sweeping around the room, lingering on each of us in turn.

The silence that followed was heavy with tension, each of us grappling with the weight of the situation.

Finally, Smitty broke the silence, acknowledging that perhaps he had blown things out of proportion. Theobold looked at Georgette, who paused and said, "We have a month left, and I highly doubt the company has the time or patience to transfer any of us at this point... I don't need, nor do I want, to know the specifics, but I would appreciate it if the two of you would figure 'whatever this is' out in Theobold's cabin and leave me in peace."

I looked at Georgette.

She is kicking me out? Can she do that? I asked myself in shock.

Smitty also looked alarmed, "Wait... So, you're pushing her into his cabin and are fine with it?!"

Georgette put up her arms, "Otherwise, I can go to HR and request a cabin change, but I'm sure they would be interested to see what I put down for my reason," she said as she crossed her arms.

Theobold's gaze grew stern at her threat, "That... is something I can figure out," he said as he looked at me and told me not to worry. "Now, there are only a few appointments left, which I will handle. I will let the three of you have the rest of the night off, and hopefully, everyone can cool off a bit."

Georgette and Smitty made their exit silently, leaving Theobold and me alone in the quiet of the gallery. He turned to me with a contrite expression.

"I apologize for everything happening like this, but at least it's all out in the open now," he said, his tone tinged with regret. The next appointment arrived, and he took them into his office, so we couldn't discuss what had just happened further.

I was mad as I left the gallery. I was mad

at Theobold for kissing me and starting all this confusion. I was mad at Smitty for accusing me and not believing most of his "story" had not happened. I was mad at Georgette for believing it and forcing me out of our cabin with a veiled threat. And I was furious with myself for allowing things to spiral so wildly out of control. I found myself walking aimlessly through the ship, my mind reeling with the chaos that had unfolded in the wake of my actions. It felt as though I had been cast adrift in a sea of uncertainty and regret. I was evicted from my cabin, Smitty was not talking to me, and the dancers were unavailable since they were busy doing the shows. I sank into a seat at the martini bar, feeling utterly lost and alone.

As I sipped on my martini, my thoughts swirled chaotically in my head, as I struggled to untangle the web of events that had led me to this moment. I thought back to my very first day onboard. The spark of attraction to Theobold had been there from the start, a flicker of desire that had been quickly overshadowed by Serge. The memory of finding myself in Theobold's bed the same night as the breakup with Serge echoed in my mind, a stark reminder of my reckless abandon.

Smitty's question from earlier lingered, haunting me: *Who even are you?*

In that moment, I realized that I had allowed "Ship Life" to consume me whole. And as I ordered another martini, I couldn't help but wonder if I would ever be able to find my way back to myself amidst the chaos that surrounded me. The constant highs and lows had drained me emotionally, and the pressure to "look the part" and try to keep up with Georgette and the other girls had changed my physical appearance. I repeated the question in my head, *Who even are you?*

I was nearly finished with my second martini when I noticed Theobold approaching the bar.

"My, how the castle has crumbled," he remarked with a faint smile, attempting to lighten the mood.

"On top of our heads," I replied dryly, my tone devoid of any hint of amusement. Theobold ordered a beer as I stirred my martini, "I'm literally homeless on a cruise ship... How does that even happen?"

Theobold grinned slightly as he joked that he had heard the sun lounges on the Lido Deck were quite comfortable.

I threw an olive from my martini at him.

"Will you stop trying to make light of this? It's not funny. I'm pretty sure Smitty hates me... Georgette definitely hates me, and we have a whole month to get through," I lamented. A few days ago, I had thought the last month would fly by, but now it felt like it would be deathly slow.

Theobold put his hand on top of mine on the bar, "They will come around. They just need some time to get used to the idea," he said.

"Get used to what idea?" I asked as my gaze shifted from our hands to his face.

He paused for a moment, seeming a bit sad. He removed his hand and told me he would go to the crew office right then and find me a spare cabin to sleep in. I thought about sleeping alone in an empty cabin, and the thought made me feel worse than I did already.

"Or you can come to mine, and we can just sleep... nothing funny. I promise," he said reassuringly. I looked up at him and saw a nervous smile as he ran his hand through his hair, tousling it.

You enjoyed kissing him, and you've been enjoying your time with him, I thought to myself.

Now that everything was out in the open, there wasn't a shroud of secrecy surrounding us anymore.

And if Smitty and Georgette already thought I was "that girl," then I might as well be.

A month-long fling with a handsome, British man from a noble lineage seems rather appealing at this point, I thought, as "Ship Life Bree" took complete control.

"To hell with it," I said as I squeezed his hand and smiled. "But we are just sleeping," I said as we left the bar and headed toward Theobold's cabin.

XXVI

CHAPTER 26

Two weeks slipped by in a haze of awkwardness and strained interactions as Theobold and I navigated the delicate balance of our newfound dynamic with Georgette and Smitty. Despite the tension, we focused on the task at hand, which provided a temporary reprieve from the discomfort that hung in the air. The art department had morphed into a silent, cold machine, its gears grinding against each other with an unsettling friction. Yet, we somehow managed to turn in a respectable number of sales by the end of the cruise.

It was a testament to our resilience, I supposed.

But as the days stretched on, I couldn't help but wonder how long we could maintain this delicate facade before it all came crashing down around us. I had moved my things into Theobold's cabin. As I grabbed my last bag from my old cabin, it felt like Georgette was an ex-lover I had just broken up with, and I asked myself if Georgette's name would be my next password.

Smitty was cordial with me, but I missed the close brother/sister bond we used to have. Guess the Price felt clinical now as we just went through the motions, and our letter printing parties had been divided into two groups. Smitty took half, and they printed them in Holiday's cabin while I printed my half with Eryn and Anna in their cabin. The girls had remained neutral through everything, but then again, Theobold wasn't their boss. As we finished the cruise, I had hoped that Georgette and Smitty would see that everything had stayed the same work-wise. I was still doing all my same duties and responsibilities. In fact, I was taking on more, trying to help them out as a type of peace offering, but it got me nowhere.

Theobold had been a great support amidst the turmoil, his presence a comforting distraction from the tension onboard. The first night I stayed over in his cabin, we didn't rush into anything physical. Instead, we simply held each other close and kissed. As our relationship blossomed in the days that followed, it felt strangely natural, as if we had stumbled upon something that was always meant to be. Unlike my romance with Serge, which had been characterized by its physical intensity, my connection with Theobold ran deeper, anchored by a shared sense of humor and a mutual understanding that transcended mere physical attraction. His infectious laughter and quick wit never failed to brighten my spirits. And as we navigated the complexities of our budding relationship, I couldn't help but marvel at the ease with which we fit together, as if we were two pieces of a melodramatic puzzle.

Theobold had somehow smuggled a Christmas tree onboard, and as we decorated it in his cabin, he told me stories about some of the amazing Christmases his family had at their estate through the years. I was surprised to hear that his mother even had Christmas cards from Queen Mary that were framed and hung on the wall. The more I learned about his family, it became clear that they were very high in society, and Theobold was in line to be the next Lord Thorne. He had mentioned Georgette's family a few times as the family estates were close to one another, but the families themselves had grown apart. There seemed to be a much deeper story about what caused the rift, but I felt it was best not to pry given the current situation between myself, Theobold, and Georgette.

Even though she had exiled me, I still kept her secret.

Theobold wanted to know all about my childhood and growing up in the South. He loved American history and the Civil War and said he hoped to get a ship assignment out of New Orleans for one contract so he could immerse himself in Southern culture. He had a child-like enthusiasm for things which was infectious. I had been spending my port days mostly with him since I didn't want to make it awkward for Anna and Eryn to have to choose who to hang out with between Smitty and I.

We kept ourselves busy exploring the breathtaking landscapes and vibrant culture of the islands. Theobold had taken me up in the mountains on Maui to the lavender and vodka farms. We wandered through the fields, inhaling the intoxicating scent of lavender and soaking in the tranquility of our surroundings. We toasted one another, sipping on a selection of vodkas infused with the freshly harvested lavender and other botanicals.

On Kauai, he rented a convertible and as we cruised along the winding coastal roads of the North Shore. In the distance, I could see waterfalls cascading through the rugged cliffs and emerald-green landscapes of the Na Pali Coast in a breathtaking display of natural beauty as we drove up to Princeville. We dined at one of the island's finest restaurants, indulging in delicious seafood and the vibrant flavors of Hawaii. Theobold suggested we visit "The Queen's Bath," a natural tidal pool notorious for its rough waters. Undeterred by the warnings of the challenging conditions, we made our way to the secluded spot tucked away along the rugged coastline. The spray from the sheer force of the ocean crashing against the rocky shoreline filled the air as we jumped in. Amongst the turbulent currents, we were greeted by massive sea turtles gracefully gliding through the water around us. Their majestic presence made it worth the risk as I gently ran my hand along the massive shell of the one that swam right up to me.

As we made our way back to the car after our unforgettable swim with the turtles, I couldn't help but chuckle at Theobold's precarious antics on the rugged lava rocks. With each step, his attempts to maintain his balance met with a series of comical wobbles and near misses. We sat in the convertible, watching a fiery sunset painting the sky in shades of gold and crimson. In that moment, with Theobold by my side and the enchanting island of Kauai as our playground, I was beginning to feel comfortable in this "new normal."

In less than two weeks, we had made some fantastic memories in Hawaii, and the selfies that we had taken during our adventures were now stuck in the sides of the mirror in the cabin. It wasn't as grand as Serge's cabin, but it had a large porthole with sunlight in the morning, large closets, and a big bed. One of the best perks was that Theobold was now in charge of the deck phone since I, and it, now lived in his cabin, which honestly outweighed the cabin downgrade. I truly detested the thing.

One night as the ship slowly sailed away from Hilo, we went to the ship's back deck to watch the lava flows. We gazed into the inky black blur of sea and land as the darkness of the night was pierced by the mesmerizing glow of a fiery network mixed with red and orange. As the molten lava met the cool waters of the ocean, plumes of white steam billowed upwards, creating a stark contrast against the dark night sky. It was a spectacle to witness. Theobold had his arm around me as I leaned on him while we watched. Lost in the moment, I felt Theobold lean down as his tender lips met mine in a soft, lingering kiss. The world around us faded into the background as we kissed amidst the backdrop of Hawaii's otherworldly grandeur. Sighing contentedly, my gaze returned to the mesmerizing display of lava flowing into the ocean. Hawaii had woven its way into my heart over the past six months, and the thought of leaving filled me with a bittersweet longing. The local Hawaiians said that once you had "The Spirit of Aloha," it never left you, and I found myself hoping that was true.

Christmas Eve arrived two weeks later. The time of year had always felt special and magical, even as an adult in my twenties, but with the tension of the current situation, it felt different this year. Smitty and I stood in the atrium running our familiar routine of Guess the Price. He put on his over-the-top, bubbly persona to get people to guess, and I smiled as he danced around the atrium in his festive, red plaid pants, throwing guessing slips into people's hands.

Anna and Eryn showed up in the atrium, both dressed in Christmas elf costumes, but they looked like they had come from a sex shop. Their boobs were falling out of the fur-lined corsets, and the red and green striped skirts were ruffled and extremely high. I did admire their knee-high, laced-up stiletto boots as they wobbled over to the table.

"Now, that's a certain type of Christmas vibe," I remarked with a chuckle, unable to contain my amusement at their over-the-top outfits.

Eryn wasted no time in introducing themselves with dramatic flair, motioning to Anna and declaring, "This is Vixen, and I am Mistle-Hoe!"

The absurdity of their chosen monikers combined with their outlandish costumes was enough to send me into fits of laughter. Anna laughed as well and said that Eryn hadn't even altered the costumes.

"I don't know what we are selling, but it sure isn't Christmas," Eryn said as she adjusted her boobs. Smitty ran over and started taking selfies with the girls, commenting on how obsessed he was with their looks.

"Just wait until you see your boyfriend!" Anna exclaimed.

Just as she said it, Holiday made his entrance in a Santa suit that seemed comically oversized for his frame. The sight of him standing there, dwarfed by the red fabric, was enough to get a chuckle from everyone in the vicinity. Holiday's expression spoke volumes as he glanced down at the ill-fitting suit, his face a mixture of resignation and amusement.

"Christmas is swallowing me whole," his words punctuated by a hint of wry humor. Before anyone could offer reassurance or sympathy, Smitty interjected, nodding towards Anna and Eryn with a knowing grin.

"Don't worry, babe. No one will be looking at you when you have these two next to you," he quipped as we all laughed.

There was a grand, velvet throne in front of the tree in the atrium for Holiday to sit on and have the kids line up to tell him what they wanted for Christmas. Holiday admitted that he wasn't great with kids, so it would be a challenge. Anna re-assured him that it couldn't go on too long because they still had to rehearse for the next day's Christmas show.

"Why are all the Christmas songs in this show so bloody old? Why can't we do a Madonna number?" Eryn asked.

"It is on brand for these outfits," Smitty said as she proceeded to sing the familiar lyrics of "Santa Baby" in a sultry tone and slapped Holiday's ass.

Smitty reacted, "Okay, Mistle-hoe...If anyone is taking advantage of Santa, it's going to be me!" he said as he walked behind his boyfriend and slapped his ass even harder, making him jump. We all laughed as an announcement sounded over the PA system, saying that Santa had appeared in the atrium to hear everyone's Christmas wishlist.

"That's our cue...Come along, Santa," Anna said as she guided Holiday over to his throne. A queue of passengers quickly formed for "Santa." Smitty and I giggled as we watched the Christmas trio interact with the passengers while their children jumped into an uncomfortable Dan Holiday's lap.

When Smitty realized it was just us standing at the table, he stiffened up.

I rolled my eyes. "Oh, come on. It's Christmas...Can we please get past this? I miss the way we used to be," I said as I walked over to the table and grabbed a wrapped present from underneath. "I know things aren't great between us right now, but I got you a present. I saw this and thought about you," I said as I handed Smitty the present.

He took it with a slight grin and began cautiously unwrapping it. It was a set of healing crystals I had bought in Kona. Smitty was very into Reiki and crystals, so I knew he would like it.

"Wow, girl...This is super sweet of you," he said as his demeanor softened, and he playfully batted his eyes at me. "I actually got you something as well...I mean, it is Christmas," he said, mocking my previous statement, as he pulled a small wrapped box out of his pocket. I squeaked with excitement as I opened it. The box had the logo of my favorite jewelry store in Maui. I pulled the top off and saw a shell bracelet. I thanked him and told him that I loved it as I hugged him.

While I was still hugging him, he said, "Don't

get too excited...I bought it before everything happened with Theobold."

I pulled away, giving him a look.

"This doesn't mean you're in the clear, but I suppose it's a step in the right direction," he said as he watched the Santa line again.

"Does it mean you will talk to me at the crew Christmas party tonight?" I asked him.

"Miracles can happen on Christmas," he joked.

I saw a large group of passengers approaching our table as they departed from "Santa's" throne. Excited children from the group rushed over, eagerly grabbing several guessing slips. Their mother explained that "Santa's elf" had informed them that participating in our "art game" could increase their chances of having their wishes granted. Glancing over at Eryn, I noticed her mischievous grin, and I couldn't help but smile myself as I watched Smitty attempting to retrieve the pencils before the kids could put them in their mouths. He shot me a look of exasperation, and I silently mouthed "thank you" at him, holding up my wrist adorned with the bracelet he had given me.

A smile spread across his face before he suddenly yelped as one of the children hurled a pencil in his direction. I couldn't help but giggle - apparently, Smitty was just as good with children as Holiday was.

I did my makeup in the mirror, adorned with the polaroids capturing moments with Theobold and me, as I got ready for the Christmas Eve party. I thought about how this was the first time I would not be home for the holidays. The thought made me a bit sad, but I realized that I was excited to make some different Christmas memories with my ship family. Theobold had a management meeting and told me he would come when he was done, so I was going to meet the girls in the crew bar. I folded a Christmas sweater I had bought for Theobold on the bed. He had mentioned it was one of his family's traditions on Christmas Eve to have an ugly sweater competition, and when I saw it in Honolulu, I had to buy it for him. I smiled at the thought of seeing him wear the tacky sweater tonight. I left the cabin and made my way to the crew bar.

Anna gave me a big hug, and then I saw Eryn, who was still wearing her naughty elf costume. She teased about flaunting it to the rest of the crew who weren't at Santa's event that evening. I laughed as she said it and looked over to the bar to see Georgette. She wore long red gloves which matched a red dress that glittered down to the floor in the light from the bar.

"Holiday Barbie arrived a little bit ago," Eryn joked as she saw my gaze towards Georgette. I gave the girls a quick smile and told them I would be back as I walked over to the bar.

Standing a few feet away from Georgette, I ordered a glass of wine from the bartender, and then, after a pause, I asked if Georgette wanted anything. She declined without looking at me and raised her martini glass to her lips. The festive spirit had not thawed her icy exterior towards me. As she set the glass down with a bright red lipstick mark on the rim, I pulled out a small wrapped present from my purse and slid it over to her on the bar. She looked down at the gift and then raised her eyes slowly towards me.

"It's just something small, but it made me think of you," I said as she picked up the present and began unwrapping it. She tore the paper open to reveal a Power Ranger action figure.

She paused momentarily and responded, "A plastic toy made you think of me, did it?"

I knew it was a dig from her cold sense of humor, and I reminded her she had mentioned that her son's favorite show was Power Rangers.

"I hope he doesn't have that one already," I said as she put the boxed figure down on the bar.

"Well, I am rubbish at keeping up with which one is which..." she trailed off, gave me a slight grin, and said she was sure he would love it.

"Look, I know things between us have been chaotic all contract, and a lot of it is my fault, but I just want you to know that I have learned a lot from you. Theobold was right when he said you are the glue that holds us together...and I also want you to know that I haven't told him anything about your secret...and I never will..." I said as her gaze softened a bit.

"I do appreciate that," she said, raising her glass to meet mine.

"Happy Christmas!" Theobold exclaimed as he appeared at the bar. I let out a laugh as I turned to see him wearing the sweater I left out. The lumpy sweater hung awkwardly from his usually tailored frame.

"I love it!" he proclaimed.

Georgette scoffed at the sweater, "Really, Theobold, an assault on my vision was not on my holiday list."

He paused, looking down at the sweater. "Oh, is this not what is usually under the tree at the Covingard estate?" he asked with a knowing grin. I tensed up.

Why is he bringing up such a delicate topic right now? I asked myself.

I was about to say something to break the tension when he continued, "I'm just kidding, ladies. It is Christmas, and I am happy to see the two of you socializing again...Although I dare say that toy may clash with your aesthetic, Georgette," he said as he looked at the action figure sitting on the bar.

"A donation for the children at tomorrow's Christmas event," she responded as she slid the toy behind her on the bar.

"Ah, I see. Well, shall we find a place we can all sit down? If you can't come together at Christmas, then when?" he asked jovially.

Georgette looked at him with a flat expression and answered, "Well, there is always next year, darling." She grabbed the action figure I had given her, gave us both a curt nod, and walked out of the bar. I gave Theobold a slight shrug as she walked out.

"I would call that progress when it comes to Georgette Day...Now shall we go find out the story of Eryn's unique choice of outfit?" he asked playfully as we walked back over to the dancers.

XXVII

CHAPTER 27

I was awakened to George Michael's "Last Christmas" as the bright sun poured through the porthole window. I looked over as Theobold finished wrapping a small box in red paper.

"Just in the nick of time!" he said with an excited grin on his face. I remembered it was Christmas morning as that wave of childlike excitement came over me.

"Happy Christmas," I said playfully, mocking his British accent.

"It's getting better," he responded to my version of his accent that I periodically tried out on him.

He jumped from the couch onto the bed, and handed me the present. I told him that I thought we had decided we were not going to give each other gifts. We had only been seeing each other for a little over a month, and my sweater gift the night before was meant to be a joke.

"I can't help myself on Christmas!" he exclaimed. I took the small box slowly, knowing it could only be a piece of jewelry. I tore the paper off to reveal a tiny ring box from the jewelry store onboard. As I finished unwrapping it, I looked up and flashed him a smile.

That smile must have changed to a look of shock as I flipped open the tiny box. I was blinded by a large, sparkly diamond ring. I stared at it in amazement and realized the last time I had seen it was on display in one of the cases in the jewelry store on deck 7. We had been perusing some of the new inventory the shops had received last week, and I had admired it.

"The second I saw you looking at it, I knew it had to be yours!" Theobold said, watching me stare at the ring. As my initial shock wore off, I remembered the costly price tag that had been attached to the ring when I first saw it.

"Theobold..." I started to say, but he interrupted me and excitedly asked me to try it on. I still sat there propped up in the bed, staring at the ring. How in the world was I holding a ring that cost more than a down payment on a house from someone I had barely been dating?

What exactly did it mean? I asked myself.

Theobold took the box from my hand and plucked the ring out. Then he took my left hand and slid the ring onto the finger where a wedding ring would sit.

It sparkled even more on my finger as I looked at it while Theobold still held my hand. Then, my shock returned momentarily when I realized we were in a stance that looked very much like a proposal. I yanked my hand away, looking from the ring to him and back to the ring.

"I don't know what to say," I finally said.

"Hopefully, that you love it!" Theobold exclaimed as he leaned in to take a selfie of the two of us and held my hand up to display the ring. I smiled awkwardly for the photo.

"Theobold...this is way too much. I can't accept this," I said slowly.

His eyes widened with excitement. "Of course,

you can! It's Christmas! I saw your face light up when you saw it in the shops. It was meant for you...and mother will love it when she sees it!"

That last sentence grabbed my full attention from the sparkly distraction to Theobold's face.

"Your mother?" I asked uncertainly.

Theobold grinned. "Well, I know we haven't made any solid plans yet, but the contract is coming to an end very soon after the new year, and I thought it would be a great surprise to bring you home! You said you have never been to the UK, and I could show you around. The Thorne estate has plenty of room, and we could have such fun together! And it will give us time to plan our next contract together," he said as if he had the whole thing planned already.

I replayed what he had just suggested in my head. It sounded so grand...and intimidating.

Not to mention meeting his mother... After only a month? I thought to myself.

My head began to spin. I started to form my response, "Theobold, I can't go home with you... I've already been away for over six months. My parents would kill me if I told them I was going to a completely different country instead of going to visit them when I finish this contract. I haven't even decided if I am going to do another contract. I told myself I would do this for a little while and then go see how the job market is in LA again."

Theobold's smile faded into a look of concern. "What do you mean you're not going to do another contract? You don't want to go back and scratch around to find a job in LA. You were meant to do this job...You are so good at it. After just one contract, you are so much better than any of the other people on my previous teams. After all our success on this ship, the company will surely give us any assignment we ask for." He paused momentarily, and then an excited look came across his face. "I could fly your parents out as well! They can stay at the estate and meet everyone!"

He was about to keep rambling on when I interrupted him. "I can't go to your estate with my parents and have us all meet your family with this ring on my finger...after barely a month of seeing each other. Do you realize how crazy that sounds? Look at this thing!" I held up my hand with the ring. "You do realize what this looks like, right?" I asked.

He laughed and said it wasn't anything like that and it was simply a Christmas present.

"Christmas present or not, it looks like an engagement ring, Theobold. This whole idea of flying to the UK and staying at your estate sounds very much like an engagement as well..." I said.

A defeated look came across his face as I said it. He appeared to be in thought for a long moment, and then he finally held up his hands, "I didn't mean to assume. It's just that things have been going so well between us, and I thought this would be a logical next step."

I got up from the bed, "Things have been fun, but this is too big of a step for me. This entire contract has been a whirlwind, and I feel like I need to go home and refocus a bit right now."

He took my hand, "So you are going to just leave and go home? What about us?" he asked, crestfallen. I glanced down at the ring quickly.

"I haven't really thought about 'us,' I guess...Honestly, I thought we were just having some fun together," I said hesitantly and then regretted it as I saw his facial expression. He dropped my hand.

"Ah, I see...well, that is not exactly what I

expected to hear on Christmas, but I suppose it's best to know the truth..." he trailed off.

I told him I wasn't sure what the next steps were for me, but the last month had been great, and I certainly planned to keep in touch with him. I felt terrible at how sad he looked. I had no idea he had all these plans. It was flattering but also very overwhelming. After all the drama with Serge, I wasn't looking to jump into a deep relationship with another man living in a different country. I slipped the ring off my finger and began to hand it back to him, feeling like I had said no to a marriage proposal.

He took my hand, closed it around the ring, and told me to keep it and have a think about everything.

"It seems like you have some decisions to make, and that is fine. But do me a favor and at least consider it?" he asked me with that signature furrowed brow and a hopeful look in his eyes. I felt too guilty to tell him no, so I just nodded and he grinned widely.

Eryn and Smitty stared at the ring as we sat in the crew mess – half in awe and half in disbelief.

"You must be magical in bed, girl," Eryn said as Smitty quietly chuckled, and I gave them both a cutting look.

"Not the advice I am looking for at the moment," I said in a tone.

Smitty took a deep breath and explained that I was probably reading too much into it and that rich people did this all the time.

"And how many million-dollar rings do you have in your jewelry box?" Eryn asked Smitty. He laughed slightly but then dove into a long rant about how this could be a pivotal moment in my life to become part of an aristocratic English family and become a duchess or countess or something. I gave him the same cutting look again.

"But I am the one who is overthinking this situation?" I asked him in a mocking tone. Neither of them was very useful in helping me sort out the situation, so I figured I was on my own. I had gotten myself into this mess and would have to find a way to sort it out.

The next few days dragged on. The time between Christmas and New Year's had always felt slow, but this was excruciating. Every time I saw Theobold, that look of excitement flashed in his eyes like I would give him the answer he wanted. I had talked with Smitty, Holiday, Eryn, and Anna, but there was no solid advice that I felt could help the situation, so I finally found myself in one of the most unlikely places.

I used my old key card to unlock my old cabin door. As it opened, I saw that Georgette had made the room entirely her own. Shoes, dresses, and accessories were all neatly displayed on my old top bunk bed. Georgette was sitting in her vanity chair doing her makeup. When I walked in, she turned her head with an air of disinterest. She raised her eyebrows when she saw the look on my face.

"My my...what have we here?" she asked as her gaze lingered on me.

I didn't say anything but held up my left hand with Theobold's ring glittering brightly. When she saw the ring, she set down her makeup brush and quickly turned her whole body to face me.

"Tell me," she said and waited, staring at me.

As I recounted the details of Christmas morning and Theobold's plans, Georgette's demeanor shifted and she turned back to the mirror. Her gaze drifted into the distance seemingly lost in the labyrinth of her own thoughts as she stared at her reflection. The room grew quiet. With each passing moment, the anticipation built, punctuated only by the soft hum of the ship's engines. Finally, after what felt like an eternity, she turned back to me.

"My advice would be to run now, darling...Once you enter the Thorne estate, it will be extremely difficult to escape it. Theobold has been under pressure to bring a partner back for some time now. If he has chosen you to present to Lady Thorne, that does not bode well for you."

I was about to ask what she was talking about when she turned back to her mirror, "Please don't think I am ignorant to what Theobold thinks about me and my family. The Thornes and the Covingards have had a rivalry for decades now, but however messy he believes my family situation to be, his is much worse...and far less of a secret."

My face must have appeared oddly surprised, and she grinned slightly, "You thought I didn't know?" I shook my head and grinned back at her. "Darling, you have had enough drama in one contract than most people have in three, and deciding to be with Theobold was not the wisest move in my opinion, but luckily, you can still salvage this."

She turned and her large blue eyes looked directly into mine, "Don't end a contract with baggage. And certainly don't carry that baggage and bring it into the next contract. Take it from a girl who has already made and learned from all the mistakes."

Before I said it, she answered my statement, "And do not feel bad about it. Theobold Thorne will find some other girl who will be perfectly content to play the happy wife in the grand countryside estate. That is not you...Otherwise, I will have tragically misjudged you."

I let out a sigh of relief and smiled. Out of all of my friends on the ship, I found it funny that the woman who had kicked me out of my cabin and iced me out with countless death glares was the one who was making the most sense and looking out for me.

She turned back to her mirror and began doing her makeup again, "And whatever the outcome is, the room is here if you need it..."

Her advice made everything click into place and instantly put things into perspective. I immediately felt relieved and confident in what I had to do. Why had I given Theobold so much power to affect my plans and make me feel bad about it? It dawned on me that I had been too focused on pleasing others, neglecting my own needs and desires in the process. It was time for me to break free from this cycle and prioritize my own well-being, even if it meant making decisions that others might not approve of.

I felt excited and emboldened as I got ready for the New Year's party. I slipped into a silver floor-length dress and put on a deep red lip as I styled my hair to drape over the right side of my shoulder. This would be the last crew party before we finished our contract, and I wanted to turn some heads with a lasting look. Theobold was in another of his long management meetings but promised to find me before midnight. I knew I would give him my answer at the party, and I was running through all the different ways I thought the conversation might go.

As I walked to meet everyone, I was still envisioning all the possible scenarios and rehearsing my responses in my mind. The ship buzzed with anticipation as passengers, adorned in their finest attire, roamed the decks. The air was filled with laughter and joyous chatter, punctuated by the festive sounds of paper horns provided by the cruise staff. It was a scene of jubilation and merriment, setting the stage for a memorable New Year's celebration at sea.

I spotted Smitty and Holiday in the central atrium next to a towering stack of champagne glasses. They were dressed in their tuxedos, standing with Eryn, Anna, and several of the spa girls, all in long glittering gowns. I joined the group just as a crew member ascended a tall ladder, a magnum of champagne in hand. With practiced precision, he began pouring, the golden liquid cascading down into each waiting glass in the tower below. The sight was mesmerizing, a sparkling centerpiece that signaled the start of a night filled with celebration and cheer.

Anna poured me a glass of champagne as I walked up to them. Smitty clinked his glass to mine and asked if everything was good. I nodded and gave him a wink.

"To the end of the year and the end of the contract!" Holiday exclaimed, and everyone cheered.

I looked around the room and observed all the couples around me – Smitty and Holiday, Anna and her boyfriend, Eryn and Brooke, who apparently were now dating...Eryn wasn't joking when she said she would take her off the market.

I looked down at Theobold's ring sparkling on my finger, and I surprisingly did not feel bad anymore. I realized that my happiness was not contingent on a romantic partner. The glimmer of Theobold's ring on my finger served as a poignant reminder of my journey up to this moment - marked by twists and turns, uncertainty, and self-discovery. I felt a growing sense of confidence in my decision to return the ring, to embrace the path that lay ahead with courage and resolve. As I stared at the ring, I felt Theobold's hands caress my shoulders.

"Happy New Year," his voice, soft and warm, brushed against my ear as he pressed a tender kiss to my cheek. My gaze shifted to see him donning one of the party favor top hats that were being passed out to the guests, with foiled lettering spelling out "Happy New Year," and I couldn't help but smile at the sight. I could smell that he had made a stop by the cigar lounge as I smelled the distinct sweet, woody smell on his jacket.

With a graceful tip of his hat to the group, he wished them all a joyous new year. He gave Smitty's shoulder a friendly squeeze and slowly led me away from the group, over to a secluded corner in the atrium. I followed him through the crowd as he smiled at me, his eyes, warm and admiring, traced the lines of my dress.

"You look absolutely stunning," he remarked as he put his arm around my waist. I told him he looked very dashing as well as he grabbed a glass of champagne from a passing waiter.

"Were you nervous that I wouldn't make it? Can't have my girl standing alone at midnight," he said with a wide grin.

I gave him a light smile. "I had no doubt you would be punctual as ever," I said, making a small attempt to deflect, but I could feel I was stalling from the actual conversation.

Theobold could sense something as well and paused before he said, "It seems like you have something more pressing on your mind..." I nervously looked down at the ring and then back to his face. He still had that confident, hopeful look in his eyes. Swallowing the lump I had in my throat, I pulled away from his embrace, slowly took off the ring, and handed it back to him. With a sigh, I found my voice, the words tumbling out in a rush of apprehension and resolve.

"I can't come back to the UK with you, Theobold. I think we have different ideas about where this is going, and I feel it would be best for both of us if I told you now. I really don't want to ring in the new year on a false note. This first contract has been pretty crazy for me, and I just really need to take some time and focus on myself and figure some things out." He took the ring from my hand slowly and turned it over in his hand a few times.

"Well...I had hoped you'd come to your senses and make the right decision," he uttered with a hint of disappointment tainting his voice. His gaze, once warm and hopeful, now hardened as it fixated on the ring in his palm. A heavy silence stretched between us before he finally raised his eyes to meet mine.

His tone took on a hint of superiority, "This new year held so much promise for you. It's truly regrettable that you've chosen to turn away from it all," he lamented. "Having the Thorne name behind you could have opened doors to exclusive opportunities," he continued, slipping the ring into his jacket pocket. I took a step back as I told him that I preferred to open those doors independently and thought he would be more understanding about the situation. His reply was laced with a sharpness that cut through the air like a knife.

"Yes, you've made it quite clear that you were merely 'having fun,' so I suppose it's for the best that I learned the truth now..." His words carried a sting as he delivered the final blow.

"Mother wouldn't be pleased with my bringing home a frivolous girl just looking for fun," his gaze bore into mine, sharp and unforgiving.

I stood there a bit stunned. The look on his face was one I had never seen before – a mix of disdain and contempt. In that moment, shock gave way to a surge of anger, fueled by the realization that if anyone had the right to be furious, it was me. After all, he was the one who had presented me with an ultimatum, relentlessly pushing for a decision.

Summoning every ounce of resolve, I retorted, my voice dripping with sarcasm, "Well then, I'm relieved I made the right choice, because I certainly have no interest in bowing and scraping to impress your mother and the rest of the Thorne legacy." My words were sharp, a mirror reflecting the cutting edge of his own.

"And let's not forget who created this entire mess in the first place," I continued, my tone escalating with each word. "You pursued me, isolated me from my friends, and got me evicted from my own cabin so I'd be forced to share yours! You've been manipulating me since the moment I stepped foot on this ship, but that ends tonight...Enjoy being single at midnight."

I saw his eyes widen as I whipped around and walked away from him, leaving him in the dark corner of the atrium. I couldn't believe how childish he was acting. I maneuvered my way through the crowd back to the group and rolled my eyes as I squeezed in next to Smitty. He gave me a perplexed look, which turned to amazement as I held up my hand and he saw the ring was gone. I picked up the glass of champagne the bartender handed me and raised it to Smitty.

"Well, I suppose I am the one who is breaking up on a holiday!" I winked at him as he gave me a huge hug and lifted me off the floor. As my heels touched the marble floor again, we laughed at the memory of the first day onboard when Smitty said he would have to break up with Dan Holiday on a holiday. Anna and Eryn joined our impromptu celebration, and I recounted the brief yet intense exchange with Theobold. Glancing over my shoulder, I realized he had vanished, leaving behind an empty space that echoed with a sense of finality.

Eryn made a toast about dropping unnecessary baggage and floating away freely before we made our way to the middle of the atrium where the guests were dancing. With each laugh and twirl on the dance floor, I felt a weight lift from my shoulders, as if the burden of uncertainty had been cast aside. As the clock neared midnight, anticipation filled the air, mingling with the infectious energy of the crowd. With each passing second, the countdown grew louder, until finally, the room erupted into cheers as the clock struck twelve. A cascade of gold and black balloons descended from the atrium's dome, enveloping us amidst the flurry of hugs and kisses from Smitty, Holiday, Anna, and Eryn.

I felt a sense of renewal wash over me. It was the first New Year's Eve in which I truly felt like I was embarking on a fresh chapter—one filled with

newfound clarity and purpose...and a new name
for a password.

XXVIII

CHAPTER 28

The day of the final auction of the contract arrived. Smitty and I smoothly navigated through our early morning setup, fully aware and excited that this was our last one. The girls at the registration table greeted us with applause as we approached the lounge that afternoon.

"The pièce de résistance!" Eryn exclaimed as we reached the table.

There was an electric energy in the air, with everyone knowing that the contract was almost complete. The girls joked about the costume room being practically empty now that Georgette had shipped her clothes back home the last time we were in Honolulu.

I hadn't seen Theobold since New Year's Eve night. After his reaction to my answer, I had taken Georgette up on her offer to move back into my old room. This final auction was the first time I would see him since I had given him the ring back. Although I wasn't particularly nervous about seeing him, I still wanted to get through the auction quickly.

By now, I was sure most of the crew would know that we had ended things, as news on the ship, especially couple drama, always spread rapidly.

Walking into the lounge with Smitty, I spotted Theobold standing on the stage at his podium. Georgette sat poised in one of the chairs in the front row, meticulously filing her nails. She wore a bright pink pantsuit that I had never seen before, and I couldn't help but admire her ability to never repeat an outfit throughout the entire contract. Theobold looked up from his podium, and a flash of anger crossed his eyes as he saw me walk in. He motioned for all of us to join him on stage and gave a quick speech about finishing the final auction on a strong note, aiming to turn in the biggest total yet to the home office. After a brief pause, Theobold turned to Smitty.

"Smithsonian, how about you get the honor of doing my final introduction?" Theobold suggested.

Smitty looked perplexed; only Georgette ever called him Smithsonian. It seemed odd coming from Theobold.

Was this his way of trying to 'punish' me by taking away my usual intro? I asked myself.

Smitty shook his head, explaining he woke up with a sore throat and felt like he was losing his voice.

"How about the fabulous Georgette Day?" Theobold asked, turning to her.

Georgette responded silently with her signature double eyebrow raise, a silent yet emphatic refusal. Theobold sighed and looked annoyed as his eyes landed on me.

With a sly grin, I quipped, "Looks like you are stuck with me," eliciting a chuckle from Smitty.

We opened the doors to the lounge and began our usual pre-selling routine before the auction. The atmosphere was charged with excitement, and the sales quickly rolled in. As I placed the final slip on the frame of an artwork I had just sold,

Theobold popped his head out from the side of the stage, behind the curtain on stage.

He motioned for me to come over and handed me the microphone, his tone sharp and slightly disgusted as he said, "Make it good, will you, darling? Go out with a bang and all that."

Anger flared inside me. He only called me darling when he was trying to stir up trouble.

Why was he behaving like such a child? I asked myself. *Was I so terrible at judging men on ships?*

"Ship Life Bree" was good at so many things that "Land Life Bree" wasn't, but when it came to men, it seemed like this was proving to be a weak point. I had the same confused feeling as when Serge had shown his true colors. Pushing my thoughts aside, I stepped onto the stage and raised the microphone to my mouth.

*Go out with a bang...*I repeated Theobold's words in my head...*I'll give you a bang, darling,* I resolved inwardly and began to speak.

"Hello, ladies and gentlemen! Thank you so much for joining us for the final auction!" I began, the crowd responding with applause. "And my goodness, are you in for a special one because when I say final...I truly do mean final. This is, in fact, our team's last cruise, which we are very excited about." Pausing for the applause to subside, I continued, "And it's also a special moment for me since this is the final time I will be obligated to introduce our fabulous auctioneer to you all..."

Smitty's eyes met mine as he heard the word obligated, a look of dramatic excitement filling them as he realized what I was about to do.

"Is he charismatic? Yes. Is he handsome? Absolutely," I continued, glancing off to the side to see Theobold standing behind the curtain, smiling at my words.

"Is he also an entitled narcissist who is aware of both of these qualities and uses them to his advantage? You bet!"

My gaze returned to Theobold, and I saw his smile fade, fueling my resolve.

"Does he use his privilege and elite societal status to further his selfish endeavors? Does he manipulate people into toxic situations where they feel like they are in the wrong when really it is him who should be ashamed? One hundred percent!" I declared, answering my own rhetorical questions with unwavering conviction.

As I looked out from the stage, I saw Smitty's

jaw wide open, and Georgette stood still as a statue while some of the passengers shifted in their seats.

"So, ladies and gentlemen, it is my pleasure for the final time to introduce you to your auction-eer... All the way from a fabulous estate in England that he never shuts up about – and where I will not be joining him... I give you the actually not-so-fabulous, Theobold Thorne!"

I finished and lowered the microphone to my side, a heavy silence settled over the room. Some people wore confused looks, while others seemed shocked. Despite the awkwardness, it felt like a triumphant moment, a cathartic release of pent-up frustration. Glancing towards the side of the stage, I caught sight of Theobold's expression, his features contorted with a mix of shock and anger. Yet, my attention was drawn to a sound—a slow, deliberate clap originating from the back of the room.

I turned back to the audience and saw Georgette, her applause ringing out proudly, a wide grin of approval adorning her face. Smitty closed his open mouth and joined her in the slow clap, followed by several others in the crowd, still look-ing confused. The claps grew louder and quicker as more people joined in. Meanwhile, Theobold remained frozen behind the curtain, his eyes burning with fury as they bore into me. Despite his silent rage, the wave of applause washing over me filled me with a sense of validation and empowerment, a reminder that sometimes speaking the truth, however uncomfortable, could spark moments of unexpected solidarity and affirmation.

Ignoring his glare, I raised the microphone to my mouth again.

"Come on, Theobold! Come out here and show them, darling!" I exclaimed, throwing his own term of endearment back at him with a playful edge, joining in the applause. As he stepped from behind the curtain and onto the stage to grab the microphone, his eyes brightened to match his fake smile. He ripped the microphone out of my hand while he smiled widely at the audience.

As I walked off stage, I kept smiling while Theobold attempted to downplay the situation with a joke about his team members becoming silly at the end of their contract. Rolling my eyes at his excuse, I passed by Georgette, who gave me a confident wink and nod of approval. I walked over to Smitty, who wore an excited grin.

I received a quick hug as he whispered, "That was savage, girl! Fucking amazing!"

Inside, I beamed with satisfaction, knowing that no one had ever confronted Theobold like that before. He finished the auction, staying in showman mode, but disappeared instantly behind the curtain afterward.

Theobold didn't show up in the gallery that night. Georgette, Smitty, and I handled all the clients, upselling every one of them. Each time the door from the crew entrance swung open, we looked up, but Theobold never appeared. Georgette remarked that he was probably sulking in his cabin after being dressed down like that.

"I quite enjoyed it," she remarked with a hint of satisfaction, her attention focused on organizing the stack of invoices we had amassed throughout the evening.

"It just goes to show that we don't need him to run the show. We can handle it all on our own...and I say that next contract, Georgette Day should be 'Head Bitch in Charge!'" Smitty declared with infectious enthusiasm.

"Let's not get ahead of ourselves, Smithsonian," Georgette grinned as she handed me the invoices. I made my final walk to the finance office and delivered the stack to the finance officer. He smiled as he flipped through them.

"The next art team coming in will have some big shoes to fill," he said, looking up at me.

"Well, they might be able to fill them, but they won't be as fashionable," I joked.

His smile broadened, and he said, "Maybe next contract, I will work up the confidence to ask you out more quickly."

Feeling a faint blush creeping onto my cheeks, I chuckled softly. "I'm taking a break and embracing being single for a while," I admitted.

"I don't blame you," he replied, his understanding gaze hinting at his awareness of the contract's drama. With a playful wink, I bid him farewell and left the office, thinking about how everyone was already talking about the next contract and we weren't even done with this one yet.

Back in my cabin, I unzipped my empty suitcase to begin packing and felt a sense of déjà vu from when I started packing back in Hollywood with all the nervous excitement to begin this new adventure. Our cabin looked empty, with most of Georgette's clothes and jewelry already packed and shipped back to England. It gave me plenty of room to open my suitcases and start packing my outfits away. As I began folding and packing my outfits, Georgette, perched in her vanity chair, offered invaluable tips on maximizing space by folding and rolling certain items. It was evident that she was a packing professional, effortlessly demonstrating her techniques as she deftly rolled several of my dresses and arranged them in my suitcase. Her grin widened as I looked on in awe, impressed by her efficiency and expertise.

"You know, Smitty is right...You absolutely should come back as an auctioneer on your next contract. You would be so fabulous and give Theobold some major competition!" I said, excitedly.

She looked up at me and smiled as she placed another dress in my suitcase and said, "I certainly have given it some serious thought...Mother is not keen on the idea...which makes it even more appealing to pursue," she grinned to herself as she said it. I asked her about her plans during her vacation, and she said she was going back to Maui to spend time with her son for a few weeks and then hopefully take him back to England to meet his grandparents.

"Any room in there for a quick trip to Hollywood?" I asked jokingly.

She grinned again, "Well, darling, there is always time for a bit of shopping in Beverly Hills." She winked at me and turned her head as there was a knock on the door. She opened the door to Eryn and Anna with excited smiles, holding two bottles of champagne and four champagne flutes. Georgette rolled her eyes, "Am I to presume you nicked those from the auction today?" she asked the girls, looking at the champagne bottles.

"Oh, come off it, darling..." Eryn said as she mocked Georgette's signature darling yet again.

Anna continued, "Besides, it comes out of Theobold's paycheck – not yours."

"Well, you are correct there," Georgette said as she held the door open for the girls to come in.

Eryn excitedly plopped down on Georgette's bottom bunk and demanded details about my already infamous introduction for Theobold, which the girls had missed.

"It was quite the spectacle," Georgette said as she popped the first champagne bottle. Eryn and

Anna laughed loudly as she recounted the auction to them. As we finished the second bottle, I was amazed at how far the four of us had come from the start of this contract to the end. We had created a sisterhood between us, and it felt good.

XXIX

CHAPTER 29

The next morning, the ship docked in San Diego for the final time of my contract. The deck phone vibrated loudly on the empty desk in the cabin. I finally didn't jump anymore when the thing sounded. After an entire contract, I had finally become used to my annoying sidekick. Security was on the other end, saying we could leave the ship. It felt surreal to think it all had come to an end as I wheeled my suitcases down the gangway of the Vivace Vision. Memories flooded back to me of my first day coming onboard and following the intimidating Georgette down the I-95 and what a complete blur the first cruise had been. I walked through the large terminal to go through the security line one final time. I saw Smitty and Holiday already in line with their luggage and wheeled mine over to join them. Smitty looked over at me and pulled his sunglasses lower to make a sad face at me.

"Oh, stop it! We are all going back to LA, so don't pretend like I'm not going to see you at the West Hollywood bars tonight," I said to him. He smiled as he popped his sunglasses back up.

"Truth!" he said excitedly.

Holiday laughed and told me that we were getting the VIP tour of West Hollywood nightlife from Smitty tonight. Holiday was coming to stay in LA for a few days and meet with his agent to see about getting some new gigs and moving to LA himself.

"Plus, it means there will be more time for both of us to convince you to do a second contract with us!" Smitty exclaimed.

I rolled my eyes lightly. "Don't you think I had enough drama in just one contract?" I asked jokingly.

"Girl, you just barely scratched the

surface...there is way more messiness you can get into," Smitty said as we moved forward in the security line. Holiday asked Smitty if he was trying to convince me or deter me from a second contract as he put his luggage through the security screener. Everyone had been asking if I would be doing a second contract, and I told them all that I felt like I needed to get away from it for a bit before I could make the decision. My indecision seemed to upset Smitty the most, but it was the truth.

As I walked through the other side of the security gate, I grabbed my heavy luggage off the belt. The weight of it pulled me forward, and it slammed down onto the ground with a resounding thud. Smitty chuckled at the noise, a deep, hearty laugh that echoed through the bustling terminal.

"You are lucky we are just driving and not flying because no amount of flirting would get the overweight fee waived on that bitch!" he said, his eyes twinkling with amusement. Holiday joined in with a laugh, the sound light and musical.

"How many new outfits did you buy on this contract? I think you outdid the dancers... Georgette's influence really rubbed off, huh?" Holiday asked.

Just then, Smitty's gaze shifted past me, and his expression brightened. "Speak of the fabulous devil herself!"

I turned around to see Georgette, effortlessly glamorous, wheeling a small designer carry-on bag. The bag's sleek lines and designer logo matched her impeccably tailored black travel outfit, complete with a wide-brimmed sun hat that cast a perfect shadow over her flawless face.

"She even travels in style," Holiday remarked, his eyes wide with admiration as he took in Georgette's ensemble. Georgette smiled and casually removed her large, oversized sunglasses.

"Always dress like you are going to be photographed, darling," she said with a wink. Her voice was smooth and confident, with just a hint of playful sass. She looked at us, her expression softening. "Well, I suppose this is goodbye..."

"For now!" Smitty corrected her. "You're coming back as auctioneer, and you are going to slay, and you had better request us for your team on your new ship...preferably in the Mediterranean... Work those contacts at the company!" he said as he winked at her.

She grinned at him. "I will see what can be

done, Smithsonian...I must say I usually do not have a problem leaving most of the crew members I meet, but I shall miss your witty attitude. Be sure not to lose it, darling."

She looked over to Holiday. "And I will miss that melodious voice of yours, Dan Holiday... Don't go getting too famous in Hollywood now," she said as she winked at him.

"No more than I will miss your flawless style, darling," he responded back.

Finally, Georgette looked at me, her eyes sparkling with a mix of pride and fondness.

"The one and only, Breeanne Bradley... What a contract you have had indeed!" She extended her manicured hand to shake mine, but I leaned in and hugged her instead. She seemed slightly alarmed at first but then embraced me warmly, her arms wrapping around me with surprising tenderness.

"Thanks for everything, Georgette. You are iconic," I said as I let her go. She smiled, a genuine, heartfelt smile that softened her usual poised demeanor.

"Keep that star of yours on the rise, and don't let anyone diminish it," she said, her voice soft but firm as she looked me in the eyes. "You have a rare talent and an even rarer spirit. Don't ever forget that."

Her phone chimed, signaling the arrival of her car. She sighed, a mix of reluctance and inevitability in her eyes. "That's my car," she said softly. She turned to Smitty and Holiday, giving them each a warm kiss on the cheek.

"Ciao, darlings," she said as she wheeled her bag towards the waiting car. The driver quickly took it and placed it in the trunk. Georgette paused, turning back to give us one last wave, her large sun hat tilting to one side as she did. "Take care of each other," she called out, her voice carrying a note of genuine affection. With that, she got into the car, her silhouette framed by the door as she looked back at us one final time. The car drove off slowly, and we watched her leave, feeling the weight of her departure settle around us. In the midst of the bustling terminal, her exit felt like the closing of a chapter.

I felt a bit sad and finally realized how close we had become...almost like sisters. My sadness was fleeting as I felt a massive hug from behind me and long red locks falling on my shoulders.

"Don't think you're getting away from me

without a final goodbye, baby!" Eryn said as she released me from behind. I turned around to see her and Anna surrounded by four huge suitcases.

"Yeah, it's ridiculous, I know," Anna said as I looked at all their bags. "Don't worry, Eryn will flash her tits at the airport luggage attendant, and we will all be sorted," she said as both of them erupted in laughter.

"It's funny because it's true!" Smitty said.

They both had changed their flights to go to New Zealand and see Erika and promised to video call Holiday when they were with her. He told them that he had already started organizing the next contract so they could all be in the same cast on the next ship. They truly were a ship family. Smitty said he would coordinate with Georgette to request whichever ship Holiday got but told him that he should press for a Mediterranean itinerary.

"Then everything will be set up when you call me and say you are going to come back!" Smitty told me excitedly.

"I get it already!" I said, hugging the girls for a final time as their Uber pulled up to take them to the airport.

"Bet you didn't know what you were getting

into when you accepted this ride!" Eryn said as the Uber driver helped them with all their luggage. The three of us laughed as we watched her and Anna get in the car and ride away.

The finality of it all was hitting me hard. I was still smiling as I glanced across the terminal and saw him.

He wore a slim black suit and wheeled one large black suitcase behind him. He didn't see me at first as he paused and took off his sunglasses to look at his phone. When he looked up, our eyes met, and that furrow in his brow appeared.

The last time I looked into Theobold's eyes, they were full of anger toward me, but now, looking into them, I saw something different. It wasn't coldness or sadness but an odd look of knowing...almost a sense of contentment. We stared at each other across the terminal, neither of us willing to break the connection. The bustling noise of the terminal faded into the background. It was as if every moment we had shared, every word left unsaid, hung between us like an invisible thread, pulling us closer even as we stood apart.

Oddly, I didn't feel a sense of anger either. It was

as if my final introduction for him the previous day had vented all my anger out. Despite the complete mess of our situation over the past month, he had played a significant role in my "Ship Life." A slight smile formed at the corner of my mouth as I lifted one hand in a motionless wave.

He lingered, continuing to look at me until a black limousine pulled up, drawing his attention. The driver got out and came to take Theobold's luggage. Before he got in the car, he turned around to look at me one final time. Our gaze held, a silent exchange of emotions passing between us—a mixture of regret, longing, and perhaps even a hint of forgiveness. His gaze lingered again, and then, finally, he nodded, popped his sunglasses back on, and got into the limo.

I watched with a mixture of nostalgia and anticipation as the sleek limousine pulled away, carrying Theobold into the distance. It seemed fitting that he was the last one I saw leaving, a silent farewell to a tumultuous chapter of my life that had unfolded over the past six months. As the car disappeared from view, a flood of memories washed over me, each one vivid and unforgettable.

I remembered the highs and lows of the

contract—the long work hours spent in the gallery and the after-hour crew parties, with their pulsing music and flashing lights. The countless hours spent laughing with Smitty and the girls, our bond growing stronger with each passing day. But amidst the laughter, there were also moments of conflict and resolution, fights and makeups with Georgette that tested the strength of our friendship. I recalled Erika's abrupt exit, a bitter reminder of the transient nature of life at sea, and the painful end of my relationship with Serge, a spark that had burned bright but ultimately fizzled out.

I realized how much I would miss all of it.

And then there was Theobold—both captivating and elusive throughout the contract. Our relationship had been a whirlwind of emotions, not as passionate as it had been with Serge, but undeniably special in its own right. Lost in thought, I barely noticed when Smitty waved his hand in front of my face, breaking me from my reverie.

"That is a really long stare for someone who didn't want to go to England," he said, amusement and a bit of concern dancing in his eyes. I met his gaze with a smile, a sense of determination coursing through me.

"Oh, I'll get there, but I'll do it my way," I replied, my voice tinged with confidence.

In the last six months, I had gained so much self-confidence, a whole new sense of style with a killer wardrobe, fantastic new friends, a brother in Smitty, a sister in Georgette, a few more zeros in my bank account, and thanks to Smitty's advice...two new boyfriends for passwords. "Ship Life Bree" had really come into her own. Now, I just needed to find a way to balance her with "Land Life Bree." I had run away from Hollywood to find something...a sense of purpose. A change of some sort, and it seemed like I had found the future career I was looking for; I just hadn't realized it yet.

Then I knew that I had made my decision.

"So next contract in the Med, huh?" I asked Smitty, a playful glint in my eye. His grin mirrored mine as he slipped on his sunglasses.

"See you there, bitch!" he exclaimed. His grin turned into a smile - a silent affirmation of the adventures that awaited us on the horizon. Climbing into our car bound for Los Angeles, Smitty launched into a spirited monologue about the drama that awaited us on the upcoming contract.

As we pulled away from the port, I watched

the Vivace Vision grow smaller in the rearview mirror, a symbol of the life I was leaving behind. But there was no sense of loss, only anticipation for the journey ahead. Through the window, I caught glimpses of the world rushing by, a blur of colors and shapes that mirrored the whirlwind of emotions swirling within me. Smitty's predictions for our next contract filled me with excitement, a rush of adrenaline coursing through my veins as I imagined the adventures that awaited me.

With a newfound sense of purpose and determination, I knew that "Ship Life Bree" was here to stay. And as the miles stretched out before us, I leaned back in my seat, a smile playing at the corners of my lips. The future was bright, and I was ready to seize it with both hands.